*Peng*

*Dandelion Clocks*

# Dandelion Clocks

## Stories of Childhood

EDITED BY ALFRED BRADLEY
AND KAY JAMIESON

Penguin Books

Penguin Books Ltd, Harmondsworth,
Middlesex, England
Penguin Books, 625 Madison Avenue,
New York, New York 10022, U.S.A.
Penguin Books Australia Ltd, Ringwood,
Victoria, Australia
Penguin Books Canada Ltd, 2801 John Street,
Markham, Ontario, Canada L3R 1B4
Penguin Books (N.Z.) Ltd, 182-190 Wairau Road,
Auckland 10, New Zealand

First published in this edition in Great Britain
by Michael Joseph 1978
Published in Penguin Books 1980

Made and printed in Great Britain by
Richard Clay (The Chaucer Press) Ltd
Bungay, Suffolk

# Contents

# KEITH WATERHOUSE

# *Albert and the Liner*

Below the military striking clock in the City Arcade there was, and for all I know still is, a fabulous toyshop.

It was a magic grotto, that shop. A zoo, a circus, a pantomime, a travelling show, a railway exhibition, an enchanted public library, a clockwork museum, an archive of boxed games, a pavilion of sports equipment, a depository of all the joys of the indefinite, endless leisure of the winter holiday – but first, the military striking clock.

Once a year we were taken to see the clock strike noon – an event in our lives as colourful, and traditional, and as fixed and immovable in the calendar of pageantry as Trooping the Colour. Everybody who was anybody assembled, a few minutes before twelve, on the patch of worn tiles incorporating an advertisement for tomato sausages done in tasteful mosaic, beneath that military striking clock.

There was me, and Jack Corrigan, and the crippled lad from No 43, and there was even Albert Skinner – whose father never took him anywhere, not even to the Education Office to explain why he'd been playing truant.

Albert Skinner, with his shaved head and his shirt-lap hanging out of his trousers, somehow attached himself, insinuated himself, like a stray dog. You'd be waiting at the tram stop with your mother, all dolled up in your Sunday clothes for going into town and witnessing the ceremony of the military striking clock, and Albert, suddenly, out of nowhere, would be among those present.

'Nah, then, kid.'

And your mother, out of curiosity, would say – as she was meant to say – 'You're never going into town looking like that, are you, Albert?'

And Albert would say: 'No. I was, only I've lost my tram fare.'

And your mother, out of pity, would say – as she was meant to say – 'Well, you can come with us. But you'll have to tidy yourself up. Tuck your shirt in, Albert.'

So at Christmastime Albert tagged on to see the military striking clock strike noon. And after the mechanical soldiers of the King had trundled back into their plaster-of-Paris garrison, he, with the rest of us, was allowed to press his nose to the fabulous toyshop window.

Following a suitable period of meditation, we were then treated to a bag of mint imperials – *'and think on, they're to share between you'* – and conveyed home on the rattling tram. And there, thawing out our mottled legs by the fireside, we were supposed to compose our petitions to Father Christmas.

*Dear Father Christmas, for Christmas I would like . . .*

'Don't know what to put,' we'd say at length to one another, seeking some kind of corporate inspiration.

'Why don't you ask him for a sledge? I am.'

'Barmpot, what do you want a sledge for? What if it doesn't snow?'

'Well – a cricket bat and stumps, and that.'

'Don't play cricket at Christmas, barmpot.'

Albert Skinner said nothing. Nobody, in fact, said anything worth saying, during those tortured hours of voluntary composition.

With our blank jumbo jotters on our knees, we would suck our copying-ink pencils until our tongues turned purple – but it wasn't that we were short of ideas. Far from it: sledges, cricket bats with stumps and that, fountain pens, dynamos, cinematographs complete with Mickey Mouse films – the fact of the matter was, there was too much choice.

For the fabulous toyshop, which sparked off our exotic and finally blank imaginations, was the nearest thing on this earth to Santa's Workshop. It was like a bankruptcy sale in heaven. The big clockwork train ran clockwise and the small electric train ran anti-clockwise, and there was Noah's Ark, and a tram conductor's set, and a junior typewriter revolving on a brightly-lit glass shelf, and a fairy cycle hanging from the ceiling on invisible wires, and a tin steam roller, and the Tip-Top Annual and the Film Fun Annual and the Radio Fun Annual and the Jingles Annual and the Joker Annual and the Jester Annual, and board games, and chemistry sets, and conjuring sets, and carpentry sets – everything, in short, that the modern boy would give his eye-teeth for.

Everything that Albert Skinner would have given his eye-teeth for, in fact, and much that Albert Skinner would never get. And not only him. There were items that no reasonable modern boy expected to find in his Christmas pillow-case – not even though he bartered every tooth in his head and promised to be a good lad till kingdom come.

The centrepiece of the fabulous toyshop's window display was always something out of the reach of ordinary mortals, such as the Blackpool Tower in Meccano, or a mechanical carousel with horses that went up and down on their brass poles like the real thing, or Windsor Castle made of a million building bricks, or Buckingham Palace with nobs on – flood-lit. None of us had to be told that such luxuries were beyond Father Christmas's price range.

This year the window featured a splendid model of the *Queen Mary*, which had recently been launched on Clydebank. It was about four feet long, with real lights in the portholes, real steam curling out of the funnels, and a crew, and passengers, and lifeboats, and cabin trunks, all to scale – and clearly it was not for the likes of us.

Having seen it and marvelled at it, we dismissed this expensive dream from our minds, sucked our copying-ink pencils and settled down to list our prosaic requests – for Plasticine, for farmyard animals that poisoned you when you licked the paint off, and for one pair of roller skates between two of us.

All of us, that is to say, except Albert Skinner. Having considered several possibilities, and taken advice on the rival merits of a racing track with eight electric sports cars and a glove puppet of Felix the Cat he'd rather fancied, Albert calmly announced that he'd given thought to all our suggestions and he was asking Father Christmas for the *Queen Mary*.

This, as you might imagine, was greeted with some scepticism.

'What – that one in the Arcade window? With all the lights and the steam coming out and that? You've never asked for that, have you?'

'Yeh – course I have. Why shouldn't I?'

'He's blinking crackers. Hey, Skinno, why don't you ask for them soldiers that march in and out and bang that clock? Because you've more chance of getting them than that *Queen Mary*.'

'If I'd wanted them soldiers I'd have asked for them. Only I don't. So I've asked him for the *Queen Mary*.'

'Who – Father Christmas?'

'No – him on the Quaker Oats Box, who do you think?'

'Bet you haven't, man. Bet you're having us on.'

'I'm not – God's honour. I've asked him for the *Queen Mary*.'

'Let's see the letter, then.'

'Can't – I've chucked it up the chimney.'

'Yeh – bet you have. Anyway, your dad won't get it for you – he can't afford it.'

'What's it got to do with him? I'm asking Father Stinking Rotten Christmas for it, not me dad. Dozy.'

'What else have you asked for, Skinno?'

'Nowt. I don't want owt else. I just want the *Queen Mary*. And I'm getting it, as well.'

Little else was said at the time, but privately we thought Albert was a bit of an optimist. For one thing, the *Queen Mary* was so big and so grand and so lit-up that it was probably not even for sale. For another, we were all well aware that Father Christmas's representative in the Skinner household was a sullen, foul-tempered collier who also happened to be unemployed.

Albert's birthday present, it was generally known, had been a pair of boots – instead of the scooter on which, at that time, he had set his heart.

Even so, Albert continued to insist that he was getting the *Queen Mary* for Christmas. 'Ask my dad,' he would say. 'If you don't believe me, ask my dad.'

None of us cared to broach the subject with the excitable Mr Skinner. But sometimes, when we went to his house to swop comics, Albert would raise the matter himself.

'Dad, I am aren't I? Aren't I, Dad? Getting that *Queen Mary* for Christmas?'

Mr Skinner, dourly whittling a piece of wood by the fireside after the habit of all the local miners, would growl without looking up: 'You'll get a clout over the bloody earhole if you don't stop chelping.'

Albert would turn complacently to us. 'I am, see. I'm getting the *Queen Mary*. Aren't I, Dad? Dad? Aren't I?'

Sometimes, when his father had come home from the pub in a bad mood (which was quite often), Albert's pleas for reassurance would be met with a more vicious response. 'Will you shut up about the bloody Queen swining Mary!' Mr Skinner would shout. 'You gormless little git, do you think I'm made of money?'

Outside, his ear tingling from the blow his father had landed on it, Albert would bite back the tears and declare stubbornly: 'I'm still getting it. You wait till Christmas.'

Christmas Eve was but a fortnight off by then. Most of us had a shrewd idea, from hints dropped by our mothers, what Father Christmas would be bringing us – or, in most cases, not bringing. 'I don't think Father Christmas can manage an electric train set this year, our Terry. He says they're too expensive. He says he might be able to find you a tip-up lorry.'

Being realists, we accepted our lowly position on Father Christmas's scale of priorities – and we tried our best to persuade Albert to accept his.

'You're not *forced* to get that *Queen Mary*, you know, Skinno.'

'Who says I'm not?'

'My mam. She says it's too big to go in Father Christmas's sack.'

'Yeh, well that's all *she* knows. Because he's fetching Jacky Corrigan a fairy cycle – so if he can't get the *Queen Mary* in his sack, how can he get a stinking rotten fairy cycle?'

'Yeh, well he isn't fetching me a fairy cycle at all, clever-clogs, he's fetching me a John Bull printing outfit. 'Cos he told my mam.'

'I don't care what he told her, or what he didn't tell her. He's still fetching me that *Queen Mary*.'

The discussion was broken up by the sudden appearance of

Mr Skinner at their scullery window. 'If I hear one more bloody word from you about that bloody *Queen Mary*, you'll get nothing for Christmas! Do you hear me?' And there the matter rested.

A few days later the crippled lad at No 43 was taken by the Church Ladies Guild to see the military striking clock in the City Arcade, and when he came home he reported that the model of the *Queen Mary* was no longer in the window of the fabulous toyshop.

'I know,' said Albert, having confirmed that his father was out of earshot. 'I'm getting it for Christmas.'

And indeed, it seemed the only explanation possible. The fabulous toyshop never changed its glittering display until after Boxing Day – it was unheard of. Some minor item might vanish out of the window – the Noah's Ark, perhaps, or a farmyard, or a game of Monopoly or two. There was a rational explanation for this: Father Christmas hadn't enough toys to go round and he'd been obliged, so to speak, to call on his sub-contractors. But the set-piece, the Blackpool Tower made out of Meccano or the carousel with the horses that went round and round and up and down – that was never removed; never. And yet the *Queen Mary* had gone. What had happened? Had Father Christmas gone mad? Had Mr Skinner bribed him – and if so, with what? Had Mr Skinner won the football pools? Or was it that Albert's unswerving faith could move mountains – not to mention ocean-going liners with real steam and real lights in the portholes? Or was it, as one cynic among us insisted, that the *Queen Mary* had been privately purchased for some pampered grammar school lad on the posher side of town?

'You just wait and see,' said Albert.

And then it was Christmas morning; and after the chocolate pennies had been eaten and all the kitchens in the street were awash with nut-shells and orange peel, we all flocked out to show off our presents – sucking our brand-new torches to make our cheeks glow red, or brandishing a lead soldier or two in the pretence that we had a whole regiment of them indoors. Those who had wanted wooden forts were delighted with their painting books; those who had prayed for electric racing cars were content with their Dinky toys; those who had asked for roller skates were happy with their pencil boxes; and there was no sign of Albert.

No one, in fact, expected to see him at all. But just as we were asking each other what Father Christmas could have brought him – a new jersey, perhaps, or a balaclava helmet – he came bounding, leaping, jumping, almost somersaulting into the street. 'I've got it! I've got it! I've got it!'

Painting books and marbles and games of Happy Families were abandoned in the gutter as we clustered around Albert, who was cradling in his arms what seemed on first inspection to be a length of wood. Then we saw that it had been roughly carved at both ends, to make a bow and stern, and that three cotton-reels had been nailed to it for funnels. A row of tin-tacks marked the Plimsoll line, and there were stuck-on bits of cardboard for the portholes. The whole thing was painted over in sticky lamp-black, except for the lettering on the portside.

'*The Queen Mary*,' it said. In white, wobbling letters. Capital T, small h, capital E. Capital Q, small u, capital E, capital E, small n. Capital M, small a, capital R, small y. Penmanship had never been Mr Skinner's strong point.

'See!' crowed Albert complacently. 'I told you he'd fetch me it, and he's fetched me it.'

Our grunts of appreciation, though somewhat strained, were genuine enough. Albert's *Queen Mary* was a crude piece of work, but clearly many hours of labour, and much love, had gone into it. Its clumsy contours alone must have taken night after night of whittling by the fireside.

Mr Skinner, pyjama-jacket tucked into his trousers, had come out of the house and was standing by his garden gate. Albert, in a rush of happiness, ran to his father and flung his arms around him and hugged him. Then he waved the *Queen Mary* on high.

'Look, Dad! Look what I've got for Christmas! Look what Father Christmas has fetched me! You knew he would, didn't you, all this time!'

'Get out of it, you soft little bugger,' said Mr Skinner. He drew contentedly on his empty pipe, cuffed Albert over the head as a matter of habit, and went indoors.

# KEN WHITMORE

# The Cream of the Country

When I got back to school after lunch I was met down the driveway by this girl saying: 'Ooh! You've knocked one of Anthea's teeth out. You're going to be in awful trouble.'

I went on my way in fear and trembling. I was very frightened of Miss Marryat. She never really did anything to be frightened of but she was a very forbidding figure.

So I met Anthea in the porch and there she was with her mouth swollen and a bit of tooth chipped off and her eyes all puffed up from crying, and we were told that when school started we had to go into Miss Marryat's study.

It was a very big room at the front of the school with a big bay window out on to the school gardens. It had once been a very big gentleman's house and this must have been the drawing-room, I imagine. It had a big Adam chimney-piece and in front of this chimney-piece was an enormous desk, at least it seems enormous to me now.

And there was Miss Marryat behind it. She always wore her academic robes and she had grey hair, drawn back, and she was a very tall, thin, beaky woman, and her eyes looked as though they'd been put in with two sooty fingers, all black all round. She always looked very sad – there was a great sadness about her.

We both hung back from telling her what had happened but gradually it came out in penny numbers. We'd been fighting about my hat.

I was a day girl at St Agnes's and every day I went home for lunch. If I didn't get this bus, the twelve o'clock, I was late getting back. And I had this friend called Anthea – Anthea Hardy – and she knew I wanted to get this bus. So I went into the cloakroom to get ready, dashing for the bus. The school was on a hill and you could see the buses, standing in at the bottom of the hill, because that was the terminus, so if one was in you could see it, just the top of it from the cloakroom windows, and if the engine was going you could see it shaking, a big red bus.

And I was getting ready when Anthea grabbed my hat.

I couldn't go without my hat. We had to always go out on the streets properly dressed, which meant we always had to have our hats on, and not at a rakish angle or anything like that. It was a blue velour hat with a blue band striped with cream.

We had straw boaters in the summer with very, very big brims – what used to be called bacon slicers. I remember this rule about wearing hats, always. I remember my boater blowing in the road and a car running over it, and Miss Magaràch, the maths mistress, coming along the street and picking it up out of the road and punching the crown back in, it was hanging out all over the place, and putting it back on my head and making me wear it.

But it was my blue velour hat that Anthea grabbed, because it was winter.

I tried to get it off her and I pleaded with her, but she wouldn't, she threw it over the rails where we kept our coats to somebody on the other side. They caught it and threw it back and Anthea tormented me dreadfully with this hat. And there was this red bus juddering away down the hill and any second it would be going.

And so I bunched up my fist and I walloped her. I just saw the blood spurting out and I grabbed my hat and ran. I ran across the road to get this bus. It was one of those old type with the open side and a handrail going down, and it was moving out, and I swung myself up by the handrail and on to it.

Miss Marryat was very put out by what we'd done and so she ordered us to go down on our knees and pray for forgiveness there and then. It was very high church St Agnes's – so high church we all knew the Magnificat backwards, bobbing and crossing, practically Catholic.

I'd only just escaped going to a convent. There were two

schools, you see, at either end of the village. There was the blue one, which I went to, St Agnes's, which was known as the Bluebottles, and at the other end there was the convent, with an identical uniform, but in brown and yellow, and they were called the Wasps. The Wasps and the Bluebottles. Mount Carmel. I always used to think it was Mount Caramel, and that's why their uniforms were brown. I remember my parents asking me which one I wanted to go to. Isn't it crazy? Well, I mean, you obviously opt for the one with the prettiest uniform when you're only eleven, don't you? The blue was infinitely prettier and more stylish. We had a very nice dark blue fitted gymslip, with a flared skirt, and a deep cream blouse and a lovely bright blue tie with a diagonal cream stripe; and in the summer we wore blue gingham frocks and our socks were deep cream with blue bands at the top. Our winter coats were lovely hairy Harris tweeds with great belts around them, double-breasted and leather buttons. They were fantastically expensive and I don't know how my father managed it.

Anyhow, here was Miss Marryat with her deep-sunk Saint Bernard eyes telling us to get down on our knees, but I was in one of my sort of I-don't-believe-in-all-that-rubbish phases and all ready to stand on principle.

Anthea was rather soft and pretty and sycophantic. She would butter up to any of the teachers and she was buckling at the knees and ready to go down and pray -- when I declared I wouldn't. I didn't see what I'd done I needed any forgiveness for. And so, seeing my resolution, Anthea decided to take a firm stand as well.

So we were let out and we were told we had to go back the next day at the same time. By then I'd established physical superiority over Anthea, so when we got outside I got her on the stairs and I said: 'I'll knock all the rest of your teeth out if you pray.'

We were hauled up every day for a week. You know how *you* were at that age – standing on principles? Well, we thought it was a fight between *us* and they had no right to interfere in it, let alone drag God into it. Between us we'd forgotten about it. We went pony riding at weekends. We were quite friends again, but we were still hauled up in order to pray.

Anyhow, the following Monday Miss Marryat took us separately and Anthea prayed for forgiveness straight away.

Then Miss Marryat called me in on my own. By now it had got to be a very big thing with me not to pray, I was picturing myself like Edith Cavell in front of the firing squad. But it had grown into a big thing for Miss Marryat, too.

'Isobel Compton,' she said, 'God doesn't like your defiance.' Her eyes had sunk even deeper and I had to lean forward to see if they were still there. 'He's had occasion to be cross with you before,' she said.

That was over my newspaper round. I used to do a paper delivery in the mornings, so I could keep my pony, Penny. I used to wear a particularly lurid pair of yellow sailcloth trousers, which were warm, and I would also on occasions wear my school blazer. I had a big canvas bag which said *News of the World* on the side.

Miss Marryat was an early riser and the boarders' hall was at the other end of the village, and she used to sweep down the main street in her academic robes just as I was sweeping past with my *News of the World* bag and school blazer and yellow pants.

And so she had me up about that. God didn't like the idea of a St Agnes's girl doing that, she said. I told her my mother thought it was a good thing for me to work – that I was going to have to work anyway. But they didn't go along with that principle at St Agnes's. Their young ladies *never* had to work for a living. In the end we compromised. I carried on my paper round, but not in my blazer.

I remember lots of nasty things about that school. My parents kept a little pottery and ironware shop and all it was was a little wooden shack and we opened the front down on chains and that was the counter, and then we pulled down a shade and set out all the wares, and we lived in a barge on the canal, this tatty old barge. My parents thought they were giving me this terrific education or whatever at St Agnes's. They thought they were doing their best for me. It was £50 a term, so it must have been £150 a year. And that was a lot of money then. They thought it was very good for me, so they went without a good deal and they lived in this barge and worked hard at their pot and pan business to send me to St Agnes's.

I remember a beastly horrible girl. I can see her now. I was walking down the drive, pushing my bike, I was on my way home. There was this beastly horrible girl with very thin fair hair. It was autumn and the leaves were very crisp and dry and they were rolling along on the ground, making crispy noises.

And this girl said: 'Hm! Isobel Compton,' to her party of cronies – in a voice that everybody could hear. She said: 'Look!' She said. 'She's so darty that even the leaves are blowing away from her.'

I could have wrung her neck. Beast. But I didn't do anything. The time I flew at Anthea over the hat was the only time I ever really got my paddy up. I was solid to look at and solid in every way. Sort of stoical. I looked it as well. It's there in all the photographs of me at that time. I had a pleasant round face and short mousey hair and a fringe, and in these photographs I always had a smile on my face.

Anyhow, here was Miss Marryat, sprinkling a pinch of bonemeal into a goldfish bowl by the window, peeping at me over her right shoulder and saying: 'God is losing his patience with you, Isobel Compton.'

I felt my heart palpitating and my fists bunching up ready to wallop her, but I controlled myself and stared past her at the lawns rolling downwards to the road. It was all surrounded by rhododendrons like a park.

'Isobel,' she said, 'don't you like it here?'

I'd never asked myself that question and for a moment I couldn't grasp what she meant. It was like asking, Don't you like it in England? Don't you like it on this planet? Some horrible things had happened to me at St Agnes's, one of them was happening to me now, but it was what I knew. It was warm and snug. I didn't feel like leaving there. I had friends. Oh, I also had enemies but I at least knew who they were.

I hated the thought of having to face new kinds of beastliness in a strange place. You might think St Agnes's was a frightful place but I'll tell you a strange thing – I liked the school. I loved it, oddly enough. And one thing it did give me – massive self-confidence. You could hardly help it. For five years you had it driven into you that you were the cream of the country's young ladies.

'Isobel? I said don't you like it here?'

I lifted my head quite proudly and looked straight into the hollows where her eyes lay buried and I said: 'Yes, Miss Marryat, I do.'

I knew exactly what I had to do.

'Then if you wish to stay you must learn to conduct yourself like a civilised individual,' she said.

I think she'd forgotten about the cause of it all – the hat.

'Our girls are moulded and groomed to grow into the women who set a standard in our society,' she said. I don't think she actually said, 'As an example to the lower orders.'

So I went down on my knees and I prayed like fury and through my half-screwed eyes I could see Miss Marryat looking – with a sort of pious relish – at my mouth working away silently.

'Oh, God,' I prayed. 'Oh, God, punish this stubborn old woman. Let her teeth drop out and her head grow bald. Let her goldfish choke on their bonemeal. Let the Governors sack her for being drunk. Let her smelly tomcat ravish her and let her have kittens at morning assembly –' and a lot more in that style.

'And God forgive me,' I prayed, 'for taking this easy way out, but praying for forgiveness for the hat would have been more dishonest still, and it was all her fault, and you know it if you know anything at all, which I doubt – yes, which I doubt – so there it is.'

And I stood up and smoothed my skirt down and looked at her as primly as I could; and she came across and shook me by the hand.

'I always knew you had the true makings of a St Agnes's girl,' she said. 'And now we're starting to bring it out.'

# RACHEL BILLINGTON

# *Sammy's Diary*

*January 20th*

My mother watches me. From behind a vase of flowers. I am not making it up. My school is just round the corner from my house and each day we walk past my house to play in a garden at the end of the road. We walk in what my mother calls a crocodile and we call a line. Each day, that is, twice a day she stands by the window and watches me go past. When I was six she used to wave and I used to wave back and point her out to my friends. Now she doesn't wave. She tries to hide and I pretend not to see her and my friends laugh at me and say, 'There she is, spying on you, Sammy.' Why doesn't she stop? After all, I am seven. Or she could go out to lunch. She used to go out to lunch very often – though not as often as she went out to dinner. Now she's in all the time.


*January 24th*

Yesterday I suggested to my mother that she go out to lunch more. She thought it very funny and laughed and gave me a hug. Usually I like it when she laughs and hugs me but this time I felt awkward. I felt like saying why I wanted her to go out but I didn't because I knew she wouldn't understand. She thought I wanted her to have a nice time which is true as well. I'm glad I didn't explain because after the hug she gave me an especially nice tea with treacle tart and ice-cream. She said I could have a friend home. She doesn't know nobody wants to come home with me.

*January 29th*

No luck. She hasn't been out to lunch once. When I asked her again she said, 'I've got a picture to finish,' and looked cross. This time I only got yucky biscuits and left-over rice for tea. I think she behaves differently from other mothers who never stand looking at their sons through windows because she is a painter. After all, it can't be much fun standing by a window watching silly little boys. My new idea is to behave very badly when I pass so that she won't want to watch. My teacher calls it 'showing off' but she doesn't understand my problems. If she notices my mother, she says, 'Oh, Sammy, look who's watching you! Better put your best foot forward!' As if it was a nice thing. Then the other children laugh more, poking me, whispering, 'Better put your best foot forward, Sammy. Which is your best foot, Sammy? I hope you know.' The teachers have definitely made things worse.

*February 3rd*

My mother was called to see my teacher. She is called Miss Storey and I did like her very much. My mother was upset. She talked to my father about it who happened to be at home. Then they both called me in to have a word with them. They were both upset. They asked me why I had crumbled up my biscuit for break and put it into her handbag. I said I didn't like the biscuit. It was yucky. I explained it was my mother's fault for never having nice crisp new biscuits. This made my father very angry. He hit me. I cried. He hit me for crying. So I cried louder. Then my mother felt sorry and took me up to my room away from my father because he was so angry. She sat on my bed and hugged me. It was nice and I very nearly told her why I had put the biscuits into Miss Storey's handbag. It was her fault really for standing at the window. Then I had a hot bath and went to bed early. My father was cross with my mother. I heard them arguing as I fell asleep. My mother said, 'He's only a baby.'

*February 4th*

Yippee! Today my mother wasn't there. Although Tommy who is nearly a year older than me and very good at football still made silly jokes, I felt very pleased. Miss Storey said my

spelling was much improved and my sums were very good.
She thought it was because of her seeing my mother. I didn't
try to explain. I didn't feel so good when I got home because
my mother was in bed. She had a headache and Tommy's
mother who had brought me home said, 'Come home with
me,' and when I wouldn't she got out my tea and put it ready
on the table. My mother's headache was better by bedtime and
she made herself look very pretty for when Daddy got home. I
was very good.

*February 10th*

I am in disgrace. I broke the classroom window. It was an
accident. But nobody believed me. I threw one of my football
boots over my head because I don't like football and the
window was in the way. Miss Storey said I shouldn't have had
them in the classroom and said, 'Can't you even say sorry?'
And when I said, 'It was an accident,' which it was, she was
very cross. I had to go and see the headmaster and the headmaster sent a note to my parents. My father said, 'You are a
degenerate. What you need is a psychiatrist!' And my mother
got cross with him. And I began to cry. In the end they
stopped arguing and agreed I was in disgrace. I only had one
piece of dry bread for tea. I am feeling very empty as I write
this. I may go down to the kitchen when they are in the
drawing-room. I think there was some left-over rice. There
usually is. I forgot to say that my mother has been at the
window every day since that day when she was in bed. Daddy
says she is upset because her painting is not going well. I don't
know why she goes on doing it at all.

*February 14th*

Because of my pocket money going to pay for the broken
window, I can never buy sweets like the other children. They
make fun of me. This morning Daddy left some money on his
desk so I took it. I bought two Rolos, two Mars bars, two
Spangles and some chewing gum. My mother hates me to buy
chewing gum. I got it out in the playground and made everybody jealous. I wouldn't give them any except Catherine who
is little and very nice. I ate so much I felt sick and Miss Storey
let me lie down during sums. I was sorry because I love sums. I

am very good at sums. Better even than Jane and Jane is brilliant!

*February 15th*

My mother still loves me despite everything. Perhaps that's why she watches me. She found the sweet papers in my pocket and I pretended that I had been given the sweets by a friend. But she didn't believe me. I think she knew all along where the money had come from. She said lying was the worst thing of all and if I owned up she would not be half so angry. I said, 'But Daddy will be.' So she said, 'I won't tell Daddy.' So then I told her about the money on the desk and being sick and everything. She was very nice. I love my mother. I drew her a picture of an aeroplane with propellers and six parachutes coming out of the bottom. She liked it very much and we had a very nice time together till Daddy came home. He was very tired and said, 'Sammy still up?' in a cross voice. My mother said, 'It's only half-past seven.' And Daddy went off to get himself a drink. I like wine, but not whisky or gin. Daddy calls Ribena Winebena but I like real wine better. After his drink he was nicer and came when I was in bed and told me a story about bears and the Empire State Building. I'm afraid it will give me nightmares.

*February 20th*

My mother and my father both love me. So does my teacher. Everybody loves me. They keep telling me that. When my father told me last night just as I was falling asleep he said, 'Have I told you that before?' And I said, 'You tell me all the time.' Then he laughed. They seem happier now that they love me so much. I'm not sure if I am. I think they have a plan. But it is nicer. No one shouts at me now even when I break precious objects or scribble on the drawing-room wallpaper or take biscuits without asking. I don't do that much because my mother has been making my best things for tea every day – like ice-cream with melted chocolate and sausages with melted cheese. Usually it revolts her. She says, 'I feel quite revolted,' and puts on a silly face. If I put on a silly face she gets cross. She used to get cross. Now she just turns away for a moment and then speaks in an extra soft voice.

*February 28th*

I've been so busy that I nearly forgot my diary. I've had
someone to tea almost every day or been out. I still don't like
football but Miss Storey says that lots of children don't like
sums which I love and you can't expect to like everything. I
like other things too. I'm nearly the best reader in my class and
the absolute best at stories when I try. Miss Storey says when I
try no one can do better. I love Miss Storey. She wears red
jumpers up to her chin and when we go to football it matches
her nose. She doesn't wear glasses like my mother which is
nice because I can see her eyes wrinkle when she smiles. She
smiled when I told her about her nose matching the jumper
and said I'd have to think of better compliments than that if I
wanted to be a ladies' man. I think I do. Even when Daddy is
nice he is loud and big and doesn't listen. Before he was nice all
the time he once called me 'A little poof' and Mummy got
very cross. I like ladies best.

*March 11th*

Tommy came to stay in a little cottage in the country we
borrowed for a weekend. We played in the stream all
weekend. Tommy got all his trousers wet and muddy the first
day so he ended up wearing pyjamas as there was no washing
machine and my mother doesn't like washing much. Tommy
and me had a brilliant time. Tommy isn't very clever at school
but he's very good at football and very good at playing. I think
he's very lucky. He has four older brothers and one younger
sister. He loves his younger sister but he pinches her when she
cries. Once I told his mother and she told me not to tell tales. I
love his little sister. She is called Marigold and has golden hair.
On the way back from the country my father gave Tommy
and me a bar of chocolate to share. He said, 'That should keep
you quiet.' But it didn't. We played Messerschmitts and Hur-
ricanes along the back window. It was lucky my father was
being nice or he would have got very cross. As it was when we
dropped Tommy home he said to my mother, 'And to think
you wanted two!' She said, 'Not for my sake. For his.' And
then they realised I was listening and shut up. They don't
realise I have nothing against being an only child.

*March 15th*

Miss Storey says that I should do really well in the exams for my next school. I don't want to go to another school. I won't know anyone. I told my mother but she wouldn't listen. She just said everyone goes to another school and that I wouldn't want to be the only big one left behind. Actually I wouldn't mind. I've been the smallest one so long. My mother is not being as nice as she was. I think it's because she's painting hard. I try and be good and quiet if she's painting when I come home from school. But I like to talk to her. And I'm hungry. Sometimes she forgets tea till it's too late to make anything except bread and butter. And she says she's tired. She often says she's tired. But when I pointed out that she shouldn't paint so hard she said, 'If you're a painter you have to paint.' And I said I painted but I stopped when I was tired which made her cross for a moment. Then she smiled and said, 'You're just like your father,' and gave me a big hug. After all, Daddy must be nicer than he seems.

*March 18th*

I was right. Daddy is nicer than he seems. My mother went away yesterday. To hospital. Just a check up to make sure she's very well. So Daddy's been looking after me. Coming home early from work and that sort of thing. We have a very funny time because he doesn't know how to cook so we are learning together. Yesterday we made the most yucky scrambled eggs which we had to throw away even though we were gigantically hungry after the most brilliant game of football. Daddy says it's all a matter of balance and since my balance is good I'll manage very well in the end once I get my kicking and tackling better. We both laughed when he reminded me how at the Sports Day last year when I was last in everything, Mummy said I would have won if the race had been longer. We both laughed so much that we had to fall on to the grass and roll around. I never laugh quite like that with my mother. I suppose it's because she wears a skirt and earrings. I'm glad I'm a boy. I forgot to say that after we laughed, Daddy was sad till the scrambled eggs.

*March 19th*

Daddy is nice but I can't help missing Mummy, I woke in the night last night. I went in to Daddy who was very nice about it and made a joke about a hedgehog because my hair was standing on end but he put me back into bed right away. I lay awake for ages. Well, perhaps not more than a few hours. But I would have liked a biscuit and a drink. This morning I was tired and Miss Storey said, 'What's got into you, Sammy?' when I didn't answer her questions. 'I hope we're not going to start all that trouble again!' She was so sharp that I nearly cried but after break she came to me in the playground and said she was sorry but she was tired and she hoped my mother would be out of hospital soon. Someone must have told her. So I said, 'Tomorrow.' And she said, 'That's good, because we don't want anything to spoil your good work, do we? Not with your exams coming up?' And I said, 'I don't care about exams,' which is true but was a silly thing to say because she cares about them more than anything and she was being nice to me. So I said I was sorry and that I was tired because I hadn't slept very well and that I promised to try hard even at neat writing which I think very boring. So it all ended very happily. The trouble with Miss Storey is that she hasn't got someone like my father to romp around with.

*March 20th*

My mother came back today. I didn't know till I got back home after school because she wasn't standing at the window. She had to lie down. She wouldn't let me hug her properly and Daddy came back like before and we made tea together. But although we burnt six pieces of toast it wasn't so much fun as when we were on our own. I think he did it on purpose to make me laugh. Or perhaps to make my mother laugh. He didn't laugh. After tea it was nice. We played Snakes and Ladders till it was time for my bath, and Daddy and I were both very pleased when my mother won because she hadn't been well. I was quite good about losing although I couldn't help getting cross when I went down the largest snake just three points before winning. At least I didn't cry like I used to when I was six. Daddy put me to bed and when he was telling me a story he said, 'It is nice to be altogether, isn't it?' And I said, 'Yes.' Because it is.

## March 22nd
A very nice time. Daddy has been in for two nights in a row. Mummy has started painting again but not for half so long.

## March 23rd
My mother's started to do a sketch of me. A sketch is a picture you do before you do a real painting. She wants to do a real oil painting afterwards. She said if I pass my exams she'll buy me an oil painting set for myself. It was boring sitting still for the sketch and even when I thought I was glued to the chair she kept saying my head was jogging or my nose twitching or something. We got quite giggly in the end. While we were giggling I suddenly thought of something and said before I could stop myself 'Is that why you watch me through the window?' She went very quiet and sort of white though she's always nearly white now. I felt myself going bright red like the girls do at school if you say 'milk, lemonade, chocolate'. You know the sort of thing. She said, 'What window?' But she knew. So I said to explain what I meant, 'To know what I look like for the painting. I suppose that's why you watch me.' Because I didn't think it was spying any more. So she said, 'I didn't think you noticed.' And I said that I did and if I promised to keep stone still whenever she wanted would she promise not to watch me any more because it made the other boys tease me. And I was so pleased to have told her that I didn't notice how upset she was for a moment or two. It was horrible. There were tears in her eyes. I said, 'Please don't cry. Of course you can watch me if you want.' And she tried not to cry and said, 'Of course I won't watch you.' And, 'I'm only crying because I'm not very well.' And luckily Daddy came in then and made her better. I was glad to see Daddy.

## March 28th
End of school. Yippee! I've got to do some work in the holidays because of these silly exams but it's easy peasy! Tomorrow I'm going to stay with Tommy's family for a week in Dorset. They have a big house near a lake and one of

Tommy's older brothers has a yacht which we're allowed to go in on condition we wear life-jackets. They are bright orange and tie up with string. My mother is packing me a special case with zip pockets. She is putting in plenty of clothes in case we get wet and my special blanket I still like at night though I don't have it put over my face any more. She says if I'm lonely I can ring her up but she doesn't expect I will be as I'm going to sleep in Tommy's room and we may even share a tent! She's taking me to Tommy's house in a taxi because she doesn't feel like driving, but she says that when I come back she'll be fighting fit because she'll have had a week with no one except my father to look after and he's out all day and only likes steak and salad in the evening because he's on a new diet. Daddy gave me 50p before he went to work because he said my report was better than he expected. He read me a bit which said, 'Despite teething troubles and a childish tendency to egocentric incivility Sammy has made great progress in all fields except sport.' I said that sport was the only thing carried out in a field and what did 'a childish tendency to egocentric incivility' mean? To which he replied, 'Being too clever by half like you've just been.' But he was quite jolly and gave me the 50p so I think he was pleased really. I am not going to take this diary to Tommy's because he might look at it and it's PRIVATE.

*April 7th*
I'm feeling very sick. I got back from Tommy's in time for Easter and have just finished my third Easter egg. It's the only time I'm allowed to eat as much chocolate as I like, but I wish I hadn't. It would have been more fun if there'd been more children around. Not just me. At Tommy's they were going to have an Easter Egg hunt. We couldn't have anyone in because my mother still isn't very well. My mother and my father were very pleased to see me when I got back but when I ate all those eggs they were revolted. Daddy said, 'You are a disgusting little pig. I'd forgotten what a disgusting little pig you were.' And my mother who was lying on the sofa said, 'Please, Lawrence,' (which is his name), 'let's have a lovely time,' and he said, 'How can I when your son's so revolting?' And then my mother went to bed. Then I went to bed and

now I'm trying not to be sick. I wish I hadn't come back from Tommy's.

## April 9th

Because it was Easter, Daddy had a day off work and he took me on the river Thames. A boat took us from Westminster near the Houses of Parliament to Kew Gardens. The Gardens were boring but we had a very big tea with as many buns as I could eat. A lady came with long hair. She was quite nice. Daddy said something about my mother not being very well but mostly they talked about plants or in French which is very rude and what grownups do when they don't want children to understand. When we got home, Daddy said I wasn't to say we'd had tea already in case Mummy had made something. And not to mention the lady either. I didn't mind because I'm always hungry and Mummy had made a huge pile of pancakes which is my best thing. Daddy tossed them and one hit the ceiling and we all got very silly. Mummy went to bed before me because she was tired. Next week we are going down to the cottage we went to before. I'm looking forward to that.

## April 15th

It isn't as nice here as it was before. I haven't got anyone to play with. Mummy isn't well enough to look after another's 'noisy little boy'. That's what Daddy said. It's not fair. My only friend is a Bishop. He lives in a barn at the bottom of a hill. He is brilliant and walks with a stick. He let me play in the church, but when Mummy found me doing a sermon with the light on and everything she was very cross. So I said, 'The Bishop said I could,' and then she wasn't so cross and she even smiled which is quite unusual these days. It is nice being with her all the time but I do get bored. Also she has started watching me again. Sometimes through the window when I'm out in the garden or sometimes when I'm in the same room, eating or something. I said, 'Do you want to sketch me?' as a hint. But she said, 'Not today, darling.' Actually she doesn't do much painting any more. I think she needs something to do. She sits about doing nothing a lot of the time. Just like the way that she used to hate when I did it. Sometimes I occupy her with a game of Snakes and Ladders. I asked her to teach me Chess but she won't concentrate. Perhaps it'll be better when Daddy comes tomorrow.

*April 16th*

Daddy hit me. I hate him. I said I was bored stiff and why couldn't I go back to stay with Tommy and then he hit me. Afterwards he shouted that I'd always been a mother's boy and now I had my mother all to myself why couldn't I get on with it and enjoy myself. Mother began to cry and he shouted, 'Now look what you've done!' which was very unfair because she didn't cry when I complained only when he hit me and began to shout. I hate to see my mother cry. I ran away into the garden for hours and I've only just sneaked back upstairs. It's quiet downstairs so I expect it's all right but I'm not going down again.

*April 17th*

After I finished writing yesterday Daddy came up and was very sorry. I was too. I didn't dare ask about Mummy. Then he said, 'Your mother's gone to bed so why don't you go in and kiss her goodnight just before you go to sleep?' So I did. And she looked not very well. But I got into bed with her and she gave me a lovely big hug like when I was smaller. And I said I wished I could sleep in her bed. And she said, 'There wouldn't be room for Daddy.' And I said, 'That doesn't really matter. He can always find somewhere else to sleep.' And she looked sad but she wouldn't let me stay. I love my mother but I wish she'd be like other people's mothers. Before she used to be painting all the time and never have any time for me and now she's not well enough to play with me. Tommy's mother does all sorts of things with her children – like climbing hills or baking cakes or making parachutes. That's what I call a real mother. Today my mother spent the whole day in bed.

*April 20th*

We are back in London and I start school tomorrow. Daddy drove us back. He is not a bad sort of father. He has bought me a cricket bat from Harrods and introduced me to the Green Cross Man. That'll show them at school. He helped me with the work I had to do too. At Harrods we met the woman with long hair – she's more a girl really. Daddy said something about tragedy but I don't know what he meant. They talked some more French. They both looked very sad. I'm fed up of people looking sad. I didn't think I would look forward to school but I am.

*April 27th*
Very busy one way and another. What with lessons, cricket, swimming, going out to tea with Tommy and David and Catherine. My mother has a smashing tea whenever I'm home which is very nice and she always sits with me whatever I want to do. Yesterday she helped me make a model aeroplane. I was better at it than her but it was great fun. I have decided not to worry about her watching me from the window this term because it's horrid being ill all the time. Miss Storey knows about her being ill and says I must be very good. I am trying but unfortunately I broke one of her favourite earrings yesterday. I was using it to do up my shirt. But she wasn't at all cross and said she had got bored of it anyway. I told her I didn't mind if she watched me from the window.

*April 30th*
Mummy started on the painting of me which is nice for her. Daddy said she is feeling a bit better but I think her face looks funny. Round and puffed-up looking. Not at all like it used to. I told this to Daddy but he said I wasn't to tell her so I won't. Daddy doesn't come back early any more so when Mummy's tired I go out to tea. David's got a new model train set he was given for his birthday. He lets me work the signals. The whole class went to his party and there was a film show of Laurel and Hardy. Grownups love Laurel and Hardy but I only like the bit when he throws nails under the enemy soldiers who dance around like mad because they've got bare feet. My birthday's not for ages – Worse Luck!

*May 4th*
My mother told me a story about a little boy who had no one to look after him tonight. I wish she hadn't. It made me very sad. It made her very sad too. I thought she was going to cry but luckily she didn't. Instead she asked me whether all my

friends had two parents. So I said Justin's mother was divorced but he still had two although he lived with his mother. And Catherine's mother is separated which means not quite divorced but she still has two. Did she mean that? So my mother said, 'Not exactly. Had any of their parents died?' So I said 'Of course not. They're much too young. People don't die unless they're old or get run over. And they're not silly enough to get run over.' Anyway that seemed to cheer her up. And she said, 'Quite right, darling. You do have a silly mother.' And then I read her a much nicer story about a car which turned into a tank and then into a boat and she thought I was very clever. She said, 'You are clever, my darling. I am proud of you.' I love my mother. I hope she never dies.

*May 11th*
My mother went into hospital again. Only for a night. But Daddy went with her so a woman I didn't know came and looked after me. I hated her. She was a liar. She kept telling lies about my mother. About how ill she was. I threw a fork at her and tipped the baked beans she'd made for me on the floor. Then I threw her handbag out of the window. When Daddy came back he was very angry with me and said, 'Couldn't I for once try and behave like a reasonable human being. Can't you see how worried I am about your mother!' So then I shouted at him and he hit me in front of the horrid woman. So then I went to my exercise books and tore out all the pages and tore them up. Daddy wasn't looking because he was giving money to the horrid woman. Now I'm in my room and I'm frightened to go to school tomorrow. I've hidden the exercise books so Daddy won't find them but I don't dare face Miss Storey. I can hear Daddy coming up the stairs again.

*May 20th*
Everything was so horrid that I gave up my diary for a bit. But now it is better. I am working hard. My mother is back and painting. Daddy is at work most of the time. Mummy still looks funny but I'm getting used to it. Perhaps it is just because she is getting older. I forgot to say that Miss Storey forgave me for the exercise books because Daddy found them in the night and we both went to her and said sorry. Daddy says it's very

important that I pass my exams so I can go to a good school with nice boys, though I don't see why. I might be a painter. My mother has nearly finished the picture of me. She hasn't let Daddy or me see it. Sometimes she is very energetic now but usually she isn't. Other people's mothers sometimes look at me in the same way my mother looks at me. I wonder if there is something wrong with me. Perhaps I have an incurable disease. Justin knows a lot about incurable diseases because his father is a doctor.

*May 31st*
Justin's father is a specialist. I wish he would look after my mother. I have not been working hard and Miss Storey is cross. My mother is in hospital again. She has been there for three nights. The long-haired girl has been looking after me. She is nice. She is sleeping in Daddy's study. It is funny having another lady living in the house. She is much keener on my cleaning my teeth than Mummy is. She makes me brush my hair too and do my homework. I would like to visit my mother in hospital but when I said so to Daddy he said, 'She isn't well enough.' I didn't ask again. Tommy asked me over to play with his new Action Man Commando but I didn't feel like it. When Mummy went into hospital she gave me a little sketch she'd done of herself in the mirror. It's very clever. It looks just like she did before she went puffy. I have put it under my pillow for the present. But I may get a frame for it. Or even make one. We're starting to learn carpentry at school and it would make a brilliant surprise for her when she comes out.

*June 3rd*
My mother is dead. She died peacefully in her sleep. There is a funeral the day after tomorrow but Daddy doesn't think I should go. I am not going on with this diary. I don't think I like diaries any more. I'll put it away with the picture of my mother. I might even bury them together. When I get to my new school I won't tell anyone about my mother. I'll pretend I never had one. I won't tell them about the diary either. Good-bye.

# STAN BARSTOW

# *Huby Falling*

I was at school with Clifford Huby. He must be the most
famous product of an establishment not given to turning out
celebrities or even fitting its sons for much in the way of
material success. Huby managed it on both counts: the wealth
through a business acumen none of us knew he possessed and
the fame through a taste for high living and a second wife who
had taken off most of her clothes in a couple of minor films and
whose breasts photographed well in a wet swimsuit on the
deck of a yacht off the Côte d'Azur. Now notoriety . . .

We were the intake of '39, entering grammar school in the
September that war broke out, most of us scholarship boys
from working-class and lower middle-class homes, with just a
few fee-paying pupils among us, of whom Huby was one. I
can't remember what Huby's father did; he wasn't a manual
worker like the fathers of most of us but neither was he very
well-off or he would surely have sent his son to one of the two
or three snobbier schools in the district, which had better
reputations and a bigger share of scholarships to Oxford and
Cambridge.

Huby was never in my set, whose activities often bordered
on, and occasionally slipped over into, the criminal. Eddie
Duncalf, who the last I heard of him, was driving a lorry, once
went to a party at Huby's house and reported that the guests
were mostly boys from the schools I've mentioned and their
stand-offish sisters. I gathered that Huby's family had solid
connections. But secondary education in those days was
limited to the bright and those who had cash to compensate for

their dullness; forms were small, and everyone knew everyone else.

Scholastically, Huby was a plodding middleweight; personally, he wasn't widely liked. He displayed a curious tactlessness in his relationships which irritated some to the point of cursing him, and there were instances of reckless behaviour which endangered not only himself but others. Yet he was not considered a brave lad. I can't, for instance, recall his ever fighting a boy his own size, but it was not unknown for him to bully someone smaller in a manner not so much viciously brutal as foolishly gleeful. 'You don't know your own strength, Huby, you daft bugger!' Well, he found out. And some of us had already found his soft centre.

Our headmaster was Dr Heathcote Jefferies, a fiery little jumping-cracker of a man whose voice when he was enraged — and he often was — could be heard half-way through the long corridors of the school. A stern disciplinarian, and remorseless pursuer of malefactors, he gave weekly addresses in assembly, remonstrating with us about our patriotic duty, which was to refrain from sabotaging the war effort by slacking, smoking, declining to disturb the brilliantined perfection of our hair by wearing the school cap, and chatting-up the girls from the nearby high school at the bus stop. Jefferies had four sons: one had studied law, another medicine; there was one in the church and one still at Cambridge. We never knew his real opinion of us — it was usually expressed in tones of blistering contempt — but we were not the stuff such achievement is made of, though we did eventually manage a parson and a handful of school-teachers on top of the foundations of clerks and mechanics. Oh, and a couple of town councillors, one of whom once fought a general election for the Tories in a solidly-based Labour constituency.

And, of course, Huby.

I realise now the foreboding that must have gripped the minds of our elders on many occasions during those first years of the war: the withdrawal of the shattered B.E.F. through Dunkirk and the anxious waiting for the Germans to invade; the savage bombing of our cities; the overrunning of Burma and Malaya by the Japanese; the movement of the Desert Army to and fro along the northern coast of Africa in an alternation of victory and defeat which seemed always to land them back where they'd started from. But to us it was all rather remote; whatever fears possessed our grown-ups, either they hid them well or we discounted them. It seemed inconceivable to us that we could possibly lose. Some of us had fathers or brothers away in the forces, which brought it a little nearer home; there were evacuees among us who spoke of destruction rained from the skies, in queer southern accents which we cruelly mocked. And uniforms everywhere, austerity, rationing, the blackout. But either morale remained remarkably high or we deplorably insensitive.

To us, young and adaptable, conditions on the Home Front rapidly became those of normal life. Food rationing gave some of us a better diet than our parents' choice and limited means would have obtained in an open market. The blacked-out nights cloaked our after-school activities. What *did* we do during those long dark evenings when no glimmer of light broke the façades of houses, when you could not tell if a shop was open or shut till you'd tried the door and stepped round the heavy entrance curtain, when elderly women stepped carefully along by the sparse glow from blinkered torches, armed with hat-pin and pepper for defence against the known enemy or that masquerading as daytime friend?

We went to the cinema as often as our funds allowed, acquiring an encyclopaedic knowledge of the Hollywood films of the period; but there were hardly any school societies and no youth clubs except the religion-tainted groups run by the local churches, which we were at pains to avoid. So we must often have been bored and in this boredom we sought and found the excitement of petty crime. But we were never apprehended by anyone vengeful enough to make an example of us, and the taint did not spread over into adult life. At least, so far as I know. One or two of those adolescent rogues standing where Huby is would tempt me to hindsight and the smug satisfaction of having seen it coming all those years ago. But Huby was not in our gang.

So it was the years of peacetime childhood which became the cloistered fantasy to be left behind, and these abnormal years through which we grew, the real world. A core of staff too old for military service held the fort among the comings and goings of men conscripted and released. We moved steadily up the school, some of us consolidating our position, others inexorably losing ground as we frittered away the advantage our County Minor Scholarships had given us in a society preponderantly made up of those doomed to leave school at fourteen for a life dominated by hourly wage-rates and the time-clock. A changing awareness of the girls down the road brought vanity, which was expressed by a facsimile of adult smartness, in pressed trousers, polished shoes and slickly-parted hair. There was no such creature as a teenager then: adolescents were adults in embryo. A great many adults were idiots but you emulated the best of them and envied them their racier enjoyments which you could indulge in only furtively. Not that we were a depraved lot. Far from it. The greater part of our time was spent with the ordinary pursuits of boyhood. But we sampled experiences like smoking, gambling and fondling girls in the shelter of long grass or the darkness of ginnels with the curiosity and awakening appetite of anyone growing through one stage of life into another which seems more pleasureful and exciting.

There had been a fire-watching duty since early 1940: a master and three senior boys sleeping in school every night – the master in the staff-room, the lads on camp-beds in an attic in the old building. They were supposed to patrol the grounds during an air raid and tackle any fires with stirrup-pumps until help arrived. We'd had in the early days a stick of incendiaries fall in the sports field and another across the roof of a nearby factory; but by the time our year was senior enough to join the rota the blitz was long over and the bombing being carried by Allied planes to enemy targets on the mainland of Europe.

The duty was voluntary, but most of us did it for the novelty of sleeping away from home and being in school but outside the discipline of the timetable. We read and yarned, played cards, had a dartboard until too many wild shots pitted the door with holes and it was taken away from us. Some of us smoked, too; always with an ear cocked for footsteps on the bare steps and a paper ready with which to waft the incriminating fug out of the window. It was an adventure and our activities, though some in violation of school rules, were innocent enough. Until I did a duty with Eddie Duncalf.

I became aware in the early hours of the morning that Eddie was not in the room. He was absent for some time. The next day I asked him where he'd been. He grinned.

It turned out – and I was not the only one who knew about it – that Eddie had somehow obtained keys which gave him access to the pantry in the kitchen and the store cupboards there. From them he was helping himself to small amounts of the foodstuffs used in making school meals: butter, sugar, cheese, tinned meat – anything, in fact, which was scarce or rationed.

I went with him once, but creeping along those dark corridors in the night, expecting at every corner to bump into the master in charge, was too much for my nerves. I could never fathom anyway what Eddie did with the stuff. There was not enough for him to trade in the black market, even if he had the contacts; and I couldn't imagine his mother accepting it without explanation. I could only assume he hid it and concocted treats for himself when he was alone in the house.

He made his last raid on a night when Huby was sharing the duty with us. As Eddie crept from the room and down the stairs, Huby spoke across the distance between our beds.

'He's a fool.'

'What?' I responded drowsily.

'Duncalf. He'll get nabbed one of these times.'

'What d'you mean?'

'Don't make out you don't know.'

I snored gently into the darkness.

But Huby was to be proved right – or partly so, for although Eddie was not caught in the act the outcome was the same. The cook had apparently known for some time that pilfering was taking place. This particular week she had taken an extra-careful inventory and when Eddie overreached himself and stole more than usual she was able to pinpoint the losses with accuracy. There was an inquiry among the kitchen staff. No culprit could be found there. Then a cleaner remembered seeing currants and raisins on the floor of the fire-watching room. Heathcote Jefferies questioned the masters first, then summoned to his study all the lads on that week's fire-watching roster.

We lined up in an arc across the front of his desk, jostling shoulder to shoulder in the confined space. Jefferies, at the window, waited till we'd settled before spinning round and reaching for a list of names. He checked us off against this without speaking, then took his stance at one end of the mantelshelf.

'There's been some stealing from the pantry.' His gaze raked across the line of faces. 'The culprit is someone who has been on fire-watching duty this week.'

No one spoke. Jefferies must already have selected the likelier suspects, for there were among us some members of swot's corner who would no more have robbed the pantry than smoke a cigarette or fail to do their homework diligently. Tolson, Lindsay and Carter did duty together and were standing at one end of the line. Jefferies began with them.

'Did you steal from the pantry?'
'No, sir.'
'Did you steal from the pantry?'
'No, sir.'
'Carter, did you steal from the pantry?'
'No, sir.'
'Did you steal from the pantry?'
'Oh, no, sir.' This was Billy Morrison, a good lad, who knew about Eddie but would never have dreamed of giving him away.

Jefferies paused here and changed his tactics.

'Do any of you boys know who did steal from the pantry?'

This was one of Jefferies' least likeable traits, his inviting you to shop someone else. Morrison spoke for all of us. 'No, sir.' I thought afterwards that it was a trick of the light, but I wanted to believe that his lip did visibly curl and that Jefferies noticed it.

Jefferies returned to the direct question.

'Did you steal from the pantry?'
'No, sir.'
'No, sir.'
'No, sir.'
'No, sir.'
'No, sir.'
Eddie: 'No, sir.'

'No, sir,' Me.

A stonewall defence. He couldn't break it. He had come to Huby, who was last in line.

'Did *you* steal from the pantry, Huby?'

'No, sir.'

We were through.

But Jefferies, stuck with all those monosyllabic denials, let his gaze linger on Huby for another couple of seconds. And Huby, unable to make do with that simple and unbreakable 'no', rushed in and sank the boat.

'I was in the room, sir.'

Jefferies pounced. 'Which room?'

'The fire-watching room.'

'How do you know?'

'I don't know what you mean, sir.'

'How do you know you were in the fire-watching room?'

'I was, sir.'

'You mean it couldn't have been you who broke into the pantry because you were in the fire-watching room at the time?'

'Yes, sir. I mean no, sir.'

'So if you didn't do it it must have been someone who was on duty with you. Eh?'

'No, sir.'

'But you've just told me that it happened while you were on duty, but it wasn't you because you were in the fire-watching room.'

'No, sir.'

'So you weren't in the fire-watching room?'

'I was, sir.'

'At the time the pantry was being burgled.'

It was no longer a question but a statement. Huby floundered. He went red. His mouth trembled. He was lost.

'Yes, sir.'

Duncalf came back to the form room alone twenty minutes later, beaten and angry, and with a threat of expulsion hanging over him which, as it happened, was never carried out. 'You absolute bloody blithering idiot, Huby. If you aren't the most useless sod I've ever met.'

But he wasn't, as he was not many years in showing.

It was working for the press that kept me in touch with Huby's early fortunes and made me aware of him again when he really started to rise into the big time. I ran into him now and then before I moved to a provincial evening paper from the local weekly. He was clerking for an uncle, marking time before he went off to do his national service. When he came back he began to do small deals in scrap metal and before long he'd branched out into war surplus materials. He made quite a bit of money, married a girl from the town and moved into a new, detached four-bedroomed house.

Then I lost sight of him until, subbing on a national daily in Fleet Street, I began to see news pars about him and, when his first wife divorced him and he married a girl fifteen years younger than himself, the occasional photograph. By this time he was going up fast; everything he touched seemed to prosper. His interests were widespread: mail order, unit furniture, domestic appliances. I don't know what quality he discovered in himself and nourished so successfully that he became a millionaire before he was forty, because, frankly, I don't understand that kind of talent. It was the business editor who ran through the list of Huby's interests for me and who later, aware now that I'd known him once, warned me of the whispers which preceded the investigation into his affairs and the eventual bringing of charges. Issuing a fraudulent prospectus is one of them, and facing the music with him are a couple of fellow directors and the secretary of one of his companies. I don't know, of course, whether Huby is guilty or not, whether his substance is solid or just a bubble blown by him or his colleagues; but a number of offences do seem to have been committed and it looks as though the real issue is who is going to carry the can?

What I'm wondering now is whether Mr Heathcote Jefferies Jr Q.C., who is to open for the Crown, is as good an interrogator as his father was, seizing on any tiny slip to force with the ruthless sharpness of his mind and the overwhelming power of his personality a breach in a solid wall of falsehood.

Does he know that Huby was one of his father's pupils years ago? Probably not, and it doesn't matter. The old man had no doubt forgotten the incident long before he died.

But I know what I'd be feeling if I were in the dock with Huby tomorrow, aware that the penalty this time will not be six of the best but more like a year or two inside and a paralysing fine. And waiting – oh, the sweaty-palmed, stomach-fluttering waiting – for Huby to be offered and succumb to that fatal temptation to enlarge.

# BARRY DAVIS

# *Going Home*

It all looked much smaller and shabbier than I remembered. From the top of Station Parade I could see the town spread out below, grey and rather blurred in the fierce heat haze; punctuated here and there by the belching chimneys of the cement factories. It's a flat place. Only the station and the bleak cemetery occupy the single hill which protects them from the frequent danger of flood water. Down in the marshes the little Norman church and the few remaining buildings of the original old Kentish market town lay scattered like a handful of children's bricks lost in the grass. As I waited for the taxi to take me home the old schoolyard rhyme ran through my head. 'A dirty town with dirty people. Bury their dead above their steeple.'

The fact that it lies below sea level and close to the broad reaches of the lower Thames makes it easy prey to the winds that sweep in off the estuary. The straggling line of poplars along the sea wall offers scant protection in the winter and none at all in the summer. Today they just stood there sadly collecting the fine cement dust that rained down from the hot, still air. Oddly, I had forgotten the dust yet it is the most distinctive feature of the town, outlining the grimy streets and monotonous new architecture with soft grey brush strokes, giving the whole landscape a matt, sterile quality. A corpse seen through chiffon. A cement shroud. The images of death multiplied in the lifeless air, self-conscious and formally phrased. They formed a barrier between me and what was waiting down there at the foot of the hill. The wait for the taxi seemed endless. My shoulderblades and armpits already felt unpleasantly damp and the new white shirt felt tight at the neck. I suppose that really I should have bought a new suit but the careful peasant in me wouldn't permit the expense. I had only worn the old one half a dozen times. Christmas, christenings and interviews had been the pattern of my formal appearance. It was far too heavy for this sort of weather; but appearances count for more than comfort when you are going to a funeral.

The back of the taxi was like an oven and smelled strongly of hot leather and the last occupant. The window seemed to be permanently fastened so I sat and sweated. It was only ten minutes to my mother's house, not worth making a fuss. We took the river road and I looked out over the estuary. It was the only part of the landscape that I remembered with any pleasure at all and that had been well over ten years ago. Then I would walk the sea wall for miles or sit studying the strings of laden barges that laboured upstream towards the Pool of London, cutting through the swell of the oil tankers with a heavy sullen air, like over-fed and listless children being dragged along by an energetic little nanny. It was *Great Expectations* country, leaden and flat. To a young imagination the thin mist often concealed prison hulks and lurking convicts, hunted like clanking animals in the grey mud of the marshes.

At weekends, in the summer, it was often possible to see the large pleasure boats, gliding down towards Southend or Margate. Across the wide stretch of water it was impossible to pick out in detail the 'kiss-me-quick' hats and transistor radios nor see the returning decks awash with brown ale and adolescent vomit. All that registered from my stretch of shore was the Mississippi elegance of the great paddle wheels churning the river into a yellow froth. The details of the picture were only filled in years later when my father used to take me bird watching. His large and powerful binoculars destroyed a lot of romance and *Huckleberry Finn* and *Showboat* were never quite as magic again after that. But a new excitement and envy took their place because the powerful lenses often brought new worlds into my focus. Trim white yachts with pristine sails making their way down towards the sea on the ebb tide. On the cabin roofs often reclined the sort of figures of which

young fantasies and popular fiction were made. Blazers and
flannels with a knife sharp crease, silk cravats and wind-tossed
curls, ice-cubes chinking in long glasses in the cockpit, the
setting sun bringing out all the lustre of tequilla and bourbon
and daiquiris swimming in passion fruit and banana. My
evenings at the Odeon had not been wasted and the inside of
my head was only too familiar with a life-style which even
then I lusted after but which was to dance always, remote and
unattainable in the wake of those little yachts bound for Mad-
rid, Monaco, or the Costa del Sol. The names had a life and
resonance in the river air which they never held in the geog-
raphy books. They promised exotic but, to my young mind,
slightly hazy promises of sun, clean linen and above all, clean
air. That particular bend in the river always represented the
escape route to other places and I would often come and gaze
down its length to the long, thin line where it met the sea. In
the other direction were the oil-soaked mud flats abandoned
by the falling tide and the gaunt pylons that brought the power
to the chalk quarries. Like crosses in no-man's-land they
marked the places where progress had raped the top soil to
feed the cement factories and left the open wounds scarring the
countryside. The raw, broken ugliness of it all was offensive
and I was glad when the taxi turned away from the view and
started to thread its way through the narrow streets of the
estate on which I had been born.

In the small front room over the shop the atmosphere was
muted. My mother and brother looked strained and uncomfortable in their black clothes. The only other relative was a
second cousin and his wife. Less mindful of convention they
had contented themselves with black arm-bands and mournful expressions. Outside in the street the neighbours' curtains
twitched with increasing frequency as the hour of the funeral
approached. Every gesture we had made, car, coffin, the
family wreath, would be assessed. Even in death one was
expected to keep one's end up.

My mother's red, wet eyes were difficult to avoid. I wanted
to talk to her but found it difficult, I always had. Unable to
contribute to the subdued buzz of clichés about a merciful
release and an end to suffering, I lapsed into a moody silence. I
was expected to talk and I couldn't nor could I relax in the

upright clasp of the armchair in which nobody but my father had ever sat. It belonged to the head of the house and I was aware of my mother's eyes upon me as my body rejected it. It was the symbol of her offer and even by sitting there I knew I had stirred hopes in her heart that I had no intention of fulfilling. The thought of coming back and taking up the reins of the small printing business that she and dad had run for so many years appalled me. I had hated that endless chain of small crises that had made up our lives; the disaster of the cancelled contract, the elation and celebration over a big run or a repeat order. Dance tickets, jumble sales, football results and embossed notepaper. Letterheads, bills, invoices and the interminable succession of Christmas paper bags. So many of them over the years that it was difficult to know where the rot had set in.

In a way, like the march of the cement factories, progress had put paid to the small jobbing printer. New and sophisticated litho and photographic techniques had slowly eroded the need for the careful pull and push of his slow endeavour, and to compete would have cost a fortune in building and equipment. Instead, my father preferred to slide gently downhill, setting type by hand in the way he loved. A good man to us; an anachronism to the world. The memory of him hung in the room prompting the first stab of real pain. I realised that I missed him. I wanted to tear back the years and say sorry, tear them back to the time when he had seemed like a king to the small boy who trotted after him across the sawdust floor, peering into one shining machine after another. I could still smell the reams of new paper and see the glint of rows of clean type packed into the forme ready for the ink roller. I remembered the excitement of waiting for the first smudgy impression to be pulled off the wet black letters and even today I take great pride in being able to recognise 14 point Ashley or Times New Roman or the squat friendly Bodoni face. Capital letters are still *upper-case* and I am boringly pedantic on the differences between bond and bank paper. As I looked down at my own stubby hands encircling the willow pattern cup I recalled the slim darting fingers of my father as he set the six point lists of football results on a Saturday evening. His intent eyes behind the rimless glasses were never more than nine inches from the work. At the memory I felt clumsy and large in the shabby little room. I saw the reproach in my mother's eyes, but it was no good. I could no more return to all this than fly.

The evening stretched ahead of me, an agony of evasion as my mother pressed me to stay. It would start in small and perfectly reasonable ways; a subtle deference to me in the matter of the estate, my advice would be sought and respected about insurance and mortgage. Then it would be my favourite meal, the cavernous armchair, the ceremonial of my father's inscribed tankard in the saloon bar of the local pub. Later tonight I would be tired. My defences would drop and she would be under them. Why couldn't I take over the firm? Didn't I want to be a craftsman? – I'd always been so good with my hands. I had such a good head for figures.

The first mistake would be to stop saying no and postpone the debate. That would mean staying on a few days; a few days in which I would lose all sense of perspective; in which I would only be able to see the outline of this room and this grey little town. The rest of the world, the future, even next week would cease to exist until it was too late. With some relief I heard the car hoot in the street outside. Assuming a suitable attitude, self-conscious, on parade, I offered an arm to my mother and led her down the stairs past the shrouded printing machines, every one a silent monument to my father. My dad was dead at fifty-five. We had had to borrow to pay for the coffin.

The funeral was a drab affair, just a handful of us gathered round the deep oblong hole in the chalky soil. Ashes to ashes; dust to cement dust. I will never understand the solemnity with which we place someone we love in a polished box, wring the necks of flowers to decorate it and express our last thoughts in phrases that haven't been current for 300 years. There is a quality of grown-ups playing charades to entertain someone who never came to the party yet, beside me, my mother was crying and was quite clearly moved by the whole ceremony. For her the afternoon had both sorrow and meaning. Not for the first time that day I felt a little guilty.

Back in the upstairs room the ritual continued; paste sand-wiches, warm light ale and sweet sherry; anecdotes and even a tentative joke, almost as if we were testing that life, our lives, were still going on. The air of sorrow and abstraction that we had all worn at the graveside seeped away through the walls of the hot little room to disperse somewhere over the mud flats. I couldn't help thinking that the Vikings had something when they pushed a flaming boat out to sea and rejoiced on the shore while it dwindled from sight. That way seemed to have a bit of dignity about it. It was the way that I wish my dad had gone. Songs, poetry and laughter. A few tears in the smoke. For a moment I had a clear image of the old man lying proudly in the prow, gliding among the tugs and paddle steamers of the Thames estuary until he finally took flight with the white winged yachts to a paradise not unlike Monaco or the Costa del Sol.

Eventually we were alone, she and I. Spread out on the table were the snapshots, letters, policies and theatre programmes that had made up their lives together. Here he was in uniform, an unlikely corporal in the West Kents. He'd jogged through it all from Dunkirk to D Day and then come back to set type for the football results on a Saturday evening. There he was, getting married in a trim three-piece suit and a bowler hat; on the beach at Broadstairs; knee-length grey flannel shorts and a grammar school cap. I handled them all very gently as I put them back into the envelope and returned it to the top drawer of the sideboard. Thirty years of their life in a bundle that I could hold in one hand.

We both sat in silence for a long time. I waited but the pressure didn't start, just the occasional quiet comment on my journey back, the time of the train, was there a dining car? Was I going to take a holiday this year? After a while even these gentle questions lapsed. The light in the room faded until she was only a silhouette against the window. I turned on the light but nothing happened.

'It's the fuse,' she said. 'It's gone. Perhaps you'd have a look at it before you go back. You always were the clever one with your hands.' She handed me the fuse wire and the blunt knife that had always done the duty of a screw driver. It might just as well have been a stick of type or an ink roller. I knew I was never going back and I had known it since the train had pulled into the station and I had seen the cement dust again after all those years.

So I mended the fuse, put a washer on the tap and had a drink at the local pub from my father's engraved tankard. As I walked home I took the river road and in the half light I could just make out one of the little white yachts heading for the thin grey line where the river meets the sea.

# BRIAN THOMPSON

# *Bunny on Location*

To have won a prize was not in itself anything very special for Bunny; he was after all, as he only half-humorously put it these days, a Blue Peter Winner in his time. Good for a laugh in a comprehensive school – a self-deprecating laugh, at any rate. He did not tell people that for some years after he sent Biddy Baxter a postcard every time he went on holiday and sometimes (not often, but sometimes), sent her a poem or a drawing.

But there were two things about this particular prize. For one, it was a public speaking prize, and the winner was offered a weekend in Paris. Bunny entered with trepidation and emerged in triumph. The man who shook his hand in congratulation also clapped him heartily on his denimed shoulder and said, quite audibly over the amplification system of the Town Hall, 'If ever I've seen a lad who can benefit from a trip to Paris, it's you!' Bunny's mates burst into spontaneous silence. The innuendo seemed to get them by the throat: a boy from Colditz going to Paris by jet, and then, in their imagination, whoring and drinking his way through Gallic hospitality. And there was more. For, in their opinion, Bunny Tabbet was a wet, and did not deserve so much as a light from the end of a fag.

He was too smart for them, too bookish and allusive. He was marked by some crippling eccentricities, in their way of looking at it. He wanted to be a film director, for one thing. It was possible – indeed it was desirable to want to be a rock singer. But to want to be a film director was over the top,

ridiculous, shaming somehow. It shamed them that anyone
should be so ambitious.

'I don't see why not,' Bunny murmured. 'Everybody starts
somewhere.' It was the wrong remark to make. The school
had produced several rock musicians, from among hundreds
who aspired. It had never once produced a film director.

· 'And I'll tell you why, Tabbet,' Mr Green said comfortably,
'because there isn't any British film industry, and if there
were, cockiness would not be enough to staff it.'

'Well,' Bunny said, 'we can't all be teachers. There have to
be a few film directors.'

Although everybody in the school hated Mr Green, who
was Smart Alec and complacent, for a man of only thirty, they
liked Bunny's answer less. What feeling there was against him
intensified after it was learned that he had won the public
speaking contest and was going to Paris. Even his few mates
wrung their hands.

'Christ, Bunny, you just seem to stroll through it as though
it were your natural right.'

'I *worked* for it,' Bunny said.

'Yes, but Christ.'

'Wouldn't you like to go?'

'I've been,' Honks said quickly.

'Not with the school, you birk. On your own.'

'What's wrong with going with the school?'

'Nothing,' Bunny said with the disconcerted voice he could
hear himself using more and more often as he approached
sixteen. So many of the conversations he had fractured, or
seemed to him to fracture, from sudden fatigue, like a plane's
wing.

For a comprehensive school student, he was, he realised,
pushing his luck. It did not do, not in this school at any rate, to
excel; it did even less to be seen to yearn for something that
was not there, within the school or within the town. What was
not already in the imagination of the community was not
worth having, or belonged to some subtle conspiracy of
wealth and language that was, in some way or another, hate-
ful. It was a school and a town strong on hate and resentment.
Putting it another way, there was little that was serene.

Serene was a word that appealed to Bunny enormously.

When his parents divorced, he took a pride in remaining, through it all, serene. It had meant being jerked out of one school and sent by cattle truck to Colditz; leaving one suburban community where the houses were owned by doctors and lawyers, art lecturers and (as it happened) a film-maker, and plunging into another where the neighbours were the patients and clients and subjects of such people. Well, the answer was to be as cool as you could be under the circumstances, and not to let go of who *you* were. He held both parents in the same cautious esteem, and tried not to judge them too harshly. It made for difficulties with his brother and sister, the divorce, and he was not always sure that he understood the matrimonial causes himself all that clearly; but he assumed they had got what they wanted, and worked on his own inner serenity. A diary helped.

He packed his diary to take to France. On the night before he left, his father rang and wished him luck. The tinny voice at the end of the line always upset him a little, but his father was a sensible sort of bloke and played it all down, asking only for a postcard, and offering only one piece of advice.

'Go to the Place Vosges.'

'Good is it?'

'Give it my love.'

'Special place of yours?'

'Just tell it hello from me.'

The more memorable feature of the flight was the landing at Orly. An unseasonable rain was buffeting the forecourt decorations of a Total garage and darkening the fields and sky behind. Bunny saw it all in a moment of *satori*, of blinding significance, before the plane touched down and stubbed itself out against the wet wind and the emptiness of having finally arrived. The clarity with which he had seen the Total garage compared in his mind with his father's account of flying into Philadelphia over the Navy yards, and seeing ships slotted into dry docks. It was the same experience.

The panic did not hit him until after he had met M Besnard, who made no secret of his disappointment at the appearance of the young public speaking protégé, consternation quickly replaced by a kind of hauteur. Lolloping along after his host, Bunny did catch a glimpse of himself in a reflective surface.

His jeans suit was a touch rumpled, maybe, and his hair was longer than anyone else's in the concourse. He had carried his Man United bag on his shoulder with a certain pride in London, which evaporated in front of M Besnard. The Frenchman ushered him into an Opel and drove off at terrifying speed.

'I had better tell you,' he said in Good English, 'that things are a little inconvenient this weekend. My wife has recently been bereaved, and there are certain other complications.'

'Strewth,' Bunny murmured.

'However, I am sure we will find something for you to do. Do you speak French?'

'Well yes. You know, schoolboy stuff. And holidays.'

'You have been to France on holidays?'

'Les Landes. Brittany. Um, Nantes. Le Golfe de Morbihan.'

'Your parents are rich, then.'

'They're divorced,' Bunny said.

He felt M Besnard look at him sharply.

But the ride into Paris was as nothing to the reception that awaited him chez Besnard. The bereaved wife recoiled a little before suffering her hand to be shaken, her white neck and breast accentuated by little black straps to a frock Bunny could tell was expensive. In the salon of the Besnard household was a complete dinner party of guests, some of them extremely distinguished looking, all of them very slightly startled.

'I must apologise, but some of my friends who wish to meet you cannot speak English,' Madame said.

'He speaks French,' Besnard said shortly.

'Ah, *bon*!'

So far so good.

'Um, look,' Bunny said, 'Mother wanted me to pack a suit, or anyway a blazer and flannels, but I didn't bring anything like that.'

'It doesn't matter. Would you like a sherry?'

'Yes.'

'This is my father, General Basonpier.'

'Oh, hullo.'

He sat down with his glass of sherry and answered a few questions in English and then a great many in French. The General asked him what he knew of French history, a gift, because for some years Bunny had been writing a book, a sort of book anyway, about Napoleon. But the old soldier waved away the idea angrily.

'No, no,' he shouted, 'I am not talking about that.'

'Are you talking about Algeria?' Bunny asked. There was the most abrupt silence, during which Besnard rolled his eyes at his wife, and she stubbed out her cigarette in a violent gesture. It occurred to Bunny, not for the first time, that a good deal of knowledge was a dangerous thing. He began to wonder how he might fare at the meal.

He need not have worried. When it came time to eat he was ushered firmly into the kitchen where a solitary place was set for him.

'I'm afraid we cannot offer you fish and chips,' Besnard said with the insolence of the rich.

'No tomato sauce either?'

But the joke fell flat. He was left to eat chicken *à la Kiev* at the white table, his back uncomfortably to the door. He ate fast, but not so fast that he wasn't interrupted. He expected Besnard back to apologise for not serving roly-poly pudding, but it was not he. A girl about his own age came in and sat down and stared at him. Bunny was too embarrassed for her to speak. She sniffed.

'Do you speak French?'

'A bit.'

'They are all pigs in there. Do you understand what I'm saying?'

'Absolutely.'

'What's that written on your jacket?'

'That's Eric Clapton's address where he was in California.'

'Is he a film star?'

'Strewth,' Bunny said.

She was not very pretty at all. She had a dark, gloomy expression, with downturned lips and a strong neck. Her clothes were not at all personalised, but a uniform he recognised from seeing similar girls on holiday – a white sweater, a grotesque old woman's bra, and a blue skirt. Round her wrist she wore a silver bangle.

'Are you poor?'

'No. How about you?'

'Yes.'

'Really?'

'Oh yes. Madame Besnard is my aunt. My mother has run away.'

'Oh, I see.'

'It's very tragic,' the girl said indolently. 'Will you be staying long?'

'Just tonight.'

'They are going to take you to Versailles tomorrow.'

'I've been,' Bunny said, thinking of Honks back in Colditz.

'Have you a lover?'

Or that's what it sounded like. He looked up from the last of his rice with a cautious expression. The girl smiled for the first time.

'You don't have to tell me. I know you don't have.'

'Oh yes?'

'You are still a baby. They will treat you like shit here.'

'How about you?'

She shrugged.

'Who cares?' she said.

He was about to try out a tricky conditional (*if you were seriously in trouble, you would not say such a thing*), when the door opened and Madame Besnard swept in, her eyes fierce and glittering, and Bunny thought, *un peu dérangé*. She made no preambles but stood over him like a conductor on a bus when he realises you've had a skinful.

'My husband thinks you must be tired from your journey and suggests you go to your room. You will find a television there.'

'Well,' Bunny said, in the pretence of choice.

'*Allez vite,*' the lady of the house said.

If he thought he had seen the last of the young girl he was mistaken there. No sooner had he set down his Man United bag and taken out a forbidden cigarette from a packet of Disque Bleue (when in Rome) than there was a timid knock at the door. He knew by its ambiguity it could not belong to any of the adults in the house, who would more probably rap on the woodwork with the butt of a sub-machine-gun. He opened.

'If you listen carefully tonight,' the girl said, 'you will discover this house is full of scandals.'

'*Absoluement!*' Bunny said fervently.

'Don't try to come to my room.'

'Oh bloody hell,' Bunny said in English, and closed the door. He lit his cigarette and studied different ways of smoking it in the mirror of the wardrobe door. The room was large and white and pretty elegant, with an attempt at serenity all right, but with nothing much personal about it. There were for example no books, and when Bunny looked more carefully, no television either. It was half-past nine. *Quelle Blague*, to be in Paris at half-past nine at night and with nothing to do but go to bed. He got out his *Rolling Stone* and read a good piece on Bob Marley and the Rastafarians, only a million light years away from his present condition.

He smoked three cigarettes in a chain, and then took off his Doc Martins and lay down on the bed. The old socks were a bit pongy, and he took them off. In the corner of the room was a wash-basin, and he ran some water and tried to wash his feet one at a time, fascinated by their length. They hardly fitted a French wash-basin, they were so long and white. He dried them on his tartan towel and then got out his diary and made the day's entry:

> Left Heathrow about six. Nun had fit in corridor going twds plane. She was an old woman. A man took off his jacket and put it under her head. Very steep climb out of take-off. At Orly, Total garage. B looks like Oliver Reed. Mrs B tricky to cast. Loonie girl. Had chicken *à la Kiev*. Washed socks.

He had got thus far when there was a knock like a butt of a sub-machine-gun and Besnard came in. Drink had mellowed him slightly.

'You know why you are here? Because I am the reciprocating organiser of the public speaking competition. A young French boy is in London now, you realise. Good. The competition is a good one. But unfortunately, certain circumstances have made your welcome less than warm.'

'Don't worry about that.'

Besnard blinked.

'Tomorrow we shall do better. I cannot tell you what is wrong, you understand, but it is all very unfortunate.'

'I'm enjoying myself,' Bunny lied miserably.

'Tomorrow you will enjoy yourself,' Besnard corrected.

'Oh, great.'

'I will say goodnight.'

'Yes, right.'

Ten past ten. Still, he thought, an early night never did anyone any harm.

He undressed and folded his clothes on to a chair. He had picked up the habit from his father of never wearing clothes in bed; and so, after cleaning his teeth and brushing his hair, he clambered into bed and turned out the light. He played his favourite game, of story boarding a film on the day's events. His current favourite director was Hal Ashby, perhaps because *The Last Detail* was his top ace film of all time. He and Hal ran over the day's rushes. The shot of the Total garage from the air would need to be duplicated from another angle: how about a long, low shot along the empty road, say at dawn, with the bunting and the plastic beach balls yammering and fluttering, a huge landscape shot, mostly grey and green? In time he fell asleep.

He had no idea what time it was when the door opened again. He sat up in bed startled.

'Um, *qui est là?*'

'Be quiet,' Madame Besnard murmured. She fell over his Doc Martins as she approached, but it was far too late to notice things like that. Bunny could tell by her smell that she had come straight from her bath. She sat down on the bed with her back to him, and a soft rustling settled into silence. After a bit, she put her chin in her hands.

'Would you like to smoke?' he asked.

'You're not smoking in bed, are you?' she said, alarmed.

'No, no.'

'Just be quiet, then. How old are you?'

'Sixteen.'

'Are you happy?'

'Happy?'

'Are you serious, then?'

'Oh yes. That, certainly.'

'Will you go to University?'

'Yes. Have you been?'

'No,' Madame said after a pause. 'Of course not.'

'You have a lovely house.'

She brushed the remark aside.

'What is your mother like?'

'Ordinary. You know. She's all right.'

'Your parents. Are they happy?'

'I suppose so. They are now, anyway. Aren't you happy?'

It was one of those conversations.

Madame Besnard stood up, wobbled a bit and faced him in the gloom. She stood with one arm across her breasts, the hand resting on the opposing shoulder.

'Move over,' she said.

'What?'

She threw back the sheets and skipped into bed beside him, seeming not to notice that he was naked, and certainly giving him no pleasure in the fact that she was an undressed woman. It flashed through his mind that it was all a complicated plot, and that the outraged husband would race in after a moment or two and shoot him through the heart. *Crime passionelle*, in fact. Accordingly, he lay very still. Madame lay on her back, twiddling the folds of the sheets between her fingers.

'It's incredible,' she said, referring presumably to some interior monologue. Bunny said nothing. The smell of her talc was too arousing for him to join in a loonie conversation. He twitched his nose. It was talc cut by a sharper scent, of lime. He experimentally sniffed at her hair.

'Have you got a cold?'

'Eh? No. No. I was . . .'

'I hate him,' Madame said.

So that's the game, Bunny thought, alarmed, and at the same time very pleasurably excited.

'Why is that?'

'He's old. And contemptible. You saw it straightaway, a boy from England. You saw it immediately.'

She was, he realised, referring to her father, the General.

'How old is he, exactly?'

'He's disgusting. Guy does nothing. You probably noticed that, too.'

'Your husband.'

'A fool.'

'Oh, yes.'

'And you, a child, nearly walk straight in and see the whole drama. Have you talked to Annie?'

'The girl? In the kitchen.'

'What did you make of her?'

'Nothing much.'

'Ha,' Madame exclaimed, in satisfaction. She rolled on to her hip and pulled him against her, his face against her breasts. With her free hand she stroked his back: but both his hands were trapped by his side, so that he was forced to lie in her arms like a stick of wood. He kissed a bit of her flesh, he had no idea what.

'Be quiet,' she whispered, 'be good.'

And incredibly, he fell asleep. It was the best way to retain serenity, he thought drowsily with his last conscious thought. In the morning, when he woke, she was gone, and only the hair on the pillow was to say she had ever been there in the first place.

One of the conditions of winning the public speaking prize was to write a report to the organising committee to say what you had done with the trip to Paris. When he got back to England, and almost by return of post from the submission of his report, Bunny got a letter saying that his report was the most lucid and entertaining they had ever had the pleasure of reading. Although he did not like to admit it completely, he was hardly surprised at that. He liked writing, he liked reading, and he liked meeting people. Moreover, he wanted to make films. It would have been surprising to have turned in a bad report, therefore.

There were a few things he could not adequately express to the organising committee, like his entry to breakfast on the morning after the night before, or the family farewell given to the mysterious General Basonpier, who made a particular point of wagging his finger in Bunny's face and saying something salty and untranslatable which had the company in stitches. The *rencontre* with the Besnards was simplicity itself. She took his hand briefly and then ignored him for the rest of his stay, and Besnard moderated his scorn on the gain side, and put a bit more treble into it, so that it came out faintly querulous. That was fine by Bunny. As for Annie, she hung about for ages before asking:

'Can I come with you today when they show you round?'

'Oh yes. Of course. Please do.'

The body of his report was an account of the sights they visited, chief of which was, for him, the Père Lachaise, the Place Vosges. It turned out to be a cloistered square, in which Hugo had his house. The day he saw it, it was hot and sunny and dusty, and quite a little bit smelly. Besnard stood him a glass of wine in a café while Madame and the troubled Annie went round the Hugo Museum. Bunny knew that nobody – *nobody* – at Colditz would grasp the significance of the events of the past night, any more than he could truly understand them himself. What he had to offer them himself, he thought, was his serenity, which had survived intact. He thought of his father, and how it was with him when he first clapped eyes on the Place Vosges, and what had gone on in *his* life the night before. He mused over the pigeons pecking in the dust and the violent bars of sunshine crashing down through the stones. When the two women came out of the Hugo Museum he felt like laughing aloud for joy, and satisfaction. Whatever the adult world was, he was beginning to think he could get its number.

From the Place Vosges to making movies was a realisable step away. He could reach out and touch it, he thought, reaching out and accidentally knocking M Besnard's glass and cigarettes from the table.

'Are you mad?' Besnard exploded.

'Sorry about that,' Bunny said serenely.

# PETER TERSON

# The Sad and Sexual
# Blackberry Trip

I never knew how the invite came about. But there we were, going blackberrying with Mr Todd on our bikes. He had a bike that was like himself, well-oiled, sensible, reliable, both brakes working. Mr Todd had hobbies. That was queer. He was the only man on the estate who had hobbies. The other men drank or went to the dogs, or just went OUT, but Mr Todd had hobbies and stayed IN.

He was all hand signals on his bike. No wobble. He had a stick with a nail on the end, tied to his crossbar, for pulling blacker bushers, and he had a tin with a wire handle for putting his pickings in.

Me and John laboured after him on our old Knacks, our ASPs. All Spare Parts. George, who had a touch of the old Mick about him with grown-ups, cycled along with Mr Todd. 'Keeping abreast,' Mr Todd called it. Mr Todd talked. About camping.

'I used to go camping a lot with my boy,' he said, 'he was a good little camper.'

We were a bit embarrassed. His little boy was a man now, or so he seemed to be to us.

'Yes, he used to collect dry bracken to use for a bed,' Mr Todd said. 'You boys go camping?'

We were going this year, we said. We'd just camped in the back garden.

'Always use bracken for beds. Keeps the cold from striking under you. That's what you should do. There's more cold from the ground than from the air, you know.'

'Never, Mr Todd,' said George.

'Oh yes, my boy was a fine camper. There was only one thing he couldn't do at camp. You know what that was? I'll tell you. He couldn't crack eggs in basins and keep them whole. Just couldn't do it.'

George looked round to us and said, 'He couldn't crack eggs in basins.'

'Oh,' we said.

'Couldn't crack eggs in basins,' said Mr Todd. 'He could do everything else, everything else. But he couldn't crack eggs in basins. I could trust him to do any other job, put a tent up, boil water over an open fire, but he could not crack eggs in basins.'

'What a shame,' George said.

We cycled on, out of our usual territory into half-country land of slag heaps and trees, and pits, and black grass. We came to a valley. The valley of blackberries. Pit heaps all about. Old iron. Torn, mangled stuff. But thousands of blackberries. We whooped around and went berserk at the sight of such juicy profusion. We charged and picked like mad things.

Mr Todd silently dismounted sedately. No hurry. Kept his bicycle clips on. Removed his stick with a nail from his cross-bar, then he took off his tin with a wire handle. He also had lots of paper bags.

'Start methodically, boys,' he said. And he started methodically. Picking, picking, picking. No rush. 'More haste, less speed, boys.'

He would pull a bramble branch towards him with his stick with a nail in it, then pick it clean. Immaculate. Then he would let it go. Then when his tin was filled he would empty it into a paper bag and start again.

We rushed about getting scratched to hell and covered in blackberry juice and getting nowhere. Just as you were picking a blacker there was always a better one somewhere else, then when you went for it, it was too far away and you tore your wrists trying to get it. Our carrier bags seemed to take each blacker with a 'ping' instead of a nice full 'plop' like Mr Todd's. We'd never even cover the bottom, let alone fill it. 'Don't be impatient, lads, be methodical, be methodical.'

We got scratched and hot and sick and tired.

'Persevere, boys, persevere.'

George picked with him. We got fed up and sloped off. We hated George for picking so sensibly. We played among the tangles of rails and buckets of pit heaps, wires, cables, all red with rust. We found some railway trucks and played on them. We ate our blackberries.

Then George came, but we wouldn't play with him. He stood between the bumpers of a couple of trucks and said, 'Look, lads, if they moved now I'd be squashed to pulp.'

We weren't taken in.

George wasn't put off so easily. He followed us around. Then when we sat down in the blackberry bushes, in a den, George said, 'Do you know what women do with men?'

We were all ears.

'Women,' said George, 'put their legs round men.'

John was angry. He wouldn't listen. His mother was a huge, fat woman, Roman Catholic, fifteen kids; John was the last of all the lads to believe that women did anything. He was loaded with sexual problems John was, but that's another story.

He said he wasn't listening to that, 'Not about mothers.'

'Oh, not mothers,' George said, 'not mothers. Think I'd be talking about it if it was mothers? Not mothers. Film stars and that.'

All ears again. He held us. All afternoon. Tales of wondrous filth. We sat listening. The sun belted down between the blacker bushes and we were mad hot. George went on, and on, from one vileness to the next. We would crawl to the bushes for a blacker and reach out, never taking our eyes off him. He would only interrupt his conversation with 'Get us one then,' and we would feed him like a great foul thing.

'Do you want to hear about Errol Flynn?' George said.

But it was no good. We were dried up.

'Do you know what Charlie Chaplin did with Paulette Goddard?'

We weren't interested.

Then George said. 'Have you heard about Toddy?'

What? All ears. Go on. Toddy. What about Toddy?

'Not heard about Toddy then? I'll tell you. Pass a blacker then.'

We gave him a handful and he sat with them in cupped hand and said, 'Toddy asked Joan Boiler to take her clothes off.'

'Never!' The estate bonny lass.

'Didn't you know then? Thought everybody knew that.'

'No, we didn't know that.'

We sucked our blacker-stained fingers and got thorns in our tongues. But didn't care.

'On the piano stool.'

No! Them piano lessons. The Boilers WOULD try to be respectable.

'He was giving her piano lessons, you see. And Mrs Todd was out. And he asked Joan to take her clothes off.'

Toddy! 'What happened, George?'

'He was doing this . . . and . . . feeling her . . . Mrs Todd came in.'

'Hooh, Mrs Todd.' No wonder he was picking blackers for her.

'Police came,' George said. 'All hushed up. Now somebody has to stay in the house with Toddy. Mr Boiler has had to buy a piano. Teacher comes to the house.'

We decided to get Toddy. Track him down. We were expert trackers. Like Indians. We blazed trails. In the back gardens. We tracked dogs. We would track Toddy. Inch by inch. On our bellies. Snake-wise. Get near him. We tried to get as disgustingly near as possible. Within touching distance of his home cobbled shoes. We were lying under him. A triumph of tracking. In the blacker bushes. We could near him rustle like a large animal after the blackers. His stick with the nail in came over and took branches towards him. He seemed to know we were there.

'You there, boys? You there?'

Still.

'You lads playing about? Come on now. Pick blackberries. Didn't bring you to play about.'

Lay as dead.

'You playing about or picking blackberries, boys?'

Without breathing.

'You boys playing about? You won't get blackberries that way.'

Like snakes.

'I've filled all my bags . . . boys.'

Not a word from us.

'What you boys doing in there, then? I know you're there. What you doing then?'

At last George said, 'We're breaking eggs in basins.'

'Come on, boys, if you're going to act the fool, it's time to go. And you won't be brought again.'

'We're cracking eggs in basins.'

Mr Todd hurried to gather up his harvest of blackberries and put them in his saddle-bag. Each paper bag was tied with a piece of string. He fixed his stick with a nail on to his crossbar and hung his tin with a wire handle from his saddle and then rode off, saying, 'Come on, boys, you're my responsibility, you know.'

We followed him. Him in front. Us behind.

'You shouldn't cycle three abreast, boys.'

Then with terrific cunning we started saying out loud, 'Seen Joan Boiler recently then, lads?'

'Joan who?'

'Joan Boiler.'

'Boiler, like in a ship?'

'Boiler as in house.'

'As in Boiler House.'

'Oh, Joan Boiler.'

'I thought you meant Joan BOILER.'

'She's a girl who plays the piano very well, I hear.'

'Does she take lessons? This Joan Boiler?'

'Yes. On a piano stool.'

'That Joan Boiler, she has a brother.'

'Yes. He cracks eggs very well in basins.'

Mr Todd seemed to realise we were talking about him and we hurried on to keep up with him. He hurried on. We hurried on. We got breathless with laughing. He was rushing on. Doing his signals. We were hurrying. His tin was banging about. We hurried on. Juice came out of his saddle bag. We shouted. 'Joan Boiler, Joan Boiler. Go home to your hobbies, Toddy. Go crack eggs in basins.'

He whipped up speed. Sitting up. Erect. Till at last we couldn't keep up with him any more and we rolled off our bikes, gasping and laughing in stitches while Mr Todd rode off. Back to his home and his hobbies.

# BERYL BAINBRIDGE

# *Grandma's Central Position*

I never took all that much notice of Grandmother when she
was alive. She was just there. I mean, I saw her at Christmas
and things – I played cards with her to keep her occupied, and
sometimes I let her take me out to tea in a café. She had a
certain style, but the trouble was she didn't look old enough to
be downright eccentric. She wore fur coats mostly and a lot of
jewellery, and hats with flowers flopping over the brim; she
even painted her fingernails red. I was surprised that she'd died
and even more surprised to hear she was over seventy. I didn't
cry or anything. My mother made enough fuss for both of us,
moaning and pulling weird faces. I hadn't realised she was all
that attached to her either. Whenever that advert came on the
telly, the one about, 'Make someone happy this weekend –
give them a telephone call,' Mother rolled her eyes and said
'My God!' When she rang Grandma, Grandma picked up the
receiver and said, 'Hallo, stranger.'

The night before the funeral there were the usual threats
about how I needn't think I was going to wear my jeans and
duffle coat. I didn't argue. She knew perfectly well I was going
to wear them. I don't know why she wastes her breath. In the
morning we had to get up at six o'clock because we were
travelling on the early train from Euston. It was February and
mild, but just as we were sitting down to breakfast Mother
said, 'Oh look, Alice,' and outside the window, snow was
falling on the privet hedge.

When we set off for the station, the pavements were covered
over. Mother had to cling on to the railings in case she slipped

tottering down the steps. The bottom of my jeans were all slushy in no time, so it was just as well she hadn't succeeded in making me wear those ghastly tights and high-heeled shoes.

I thought maybe the trains would be delayed by the snow, but almost before we reached the station it was melting, and when we left London and the suburbs behind, the snow had gone, even from the hedges and the trees. The sky turned blue. I was sorry on my mother's behalf. You can't really have a sad funeral with the sun shining. She looked terrible. She looked like that poster for 'Keep Death off the Road'. She'd borrowed a black coat with a fur collar from the woman next door. She had black stockings and shoes to match. She doesn't wear make-up, like Grandma did, and her mouth seemed to have been cut out of white paper. She never said much either. She didn't keep pointing things out as if I was still at primary school, like she usually does – 'Oh look, Alice, cows . . . Oh Alice, look at the baa lambs.' She just stared out at the flying fields with a forlorn droop to her mouth.

Just as I'm a disappointment to Mother, she'd been a disappointment to Grandma. Only difference is, I couldn't care less. Whenever I have what they call 'problems' at school, I'm sent to the clinic to be understood by some psychologist with a nervous twitch, and he tells me it's perfectly natural to steal from the cloakroom and to cheat at French, and anyway it's all my mother's fault. They didn't have a clinic in Mother's day, so I expect she's riddled with guilt.

Apparently Grandma was very hurt when Mother got married and even more hurt when she got divorced. First Grandma had to go round pretending I was a premature baby and then later, she had to keep her mouth shut about my Dad running off with another woman. She didn't tell anyone about the divorce for three years, not until everybody started doing the same thing, even the people in Grandma's road. Actually, I don't think Grandma was hurt. It was more likely she didn't care for the sound of it.

There were a lot of things Grandma didn't like the sound of, my record player for one, and the mattress in the spare-room for another. If we went down town for tea, she used to peer at the menu outside for ages before making up her mind. It drove Mother wild. 'I don't think we'll stop,' Grandma would say, and Mother would ask irritably, 'Why ever not, Grandma?' and Grandma would toss her head and say firmly, 'I don't like the sound of it.' And off she'd trot down the road, swaying a little under the weight of her fur coat, the rain pattering on the cloth roses on her hat, with me and Mother trailing behind.

Once I went on my own with Grandma to a restaurant on the top floor of a large shopping store. We were going to have a proper meal with chips and bread and butter. The manager came forward to show us where to sit and we began to walk across this huge room to the far side, towards a table half hidden behind a pillar. My mother always moves as if she's anxious to catch a bus, but Grandma took her time. She walked as if she was coming down a flight of stairs in one of those old movies. She looked to right and left, one hand raised slightly and arched at her wrist, as though she dangled a fan. I always thought she was waiting to be recognised by some-body or expecting to be asked to dance. She went slowly past all these tables and then suddenly she stopped and said quite loudly, 'I don't like the sound of it.' She turned and looked at me; her little red mouth quivered the way it did when she'd run out of peppermints or lost at cards. I was sure everybody was looking at us, but I wasn't too embarrassed, not the way I am when Mother shows herself up – after all Grandma had nothing to do with me. The manager stopped too and came back to see what was wrong. 'You're never putting me there?' said Grandma, as though he'd intended sending her to Siberia. She got her own way of course, somewhere more central, as she put it. Grandma settled herself down and took out her cigarette case. When she opened it, it played a little tune. 'I don't like my light being hid under a bushel,' she said.

I wasn't really looking forward to the funeral. I'd been in a church once before and I didn't think much to it. I wasn't the only one either, because the next time I passed it, they'd turned it into a bingo hall. When we were nearly at Liverpool my mother said if I behaved myself I could go to the graveside. 'You mustn't ask damn fool questions,' she warned. 'And you mustn't laugh at the vicar.'

'Are they going to put Grandma in with Grandpa?' I asked. I knew Grandma hadn't liked him when he was alive. She said he was a bounder and a moody old beggar. They hadn't slept in the same bed.

My mother said, yes, they were. There was a shortage of space. It seemed a bit unkind to me.

'Do you know,' my mother said, 'your Grandma was madly in love with a man called Walter. He played tennis on the Isle of Wight. He married somebody else.' It was a riveting thing to tell me and I was dying to ask questions, but the train was coming into Lime Street Station and Mother was doing her usual business of jumping round like a ferret in a box and telling me to comb my hair and pull myself together. She led me at a run up the platform because she said we had to be first in the queue for a taxi. We had a connection to catch. The awful thing was they'd changed the city or something – there was a one-way system for traffic that Mother hadn't known about. If we'd walked, all we'd have to do, she said, was to sprint past Blacklers and through Williamson Square, and then up Stanley Street and we'd be there. As it was we went on a sort of flyover and then a motorway and it took twenty minutes to reach Exchange Station. She was quivering with anxiety when she paid the cab driver. We hadn't bought tickets for the next train and the man at the barrier wouldn't let us through. 'But they're burying my flesh and blood,' shouted Mother. 'At this very moment,' as though she could hear in her head the sound of spades digging into the earth.

'Can't help that, luv,' said the porter, waving her aside. Then my Mother did a frantic little tap dance on the spot and screamed out, 'God damn you, may you roast in hell,' and on the platform, echoing Mother's thin blast of malice, the guard blew a shrill note on his whistle, and the train went. I kept well out of it. The only good it did, Mother making such a spectacle of herself, was to bring some colour back to her cheeks. When the next train came we had to slink through the barrier, without looking at the porter. On the journey Mother never opened her mouth, not even to tell me to sit up straight.

We weren't really late. My Uncle George was waiting for us at the other end, in his new Rover, and he said the cars weren't due for another half hour. 'Mildred's done all the sandwiches for after,' he said, 'and the sausage rolls are ready to pop in the oven.'

'That's nice,' said Mother, in a subdued tone of voice, and she leaned against me in the back of the car and held on to my arm, as if she was desperately ill. I couldn't very well shake her off but it made me feel a bit stupid. My Uncle George was a bit of a maniac. He said I was a bonny girl and hadn't I grown. The last time he'd seen me I was only six so you can tell he wasn't exactly the Brain of Britain.

It was funny being in Grandma's house without her knowing. She was very houseproud and usually she made you take your shoes off in the hall so as not to mess the carpet. My Auntie Mildred was dropping crumbs all over the place and she'd put a milk bottle on the dining-room table. There was dust on the face of the grandfather clock. Grandma was a great one for dusting and polishing. She wore a turban to do it, and an old satin slip with a cardigan over. She was once mistaken for a cleaning woman by the milkman, who hadn't seen her before without her jewels or her cocktail dresses.

I wasn't sure where Grandma was and I didn't like to ask. When the cars came I was amazed to find Grandma had come in one of them and was waiting outside. There were just two bunches of flowers on the coffin lid. 'Why aren't there more flowers?' asked my Mother. 'Surely everyone sent flowers?'

'I thought it best,' explained my Uncle George, 'to request no flowers but donations instead to the Heart Diseases Foundation. Mother would have preferred that, I think. She always said flowers at a funeral were a waste of good money.'

My Mother didn't say anything, but her lips tightened. I knew that Grandma would be livid at so few flowers in the hearse. She did say that flowers were a waste of money, but she was talking about other people's funerals, not her own.

I don't remember much about the service, except that there were a lot of people in the church. I thought only old ladies went to church, but there were a dozen men as well. At the back of the pews there was an odd-looking bloke with a grey beard, holding a spotted handkerchief in his hand. He seemed quite upset and emotional. He kept trying to sing the hymns and swallowing and going quiet. I know, because I turned round several times to stare at him. I kept wondering if it was Walter from the Isle of Wight.

For some reason they weren't burying Grandma at that

church. There wasn't the soil. Instead we followed her to another place at the other end of the village. The vicar had to get there first to meet Grandma, so we went a longer route round by the coal yards and the Council offices. It was a big graveyard. There were trees, black ones without leaves, and holly bushes, and marble angels set on plinths overgrown with ivy. Four paid men carried Grandma to her resting place. Ahead of her went some little choir boys in knee socks and white frilly smocks. They sang a very sad song about fast falls the evening tide. It wasn't even late afternoon, but the sky was grey now and nothing moved, not a branch, not a fold of material, not a leaf on the holly bushes. It was as if we were part of a drawing done in pencil with a frame round us, and we were under picture glass. The vicar followed Grandma and then my Uncle George supporting my mother at the elbow, and then me and my Auntie Mildred. We went up the path from the gate and round the side of the church and up another path through a great field of grey stones and tablets and those angels with marble wings. But we didn't stop. The small boys went on singing and the men went on carrying Grandma and we reached a hedge and turned right and then left, until not many yards distant there was a new plot of ground, so out of the way and unseen that they'd left bricks and rubble lying on the path. I didn't know how we kept on walking. Someone should have cried out, wait, some great voice from up there in the pale motionless sky should have told us to stop. I thought of Grandma in the restaurant, eyeing the distant table with a jaundiced eye, refusing to budge from her central position.

After she was put in the ground, before they hid her light under a bushel, we threw bits of earth on top of the coffin.

I didn't like the sound of it.

# DON HAWORTH

# *Memories of a Childhood Friendship*

The recreation ground was a plain of cinders bounded on the
far side by a stream. Beyond lay fields and the bluebell woods
and beyond again the moorland hills criss-crossed by walls
and dotted with farms. On fine summer mornings on the rec
when the wind was the right way you could sometimes hear a
farm dog bark so distant it sounded like a memory and from
the town side you heard the industrial hum channelled
through terraced streets where chapels frowned and Co-ops
bantered and the ambulance came for old people taken badly in
the corner shop.

We stopped playing football to see somebody lifted into the
ambulance, a mob of children crowding between the door and
the ambulance, falling over each other to clear a passage for the
stretcher.

'His tongue were lolling out.'

'He's Boggy Buggins's grandad.'

'It were all purple.'

'His number's up.'

'He's a goner.'

And we ran back to the rec and belted the ball about with
shouts of laughter because at eight you know your fate and
those of us who were allowed out on the rec every night knew
we would live forever.

Recreation grounds ought to be made of cinders. It was a
bad move when the authorities replaced cinder recs with playing fields which are too sloppy in winter to play football
properly and too bumpy in summer for a decent game of

cricket. A football plays true off cinders and a cricket ball fairly true; and cinders drain well. We used to play every daylight hour except when we were at school and except on Sundays when the rec was left empty out of respect for God.

In the short winter evenings between school and darkness there were only boys on the rec, scores of them but only boys, grabbing an apple or a jam butty after school and running out with it to kick a ball until the light had gone and the gaslamps shone along the streets and the ball came up at you like a leap of solidifying darkness.

Sometimes our gritty football hurtling out of the night unfortunately floored passers-by, adults who took short cuts across the rec, and we would judge from their demeanour as they rose on to all fours whether to apologise or to run.

In summer men came out to play, practising cricket, and some nights strode up with canvas bags full of tackle to play Sunday School league matches. There could be a dozen matches going on at once, and twenty or thirty sets of men and boys practising, bowlers charging in every direction, batsmen crossing, balls flying everywhere. Cinders take spin and spin bowlers abounded, they were quite old some of the bowlers in the Sunday School league, delivering with a grotesque contortion of the wrist a ball which usually turned a little but occasionally broke ferociously.

'How is he?'

'Bloody hell, it hit a brick.'

'It were my googley.'

'It hit a sodding brick.'

'They all count in this league.'

Oh yes, you could be out just like that, but on the other hand you could hit a fourteener. With all that mob milling round in different games there could be no boundaries. You had to run them all and the game was to clout it into the river and run up an astronomical score while a fielder with too great care for dry feet teetered on stepping stones after the ball. Terraced houses stood along the other two sides of the rec and a few of them had their windows broken every summer. The most spectacular shattering I saw was done by a youth who went so far back to take his run that you lost him in amongst all the other matches. Then you'd see his plume of dust and he would appear, skittling over cyclists and women with prams, sending dogs and children rolling in the dirt, whipping past the wicket-keeper of another game and letting go a delivery which would flatten anything in its path. He uprooted wickets, he laid out batsmen, wicket-keepers, pipe-smoking strollers, and square leg umpires, and one evening his outswinger flew straight through the downstairs window of an overlooking house. The family sat with their irons poised over their steaming dinners, all looking towards the new hole in the glass as though they expected to be photographed. Few of the inhabitants were transfixed in this manner. Perhaps by a process of natural selection the houses overlooking the rec had come to be inhabited by quick ferrety little men who shot out of their happy homes like greyhounds out of a trap at the first crash of glass. They were mentally flexible as well, ready equally to accept apologies and argue compensation with those who stood their ground or to pursue and batter those who ran. 'Only the scum runs when they bust a window,' the lads said.

And indeed the rec was ruled by law and propriety. The broad outlines were conveyed by boards which said in big letters: 'No stone throwing, No betting, Commit no nuisance,' and there were other boards which bore the bye-laws, two-square-feet of small type, compared to which the Beatitudes and the Ten Commandments were the merest rule of thumb for human conduct.

And there was a rec keeper, distinguished by a peak cap, an official, indeed an officer, not a groundsman because a rec needs no groundsman. In winter he and his cronies coughed over a brazier in his stone hut. In summer they sat, four of them, on a stone bench impassively maintaining law and order over the entire rec. One of the old men died and they left a gap where he had sat, so the bench and the three who remained looked like an old man's lower jaw with one tooth missing. Batsmen used to say they would cut one through the gap, but nobody ever did out of respect for the law.

James, whom I want to tell you about, was neither a footballer nor a cricketer. He was unemployed. The unemployed could, of course, have played either game but by and large they stuck to one of their own which was called buck and stick because it was played with a buck and a stick. The buck was like a wooden spinning top two inches long. It was placed on a flat stone and rapped on the point with the edge of the stick so it spun up into the air, and the man with the stick then smote it as far as he could. His opponent measured the strike, stepping out with a long swinging stride to make the count as low as possible. Then they changed roles and whoever had the longest strike had won a point. There was a certain knack in timing the spin of the buck to catch it a good crack but that's all there was to it, and I suppose the reason why it was played by the unemployed is that you'd have to be unemployed to be reduced to a game like that. It was all right during the day, especially in term time when the rec was clear of children, but it wasn't really approved of in the evening, when the wooden bucks spun head high through the throng of sportsmen. 'It could knock your eye out,' everybody said. James came to be a friend of mine because he clouted the buck that nearly knocked my eye out. A horse and cart were passing beyond the railings in the street and the buck hit me so hard beside the eye that for one daft moment I thought the horse had whipped round and sideswiped me with the cart.

'I'm sorry, cock. I'm sorry cock. I'm right sorry.'

I was sitting on the cinders. He stood me up and nursed my head against his thighs. His smell surprised me. Half of the unemployed were gritty with coal and the other half smelled sourly of cotton but James smelled differently. He smelled of leather.

He would have hoisted me up but the games had stopped and everybody was watching and he respected my wish to walk. 'He's been blinded,' somebody said, but I hadn't because I could see the sparkling cinder surface of the rec. 'He's had his eye put out.' But if so, it was only one eye because I could see the flagstones and the cobbles as I crossed the road holding his hand. But I can't have been all there because I only half remember James handing me over to my grandmother. They both said I was brave while I stood in the living-room with my head singing and my face bulging like a cat's, then she closed the door on him and I had a good weep. She put a hot poultice of cumfrey on my face and water ran down my neck. She had great faith in the vegetable. There was a herb of the field, she said, to cure every malady of man. Why then, I asked, had Boggy Buggins's grandad snuffed it? There was a herb, she repeated, to cure every malady, but not all had yet been discovered; cumfrey had and to that extent it put us one up on Boggy Buggins's grandad who, through lack of diligence on the part of herbalists in the field, had been allowed to slip away.

The accident brought me some distinction. I could see the lump when I looked sideways and I was pointed out at school as the boy who had been hit by a buck and stick. A lad who wore specs said if I'd wore specs they'd have been bust. Some yobboes tried to say my grandmother had hit me with the rolling pin, but it was well-known how I had suffered my injury and the matter was treated with respect, and calculations were made about how nearly I had come to have my eye knocked out. The headmaster said I was very fortunate still to have binocular vision and his pedantic joke gave him a good laugh and all the children laughed, including me, without quite knowing what we were laughing about. They were heady exciting days at the centre of attention. Groups formed round me in the school yard and escorted me home.

'If it had copped thee behind th'ear it'd have given thee meningitis.'

'If thou'd have turned quicker it'd have knocked thee conk off.'

'Why didn't thou duck down?'

'I didn't see it coming.'

'Didn't thou hear t'woosh on it?'

'How fast dost thou reckon it flies?'

'Sixty miles an hour.'

'Sixty million billion mile an hour,' a little boy said, and Jim Cryer who had appointed himself to be my handler, or PRO said, 'That's bloody daft.'

'Did you cry?'

'Course I didn't cry.'

'I bet you cried when you got in your granny's.'

'No.'

'Were it sharp end as copped thee or t'blunt end?'

'He's not answering no more questions today,' my PRO Jim Cryer said. 'So bugger off.'

At home James was waiting for me, sitting on the sofa in his Sunday suit and my grandmother had given him tea with the best china. She explained that he was offering me a trip in a lorry in consideration of having raised a bump on my head.

'And can I go?'

'If you want.'

So next day at school I was able to announce that I was getting a trip in a lorry off the bloke that had nearly knocked my head off with his buck and stick.

'Stand back,' Jim Cryer shouted. 'He's getting a trip in a lorry off the bloke that nearly knocked his head off with a buck and stick.'

'What sort of a lorry is it? Is it a Leyland?'

'No, it's an egg lorry.'

'That's not a kind of lorry, you blockhead.'

'He knows it isn't, you stupid buggers,' Jim Cryer said. 'He's telling you what it carries.' And he cuffed two or three of them to help the point home.

'Is it going to Manchester?'

'No.'

'Liverpool?'

'No, Yorkshire,' I said, 'picking up eggs.'

I couldn't sleep for the thought of Yorkshire. I had never been there. I had never been anywhere really. I lived inside a sort of triangle. The rec was the boundary on one side, and on the others the football ground and the Sunday School which was also the day school. I sometimes went beyond, of course, to the bluebell woods or the pictures or the town centre and I had been to Blackpool and Southport and to Bacup where my other grandmother lived, but never to Yorkshire.

The lorry stopped at the end of the street at quarter past six in the morning and I climbed up on the juddering step and into the cab between James and his brother-in-law who was the driver.

'I'm called Fred Parker,' he shouted, nipping my leg with the gear lever. 'It's a fair crack you got. What school do you go to?' He said he'd been there but he'd wasted his opportunities. 'It's a useful thing is education. What's four times seven?'

We ran out of the town and up through the Forest of Pendle which is not a forest at all but a great spread of fields and moorland where centuries ago they hanged some ignorant old women to safeguard Christendom from witchcraft. And I answered questions of multiplication and of dates in history that Fred Parker put to me and he gave me sweets as a reward, lemon with fizzing sherbet centres, and at the top of the hill the sun broke through the mist and Fred Parker said, 'We're in Yorkshire now.'

Rapid streams, broad rivers, meadows of the gentlest green, divided by white stone walls and rising to flat-headed outcrops of limestone. At places farmhouses were dug high into the hillside, approached by grass roads whose course from the main road was lost in a muddle of walls and outcrop. Some hill farmers left their egg boxes for us on wooden platforms, built to take milk churns, by the road, but at most places we drove right up to the farms. We lurched slowly along roads, splashing through fords, and passing beneath crags where sheep would suddenly appear like Indians in a Western film. At one place they fed us. Fred Parker penetrated the darkness of the kitchen and greeted a man in there with a great bray of laughter.

'Who's the lad?' the man asked.

'He's a lad,' Fred Parker said, 'who nearly had his eye knocked out with James's buck and stick.'

James smiled.

'That's a right shiner,' the man said. 'Sit down and reach up.'

Several men were already sitting round and the table was laden with jam and bread and cheese and pies and cakes, and a strong woman came in with a huge two-handed teapot and said, 'Have a cup of tea.' Then in the darkness I noticed a very old man sitting under a grandfather clock listening, if he still heard it, to the pendulum, beating away the seconds of his last days. Kittens in the hearth scratched at his boots and he prodded them off with a stick. Two small children came to play, his grandchildren or his great-grandchildren, and he prodded them off too, without affection and without annoyance.

Nobody took any notice of him. We ate in gales of laughter. The men told a story of somebody who had gone to Leeds Infirmary and been operated on in error. Fred Parker told of the follies and misfortunes of his boss and the woman leaned against the doorpost and joined in the laughter and James winked at me and said, quietly, 'Are you all right, then?' Then one of the men said something brief I couldn't understand at all and we all got up in a bellow of crumbs and laughter, leaving the table strewn with the remains of the food and the old man sitting unheeded by the grandfather clock.

We drove on to several more farms, then we had our lunch sitting on the edge of a disused and overgrown quarry. James had brought sandwiches wrapped up not in paper like Fred Parker's but in tea-cloths which kept them nice and moist. One of the cloths was for me and he opened it on a flat stone, salad sandwiches and cheese and a boiled egg and a piece of fruit cake wrapped in tissue paper. He filled the cup of a vacuum flask and set it beside the sandwiches. Small flies fell into the tea and wallowed. 'They've come for a steam bath,' Fred Parker said, and some of them drowned before we could fish them out.

James paid for us to go through a show cave. We saw waterfalls and smooth shoulders of rock which films of water crossed in surges. We saw stalactites and stalagmites and the guide explained how they were formed: dripping water left behind the minutest grains of calcium and it had taken millions of years to grow into the formations we saw. We were not to be misled by the small stalactites forming above the light bulbs. The heat of the bulbs evaporated water and speeded the process on a scale inconceivable in nature. These formations had started at the beginning of time. We weren't disposed to argue and, seeing we had assimilated fact so readily, the guide proposed an exercise in fancy. Could we see in this formation the likeness to a bear?

Fred Parker said which way up? The guide said the way up you're standing.

Fred Parker readily divined its eye and its snout and its ears and he agreed how the ribs of limestone could well be thought to resemble a bear's fur. He perceived other animals that were pointed out to us, an elephant and a monkey. He went on to envisage a whole menagerie as we tramped round. It simply didn't penetrate that we'd finished with animals and we were now required to perceive totally different kinds of things, such as cathedrals, forests and cities. Fred Parker continued to see rhinos and giraffes quite beyond credence and at odds with the fancies commended by the guide.

'It's not a dinosaur, it's a wishing well,' the guide said. 'We're not in here to act the goat.'

'All right,' Fred Parker said, 'what's this supposed to be then?'

'Snow White and the seven dwarfs,' the guide said, and he snapped the light off inside the grotto and stumped on to the platform that marked the end of the part of the cave open to the public. A rapid river disappeared into the darkness beyond the lights. The guide stood silent, in a huff at Fred Parker's conduct, then the offence wore off and he said the cave ran another three miles under the mountain. The passage narrowed to eighteen inches and the narrowed stream then would run above the height of a man's head. Beyond that you reached a waterfall thirty feet high and when you'd climbed that there was a long crawl, then a wider passage which suddenly opened up into a lake you'd need a boat to cross. Beyond that was a second lake and on the far shore an underground chamber like a cathedral.

Outside the sunlight was blinding. Many of the fields were full of haymakers – farm labourers, children, old men, anybody capable of handling a rake or a fork, and horses with jingling harness that on the steeper slopes pulled sledges instead of carts. In those days the hay was raked into cops and the cops gathered into pikes shaped like tents with a point on the top six or seven feet high. They shed the water and stood out for the duration of the summer. It all looked like a child's painting, the yellow pikes, the green grass, the white walls, the farm buildings low at the foot of the fells and the cumulus clouds changing shape above the summits. I remember some children kicking up the white dust of the lanes as they came home from school and a shy girl who watched us load the egg boxes from an arch in a farm building, and an old parson with a shining face and a gold watch chain and boot soles an inch thick who was trudging off, we were told, to say a last prayer with some parishioner whose day was done.

And so, nearly, was mine. Driving back Fred Parker considered how you'd get a boat down to cross those big black lakes. What you'd have to do would be to take your boat through in pieces and nail it together on the underground shore. He wondered if there'd be any fish. If so, they would be numerous because there would be no anglers. Perhaps the fish, undisturbed for millions of years, had grown to an enormous size. That didn't happen with animals but it did happen with fish because they didn't need legs to stand on. A cavern chamber like a cathedral. What the guide meant was space. We understood this, but all the same the picture was of a building, nave and transept, stained glass windows, altar and choirstalls, evensong, on the far shore of the black lake.

The lorry dropped me at the end of my street. I was so sated with the events of the day that when my grandparents asked me what I'd done and where I'd been, I could only say, 'In Yorkshire.' And yet when I woke in the night it was not the places or the events I remembered, nor Fred Parker's dominating performance, but James who had done little but smile a diffident smile and mark himself out by his quietness. I remembered climbing down from the lorry and the anguish of seeing it go, knowing that I had been more than compensated for the crack with the buck, and that if I met him again it would be a nod or a wink, or perhaps nothing.

I played at the other end of the rec so he wouldn't think I was hanging round him. Then one day some lads had chucked me out of a game of cricket for arguing and I was sitting with my back to the railings and he came behind me on the flagstones leading a greyhound. I said it was a grand dog. He said in his diffident way, 'I'm exercising it for the folks next door. Want to come?'

And so I went. I went to all sorts of places with him in those weeks and I learned all sorts of surprising things. We took the greyhound back to its home, a scruffy house with some of the wallpaper held up by drawing pins, and the folk made the dog a slap-up dinner with meat and two beaten eggs while they themselves ate tripe swimming in vinegar. It was surprising to find that James lived in such a scruffy street. When this dog had a win we all went shouting down to the chip shop. It was so uproarious that I started laughing without knowing what the joke was and apparently it was an indecent one because all the women screamed out when I laughed and one

of the men said, 'He's a well-advanced lad is this. Have
another fish, cock.' Without in any way disapproving James
did not join in and it was noticeable that they all took on a
more decent and sober tone when they spoke to him. His
shyness and constraint distinguished him. He was also distinguished by occupation. They were unemployed cotton weav-
ers and coal miners but he was an unemployed shoe repairer.
What's more, when he was in work he wasn't just an ordinary
benchman hammering at a shoe roped on a last, but a
machinist. A man working such a machine in the window of a
shoe shop rapped on the glass one day when we were passing
and, in the lip language which was learned in the racket of the
cotton mills and widely used outside, he asked, 'Are you
playing?' The word means exactly what 'resting' means to an
actor – out of work, on the dole. He turned back to the
machine and James pointed out to me the cutter and the setter,
the carborundum wheel and the polisher and the stitching
machine beyond. The machinist got black flecks on his face
from the whirling wheels.

'Do you have a black face like that?'

'When I'm working.'

'Do you go round with your face black?'

'Till I get home. I wash it off at home.'

'Can you see it when you've got a black face?'

'If I look in the mirror.'

'Does it taste like it smells?'

'Something similar.'

I didn't ask anything more about being a machinist because
my grandmother had told me that I mustn't hang round him in
case he didn't want me – which I didn't do – and that I mustn't
badger him with incessant questioning. I knew I did this and I
tried to stop in case it got too much for him and he dropped
me. I knew he had a hullabaloo to put up with at home because
when we went a walk he'd stop at his street end and say, 'Let's
have a rest before I go in.' I had never before known anybody
who rested standing on the corner of the street to brace himself
to brave the happy home. It did not occur to me until years
later that he was out so much and I was able to enjoy his
company so often because of the domestic uproar. He had God
knows how many sisters and a fat mother and a father with a

pale, bald head, who hadn't had a job for donkey's years. They sat round with the wireless at full blast cheerfully bawling at one another and swigging pint pots of tea sweetened with milk from tins which made innumerable rings on the newspaper spread on the table top.

My grandmother didn't like those kind of families and she didn't like my going down to the dog track in the morning. When I went running home with a ticket James had bought me for a raffle of a cricket bat, she said I imposed too much on his generosity, and I had the frightful feeling that she and my grandfather were talking things over when I was in bed and that I would be forbidden to see him.

It was at this critical moment in our friendship that James and I were publicly thrown out of the tin tabernacle. Normally the gospel was preached there to a congregation of feeble-spirited sinners but on this afternoon it had been let to some Popular Front organisation as a platform for a man who was advertised as a celebrated anti-Fascist. J. Farrington Pope he was called or something like that, the kind of name you would expect to contribute bird noises to Children's Hour. James and I went because it was raining and I recognised a fair number of acquaintances of my grandfather, who was in favour of any good cause that cost nothing and had thus been enlisted in the Popular Front. The tabernacle was nearly full and there was something of the excitement that precedes a Cup Tie. At the end of our row an idiot was sitting with his hands under his knees, slowly rocking backwards and forwards. I plied James with questions which he met with his slow smile and allowed other people sitting round to answer.

'And this chap that's speaking,' I asked, 'will he have a black uniform?'

All hell broke loose. Faces reared in front of us, bent round the back of us, glowered over us. Affronted, outraged faces, many circles of indignant mouths all saying, 'Oh no, oh no.'

'Does he not know the difference between a Fascist and an anti-Fascist?' somebody demanded.

'Ignorant little bugger,' the idiot said.

'Have you not taught him such a rudimentary distinction?'

'Ignorant little bugger.'

'J. Farrington Pope is an eminent Esperantist.'

'Ignorant little bugger.'

'Look,' said James – and it was the only time I ever saw him cross – 'he's too young to know, so if you'll just let us sit here quietly.'

'The lad should be put on right lines,' a man said.

'The lad should be left alone,' James said.

'Ignorant little bugger, ignorant little bugger.'

A civil old man gave the idiot a humbug which silenced him and, turning back to the hubbub around us, said, 'Could I just have a word, please?'

Everybody went quiet and he said, 'Just to put you on the right lines, son, J. Farrington Pope will not be wearing a uniform because he is a man of peace. It is men of war who go about in uniforms, Hitler and Mussolini and the generals and air marshals. J. Farrington Pope will be dressed just like any of us.'

Well, he came on the stage, and he wasn't dressed like any of us. He wasn't out at the arse and elbows like us. He had a tweed suit with small twigs woven into it and he wore a red cravat. He was bald and tall and when called upon to speak and applauded in anticipation he launched himself in a high-pitched voice with a testimonial for the international language Esperanto. He had fallen ill in a country which only a few years ago had been considered an enemy of our own, and Esperanto-speaking natives had nursed him back to health with strengthening broths. He derided armaments – the reeking shard and iron tube, as he call them – and somebody shouted out a brisk question to which he replied with a schoolmaster's smile that he would not ape the dictators in barbarism but appeal over their heads to the German and Italian people. He made a looping movement like somebody playing ping-pong.

A kind of restiveness spread through the tabernacle and I thought that everybody else was beginning to find the forms hard sitting. I now understand it was not from physical discomfort but from mental agitation that their murmurs of disquiet arose. J. Farrington Pope was an imposter, an old-fashioned pacifist, now so far adrift from the party line that he ought to have been and no doubt soon was, deprived of his licence to practise as an anti-Fascist. Of course I understood nothing of this, but the unrest unsettled the idiot who had finished his humbug and craned forward to look at me down the row. 'Ignorant little bugger,' he said. 'Ignorant little bugger.'

Faces whirled round and said, 'Shh', more at me than at him and in self-defence I said, 'He's not dressed like us anyway,' and immediately shouts were heard from all over the hall, as I now understand, of dissent at J. Farrington Pope's deviations, but as I then thought of protest against my outburst. The chairman thumped the bell and altercations broke out all over the tabernacle and the chuckers out pushed through to the end of our row and some clown said, 'It's them two, a nest of Fascists.'

One had me by the ear and James punched him, then James was dragged down and forms were knocked over and everybody was sent sprawling and I was hoisted over their heads with barely a chance to get a decent kick at the idiot as I was whipped past, and scuffling was going on all over the place, and James and I were dragged to the door and pitched down the steps, over and over, ten wide steps, and we sat up at the bottom like a pair of knockabout comedians under a poster which said, 'God Is Love.'

James dusted me down. 'What'll happen if your grandfather gets to hear? He'll happen stop you coming with me.'

He was likely to get to hear because many of the audience knew him and as we walked along the street I thought up and proposed to James a whole variety of lies and alibis.

'No,' he said, 'we must find your grandfather and make a clean breast.'

My grandfather was an insurance agent covering the whole town but there was no difficulty in finding him. Many people were unable to pay their weekly premiums so he put in the money out of his own pocket whenever there was danger of a policy lapsing and in this way and at the cost of accumulating a debt which later reduced us to penury, he was able to finish his collecting and repair to the billiard saloon about three o'clock. That day he finished his game then he and James talked under the scoreboard, quite easily it seemed on both sides. My grandfather called me across and made a joke about our being in the wars at a peace meeting and said James would be coming round for a talk in the evening with himself and my grandmother.

It did not, of course, occur to me that this was in any way an unusual sort of conference, but it seemed ominous that it should be held in the evening. The only evenings James ever passed in my company were when we returned late from our trips in Fred Parker's egg lorry. On other evenings he walked out with his girlfriend who like him had a distinguished occupation. She was an unemployed cinema usherette, and she had been in work so recently that I remembered her in the Regal squirting from a hand pump the exquisitely scented disinfectant that hung about the place and made it and her seem part of the enthralling world of the silver screen. If James was to give up an evening with her matters were obviously serious, and when we had eaten tea my grandfather sent me off to the bluebell woods and asked me not to return before eight.

James had gone when I got back. My grandfather showed me a chair and prepared to announce their findings. He started by praising James's qualities, his quietness, his kindness, his slow good nature, and I feared the worst. I knew all good things came to an end and the best things only last a short time. But my grandfather was saying that they thought James could only be a good influence on me and that if we kept clear of political meetings and the dog track he thought it well that our friendship should continue.

My grandmother leaned forward to say a word. She said it was rare for anyone in this world so much to like the company of another as constantly to seek it, and almost unheard of for a young man to seek the company of a child.

'Why does he then?' I asked.

My grandmother said we must be thankful for grace and not question it. Seeing I did not understand, my grandfather said, 'Because of your incessant chatter.' But my grandmother would not have that. She said we must not question the gifts of providence.

All this now seems very odd but it is how it happened and I remember the thrill, the tightness in my chest and the tingling in my spine, at knowing that I, I myself, nobody else, was sought out, and that James delighted in my company exactly as I delighted in his.

Through the long summer holiday we went to the dales with Fred Parker, we exercised the greyhound, we went together and collected James's dole which was paid out by a hunchback nobody liked. One day, the story went, when a tradesman inquired for work, the hunchback said insultingly, 'They want navvies in Bolton,' the tradesmen replied, 'Aye and they want camels in Egypt.' He had his dole stopped for a period that differed according to who was telling the tale.

We went errands for cigarettes and tinned milk for James's dad, we went on the rowing boats, we played on the rec, we had dinner at his house and tea at mine, we went long walks in the country and he introduced me to his fiancée who did actually smell of the scented spray they used in the pictures. We seldom arranged to meet. We would both be down at the rec, I with the boys and he with the unemployed men, then more often than not we would drift off together. Not every day, so that when he ceased to come, I thought he had given it a miss just for one day and then for two, but by the third day I knew something was wrong. I walked out looking for him to where we usually exercised the dog, I went to the employment exchange, to the garage were Fred Parker kept his lorry, to where the boats were anchored, all over the place in a desultory sort of way. My grandfather had told me to let him be when he wished, not to myther him, so I did not inquire after him, not even when I went to his house. I could see his relations in the dark interior boozing tea and I'd heard their hullabaloo even before I reached the corner where he usually stopped for a rest.

It was nearly tea time. I kept thinking I had better go. Then I would give it another couple of minutes until finally it had gone past our tea time and I simply gave up to going home and sat down on the edge of the pavement not far from James's door. I poked with a stick at the tar between the cobbles and he was nearly on top of me before I saw him. I immediately understood that a tragedy had happened, and that it was all over – the boats and the Yorkshire dales, the old man beneath the clock, the greyhounds, the meals together, the crotchety hunchback who paid the dole, Fred Parker's lorry and the cathedral on the far shore of the underground lake – all finished.

James had black flecks on his face and he said with some embarrassment, as though he expected to be congratulated, 'I'm in work again. I've got a job.'

# PETER HAWKINS

# *The Son of the Farfield Lane Flyer Rides Again*

I often wonder if my dad really liked cycling any more than I did. I suspect he did, for he was a lover of punishment. And when fair weather came, because he loved me, he punished me. He'd get out the map, study it and say: 'Nah then, lad – where arta baand today?'

And off I'd go into the shed to pump the tyres up and root around for my cycle clips. See here. I've got a platform ticket from Otley station. Now that's worth something, for there's only ferns and brambles along there now. Every time I went out cycling, while my mother cut sandwiches, he scanned the route – every inch of the way. And to make sure I went there, I had to bring something back. One time it was a bottle of sulphurated water from Harrogate. That's a souvenir I never kept. But here in this drawer I still have lots of them. Platform tickets mostly, postcards, the odd ashtray, Brontë perfume, Harrogate toffee, Pontefract cakes . . .

My mother tells me that after I set off he used to sit back in his chair and close his eyes. Every now and then he'd take his watch from his pocket and say: 'He'll be well past Heckmondwyke by now,' or, 'He'll be coming up to Arncliffe. That's a climb. He'd better tek it fast, mind, or he'll never get up it.'

And as I plodded along I seemed to have him by me or – more often than not – away ahead of me. Sometimes I'd see the ghost of a lad – about my size but in peak condition – towering ahead of me on the ghost of a penny-farthing. Try as I might, I could never catch up with him.

Then when I came home, Dad would go over the route again, discuss the gradients, and plan my next route.

'Up bi Wood'us Moor, look out for a stone staircase. It's just over t'road from that statue they've put up for t'queen. It's nobbut a yard high and they used to use it for mounting horses wi'. I used it sometimes for getting on t'penny-farthing.'

In a flash he was the young, robust ghost who accompanied me on my journeys.

'I used to mount 'em from behind. My left foot on that little step and – up! And it were swaying like a great leaf but I held it and then I were off. How did I stop it? Well, there were no brakes i' them days. You just stepped forward. Walked into the air and hoped you'd land on your feet. Well, we mighto' hurt oursens but never much. Then we'd be up again and soon we'd be going tiddley-pom, tiddley-pom down t'cobbles and if we fell off, well, we got on again.'

Then he'd get out his trophies for racing. Those were after his penny-farthing days, of course. Bikes were not as crude then as you might think. After all, they shipped fold-up cycles to the Boer War, didn't they? My dad was known as the Farfield Lane Flyer in his day. He won silver cups and even a tea service for long distance. And he had a gold medal presented to him by the Horbury Cycling Club in 1897 for good attendance. If it hadn't been for his affliction . . . That's what took him off his bike for good.

He fought against his affliction like the strong man he was but in the end it put paid to his cycling days. Instead he accompanied me on my long journeys only in his mind.

My mother says he was always sad and distant while I was away. He kept his map close by and reached for his watch out of his waistcoat pocket, checked it, clicked it shut, put it back and closed his eyes again. He seemed to know every yard of the road he sent me on.

'Didstha see t'stone staircase?'

'Aye, Dad.'

Well, I can't say for certain, but if it was there in his day, as like as not it was there in mine.

'Nah, then,' he'd say, 'what hastha browt back for us?'

I drew out a picture postcard of Headingley cricket ground.

'Why, man,' he said, 'that's hardly out o' Leeds. I want thee to see t'country. I tell thee where I'm baand to tek thee next time. See here.'

The map was by his seat, just as it had been when I left that morning.

'Now tha sees there's a long hill here. Now that's Otley Chevin. It's a steep incline. I took it at t'bottom fast but never once did I get to t'top wi'out having to get off. But it made me fit. I were tingling and aching all over! And coming down . . . ! Oh! Cause I told you we had no brakes, didn't I? I tell thee what, lad, there were a copper stopped me once and took me name and address for speedin'.' It was the year of the great summer when all the folk were complaining on account of it being too hot. 1911 was it or 1912? I remember I rose early and wearily took down my cycle clips after a heavy breakfast. He was waiting with the map on his lap.

'Nah then. I want thee to climb to t'top of t'Chevin and bring us back a breadcake. Bring it back fast, mind. I don't want it to be stale when I come to eat it.'

'Where would I get a breadcake, Dad?'

'Tek a look. Here.'

There was a pencilled cross on the map.

'From up here you can see right across t'Wharfe Valley. Over to t'left you can just mek out t'Cow and Calf agin Ilkley Moor like a couple of pimples on t'side of a cliff. Across in front of you there's Farnley Hall just among t'trees. Farnley Hall! T'bugger there chased me many a time. Up to t'right on t'sky line there's Arncliffe Crag. You can see all that and sup tea at t'same time. Because looking out across that view is Jenny's Cottage. You won't have heard of that, will you? Well, Jenny's Cottage is where they serve t'finest breadcakes i' Yorksher. I want thee to climb up there and tek in such a sight as you never took in in your life. Breathe it into your body and into your bones. And bring us back a breadcake for me tea.'

So I was on the bike again, my flask full of lemonade and my heart full of the morning. The bike seemed a part of me as it often did on those mornings. If I could keep up a good pace I could reach that café with the dew still on me.

I started to have my doubts a while later as I neared Otley and became aware of a rocky hill sheering up to my left. Then I came to the edge of the town and turned into a narrow road

that humped over the railway and then rose up and up and up.
I should not have cursed my father, but I did as I considered
that long, hard incline. I cursed again as I tried to gather speed
over the railway bridge and my legs pressed into the pedals.
My head was down, seeing only inches of the ground ahead
and sweat was running into my eyes. My heart hammered into
my chest and my shins were like lead beating out blood. My
lips were muttering foully while there was breath to mutter.
And when I twisted my neck up, all I saw was road and road
and more road and my shirt dripped against my body.

Then as I forced each inch up the hill it seemed there was the
shadow of a penny-farthing racing ahead of me and on it,
bursting with energy, a young lad, his cheeks weather-blown
and rosy. And I could see myself red-faced and puffing behind
him. The harder my efforts, the more the gap between us
widened.

It got so my legs could not take the aching any more. I
stopped and pushed my bike under a bush. Then I sat down
and rubbed my legs. Below me, though not far enough below,
lay the small town. A toy train was steaming out of the station.
It passed beneath me and I watched it crossing the valley
towards Leeds. I took a drink from the saddle-bag and then
pulled myself up. There was still that breadcake to get. The air
felt still and heavy as I foot-slogged up the hill. Each time I
seemed to near the top it seemed to stretch away again. And to
make things worse, I still saw through the haze my father,
forging ahead, still on wheels and nearing the summit. But *I*
got there too and threw myself down. The view, as far as I
could make out, was as he'd described it. It lacked one thing.
The café. So with stiffening legs I roamed that hill-top, now
sick with hunger. I met a horseman, trotting casually and
envied him silently as I asked him if such a café existed. Of
course it did, he informed me, a mile or so away.

'But aren't I at t'top?'

'Oh, yes – you're at the top all right. But you're at the
wrong end, young feller,' and he directed me. 'You can't miss
it.'

After he'd faced me in the right direction he said: 'Have you
a bike with you?'

I hadn't the cheek to turn back the way I'd come until horse and rider were out of sight. I was determined to go no further. My father could say what he liked. But my head hung sheepishly as I retreated down the Chevin.

The steep descent made my legs go taut. My calves were throbbing and I was dizzy with hunger, the heat and the heavy feeling of failure. Soon I was pulling the bike out from the bush and free-wheeling down the hill. For the first time I felt a breeze and I felt lighter.

'Brakes? I never had no brakes! Once a copper pulled us up for speeding!'

I bumped over the railway bridge and slowed down to meet the main road. There was a new strength in me, a new feeling of determination. I was going to find my own Jenny's cottage.

Across the road I leaned my bike against a wall. Then with a courage that had never gone into my cycling I braced myself and knocked on a door. I was lucky. The lady who opened it was elderly – well, perhaps middle-aged – and she looked kindly enough. She greeted me and I paused long enough to choose my words with care. Then, as she began to look puzzled, I went into action with scarcely a breath.

'Please, missus, could you let me have a drink o' water, please? I've cycled all t'way from Leeds and me dad made me go reight up t'Chevin and I've had nowt to eit sin breakfast.'

There was a short silence. She didn't shut the door. She smiled.

'Why me little doy,' she said. 'Tha looks fair weshed away. Come in and sit thissen down. Wiltha have a piece o' parkin?'

'Well, me dad said I wasn't to eit owt before I got back,' I lied.

'He won't begrudge thee a piece o' parkin and a drink o' tea,' she said. 'Come in, lad.'

So I had parkin and tea and a sit-down and a talk. I even dared to ask her for a breadcake before I left. She took no offence, but I got no breadcake either. I cycled half a mile, then, along the glorious flat, and up a gentle slope to Otley station. I wheeled the bike in and bought a single ticket to Leeds. I also bought a platform ticket . . .

'What did tha see, lad?'

'I saw Arncliffe Crag all reight. And I med out a building closer in and I reckon it were Farnley Hall.'

'Farnley Hall! Did I ever tell thee about Farnley Hall?'

'Aye, dad.'

'Now what about that café. Wern't it grand? What about Jenny? Was it her as served thee?'

'I . . . reckon it were her.'

'What's she like – eh? Tell us everything! Ha-ha! When *I* went there she were nobbut a young lass. But she were bonny! Tha shoulda let slip my name, just casual-like, and watched her face. I'll tell thee a tale one o' these days, a tale I've never told thi mam. She were a woman were Jenny. Nah-then – where's that breadcake?'

'Breadcake, dad?'

'Aye. Let's have it.'

'They . . . never had any left.'

'Eh?'

'Aye, that's reight. I got there a bit late, tha sees, and . . . they never had any left.'

'Oh, dear,' he said. 'That's bad. Times have changed, I see. They'd never have allowed that in my day. They took a pride tha sees. That Chevin place has gone reight down hill.'

'I tell thee what I *have* got, dad,' I said, and I fumbled for it in my trouser pocket. 'There – a platform ticket from Otley station . . .'

I still have it here in my drawer. It was my ticket, I suppose, to growing up. My father could never truly dictate to me after that. Not that I opposed him, but I learnt to play the game against him. I was never dishonest with that sad, proud old man. Well, perhaps I was. I learned the use of thorough reading of a map. Study your contours, see where the lines tighten together, and soon you can define your high crags and calculate exactly what you will see from a given point. After that, your imagination will never take you far wrong. Not when your father longs to see the things you see for him.

The café that eluded me that day has disappointed many travellers since. Once I saw it with its roof caved in and its windows gone, gazing across the Wharfe Valley like an empty skull. Years later I went again and it had gone. Someone had done an improvement job, cut a few pretty paths into the hill and wiped the old cottage off the summit. So I never got to taste a breadcake there. And I never brought *him* one to colour his tired imagination. But I like to think my map-reading fed him better than any breadcake.

After that journey, whenever he sent me off on a mission it started as it had always started. But the bike took me to the station where I packed it into the guard's van and continued the journey in a third-class non-smoking compartment. On my return I fed him with traveller's tales and panoramic views and generally threw in a platform ticket too. And he never caught me out. If you feel it was wrong of me – remember this.

My father was failing fast. I was his eyes and his dreams. I carried him back to his golden youth, while he looked forward to nothing. I became what he wanted me to be: a robust, honest son who matched the lad who once, on a wilting summer's day, penny-farthinged down the Chevin without brakes. That was the crown of his ambition for me. I never let him down.

# NORMAN SMITHSON

# *The Tuppenny Rush*

There's me and Young Tush walking up their street wondering about how we could get in the Tuppenny Rush tomorrow
afternoon. 'It's all Chinese Charlie's fault,' said Young Tush.
'He's got it in for us and I don't know what for 'cos we've done
nowt to 'im 'ave we?'

'No, we 'aven't, it's just that he dun't like us much.' Chinese
Charlie looked like a Chink with glasses and bow legs and he
was one of the chucker-outs at the Tuppenny Rush, a special
picture show for kids at the Queen's every Saturday afternoon
where you nearly get your ribs crushed in queueing for your
tickets. Last week Chinese Charlie had thrown me and Young
Tush out for too much shouting – so he said anyway – and had
told us not to come back until further notice.

'I'm not bothered much about going really, except I've 'eard
tell *The Three Stooges* are on tomorrer,' said Young Tush.

'*Three Stooges?*'

'Yer, man.'

'Who ses?'

'Jebbers.'

'How does he know?'

'From that feller that works there.'

'Aw, yer.'

'And Jebbers ses the big picture's got Buck Jones in it an' all
. . . Best show they've had for years, man, and there's us can't
go.'

'Course we can go, man, wi' masks on.'

'Masks?'

'Yer, them masks we got at the school party. Put them on and hide near the wall in the queue and Chinese Charlie'll never know the difference cos he's short-sighted to start with.'

'Good idea, man.'

'Eh, look at that.'

'What? Where?'

'Daft for looking.'

'That's got whiskers on. Race yer to t'schoolyard.'

Young Tush just beat me by his big conk though we called it a draw and then, while we were still panting, he said, 'Right, a wrestle.'

'Right. I'm King Kong.' I hunched my shoulders and let my arms dangle like a gorilla.

'And I'm The Bull,' said Young Tush and he put his head down and walked bow-legged. The Bull was another of the chucker-outs at the Tuppenny Rush, the big white chief, and Young Tush was always The Bull when we had these wrestles. We circled round each other making bull noises and gorilla noises and then Young Tush dived on me and we rolled off the flags and on to the cobbles. We often had friendly wrestles, but sometimes, if we got a bit too tough and lost our tempers they finished up in real fights. It seemed to be getting that way now when Young Tush got me in the dithering scissors, but then his mother must have seen us from their front window because she came storming out of the house and grabbed hold of him and shouted, 'What did I tell you about looking after yer new trousers? You never take a bit of notice of what I tell yer. Rolling about in the dirt like a little hooligan. Get inside this minute.' She slapped him on his backside and dragged him into the house.

'See yer tomorrow, Knocker,' he shouted, just before he disappeared, but before I had a chance to shout back his mother turned on me then. 'No he won't,' she shouted. 'Every time he goes with you he starts fighting.' She was only little, but she was like a blinking stick of dynamite when she lost her temper.

'We were only playing,' I said.

'Don't talk back to me,' she snapped. 'Get off home where you belong.' I thought about giving her some lip, but decided not to because last time she took it out of Young Tush. So I turned away and began to walk off, but then she called me back. 'Come back 'ere and let me brush you down, or else you'll be getting a good hiding when you get home as well.' So I went back and she dusted me down with her flat hands, and when she got to me backside she dusted me a bit harder, but it didn't hurt and then she said, 'Now pull yer socks up and go home looking respectable.' She gave me a last slap on the pants and then I went off, by the short cut, round by Mr Baxter's who lost all his money on the horses, over the wall near the old stables, past Mrs Thompson's, who lays 'em out for one and a tanner, and when I got to the top of our street I thought what with Chinese Charlie and Young Tush's mother I bet we never get in the Tuppenny Rush at all tomorrow.

Anyway, tomorrow comes and after dinner I calls up for Young Tush as usual. His father came to the door and I thought that's good, maybe his mother's had to go to Mrs Rawling's funeral. 'Come in, lad, he won't be a minute.' Young Tush's father was a little chap who hardly ever took his cap off. He followed the Rovers Rugby team all over the place and was always wanting to shoot people. If you went to the match with him and one of the players made a muck up he'd shout, 'He wants shooting.' And once he got into an argument with another feller and he said, 'If I had my way I'd shoot all the players, put the directors on a free transfer and dig the pitch up for rhubarb.' Another time he ran on to the field and clocked a touch judge and had to spend the night in clink at the Town Hall. He's Rugby mad and he often says that when he dies he wants his ashes putting in a Rugby ball, alongside a pint bottle of best bitter, and then buried under the Rovers turf, near the goal-posts.

'So yerroff to t'flicks with our Ronnie, are yer?' he said when I got inside with the house smelling of meat and tatie pie and new cake straight from the oven.

'Yes,' I said.

'He means yes if he's lucky,' said this voice and it gave me a bit of a turn because it was Young Tush's mother's voice as she came into the room from the stairs' steps.

'Why, what 'ave they been up to now?' said Young Tush's father.

'Oh, fighting and carryin' on,' she said. 'I think our Ronnie teks after you for that.' Young Tush's father seemed a bit upset at this but before he could say owt their Billy, who was slicking himself up with hair-oil and that in front of the sideboard mirror, turned round and said, 'I've heard that they carry on like little 'ooligans. That's right, isn't it, Young Knocker?'

'Who told you that?' I said, and thought I bet it's Chinese Charlie's lass that's been telling him. He was a bit struck on her.

'Never mind who told me. Just behave yerself in future, that's all.'

'And you behave yourself an' all,' said Young Tush's mother. 'You've a lot of room to talk I must say.'

'Ay, you needn't say owt,' said Young Tush's father. 'I suppose yer doin' yerself up to do a bit of birding. Tha's not right in the 'ead. Walking round town shopping of a Saturday afternoon with a lass. If you had any sense you'd be off to t'match wi' me.'

Billy just laughed and slapped another dollop of oil on his hair. Then Young Tush's mother said, 'Our Ronnie won't be long, luv. He's just gone to the shop.' So I thought, oh that's good, she's calling me luv again so everything must be all right and then Young Tush came in whistling and that and swinging the shopping basket around.

'Iya.'

'Iya.'

'Where's yer mask?'

'Can't find it.'

'No, can't find mine either.'

'Still. It'll be all right though.'

Young Tush's dad said, 'What d'yer want masks for?'

'Scare kids with in t'pictures.'

'Huh, yer don't need masks to do that,' said their Billy. 'One look at you two's enough to make anybody jump.'

'Aw shurrup,' said Young Tush. And then to me he said, 'He's funny our kid isn't he?'

'Yer.'

'And you'll be funny as well if you don't hurry up and get yourself washed,' said Young Tush's mother. She was always making him have a wash. Anyway, after inspecting his neck and a bit more waiting his mother gave him his tuppence and then we were off. Soon as we were clear, down the street, Young Tush said, 'D'yer think Chinese Charlie'll be looking for us?'

'Don't know. Might've brought the cops with 'im as well.'

'Might not. Might've got knocked down with a bus.'

'Yer. Hope so.'

'Anyway, if he does say owt we can say we forgot.'

By the time we got to the Queens there was a big queue, all shoving and pushing, but there were no fights yet because The Bull was there keeping everybody in order. We couldn't see Chinese Charlie anywhere, though he might've been inside throwing his weight about. The Bull was the boss chucker-out, a massive feller with a bald head and a thick neck like a house-side and we only called him The Bull when he wasn't listening because if you gave him any lip he could pick you up with one hand. But he was all right when you got to know him and was one of our mates like, so we went up to him and asked what was on.

'Wait and see,' he said, 'and don't be so cheeky.'

What with being in trouble with Chinese Charlie already we didn't argue, and anyway we'd seen The Bull wrestle a few times in Professor Roscoe's booth at the fair. He called himself Karl Bolonski, or summat like that, the Russian Terror, though Young Tush's father said he was bred and born in Woodthorpe.

If The Bull had been in a good mood we could have gone up to Jebbers, who was right at the front of the queue, and told the other kids that he'd been saving our places while we'd been to the chemists for my grandmother's medicine. But it was no good trying it on with The Bull being grumpy so we just shouted, 'Save us two seats next to you, Jebbers,' and then went up to the back of the queue. Well, everything was going all right, no trouble nor nowt and no Chinese Charlie, until we got halfway to the pay box and two kids tried to push in in front of us.

'Eh, get to t'back.'

'Yer, get to t'back or else we'll do yer.' We always acted tough at the Tuppenny Rush because if you didn't you never got a seat.

Anyway these two kids turned round and one of them said, 'Oh, yer'll do us, will yer,' and the other kid said, 'Oh yeah, you an' whose army?'

'We don't need no flipping army. We've had to queue, so'll you.' Me and Young Tush hadn't lost a fight at the Tuppenny Rush yet. Then one of the kids said, 'Aw, mind yer own business,' and they both turned their backs on us and started chatting to their mates. So, me and Young Tush looked at each other and then, right, I grabbed one kid's arm and Young Tush got the other kid and we slung 'em out of the queue.

We were ready for 'em when they rushed back at us, and one of them nearly knocked my teeth out with his nut, but then I got him in the head lock and put the screw on. By this time all the other kids in the queue were shouting. 'There's a fight, there's a fight,' and then I got a right punch on the back of the neck. I saw stars and staggered about all daft and the next thing I remember there's me and Young Tush being dragged up the queue by The Bull, by our coat collars. He dumped us right at the back and said, 'If I 'ave any more trouble from you two, yer won't come in at all.'

'But it wasn't us, Mister,' said Young Tush, 'it were them others pushing in.' But The Bull just waved his big picture torch at us and said, 'I've told yer, no more trouble. And don't be so cheeky.' He started to go off down the queue and then suddenly he stopped, turned round and came back to us. 'Ere,' he said, 'didn't we 'ave some trouble with you two last week?'

'Who? Us? No, we didn't come last week. Did we?'

'No, we went to t'match last week.'

'Oh,' said The Bull. 'For a minute I thought you were the two Charlie Dawson had put out. Anyway, remember what I've told yer. We've no favourites 'ere.' And then he went back down the queue and Young Tush said, 'I thought we'd had it then, man.' By the time we got our tickets and got inside there was a right commotion going on, and lucky for us we spotted Chinese Charlie down among the front rows looking for trouble. So, we hung back a bit and then we saw Jebbers, bang in the middle of the red plush seats, shouting and waving to us. If you wanted one of these seats you had to start queueing about breakfast time. At night, when the real people came, it cost sevenpence to sit in these though it was tuppence all over on a Saturday afternoon. Normally we finished down among the baking boards.

Anyway, we pushed our way along this row of seats and just as I was plonking myself down a piece of orange peel whanged me on the 'ead. It didn't 'alf sting an' all, but it was no good trying to find out who did it because everybody was slinging orange peel at everybody else. Soon as we sat down Young Tush said, 'Oh I've got a flea,' and began scratching his neck and Jebbers said to him, 'Don't be daft, man, it's yer imagination, yer don't get fleas in t'sevenpenny seats.' This seemed to cool him down a bit and then Jebbers said he'd had six fights saving these seats for us and while he was telling us about them the feller with the spray gun came round squirting disinfectant to kill all the bugs up in the air. It was worse than flipping scent and we all smelt like cissies but the lasses round about thought it was lovely.

Then I saw Chinese Charlie coming up the aisle from the front and looking at the lads on each row, as though he was searching for us. 'Eh up, he's after us, man,' I said to Young Tush and told him what was happening, so Jebbers said, 'Bend down on the floor as thou yer've dropped yer 'anky and I'll tell yer when he's gone.' So, we waited till he was about three rows away and then we got down, with Jebbers saying 'Keep down, keep down, it's our turn next,' and then he started cheering with all the others because the lights had gone out and the flicks were starting. So we had a look up, and just saw Chinese Charlie on his way back to the front, and everything was all right, for now anyway. So we sat down again and when we saw it was *The Three Stooges* coming on, Young Tush said, 'Told yer, man, didn't I?' and we all cheered again because they were our favourite film stars and me and Jebbers started laughing already. We'd seen this one before a few times but that made it better because we knew what was going to happen. Jebbers laughed his hat off and when the Three Stooges began clonking each other with hatchets he waves his arms about and kicked me on the nut with his fist in fun. Then he turned to the kid on the other side of him and did the same, but this kid didn't like it and wuffed him one back, so Jebbers said, 'Right,' and was just going to have his seventh scrap when The Bull came, shone his torch and said, 'Nah then,' and gave him his first warning. Three warnings at the Tuppenny Rush and you were out.

After *The Three Stooges* the curtains came to, but then when they tried to put the next picture on they stuck half way. So, we all cheered and then The Bull got this long pole and pulled back the curtains with it. Not that it mattered much because this film that they put on now was a travel thing about Paris or summat and this kid in front of me started flicking little silver pellets up into the light to make it sparkle and that. But The Bull soon saw him and clonked him on the nut with this long curtain pole and gave him his first warning. Good job for us The Bull was looking after these seats and Chinese Charlie was up at the front, else we'd've been out long ago. Anyway, about halfway through this travel picture we all started booing so they took it off and put the big picture on with Buck Jones in it, just like Young Tush had said. It seemed all right as well, but then it started breaking down every few minutes and coming back on upside down and that. So, we all whistled and stamped our feet and Jebbers shouted, 'Put a shillin' in,' and The Bull was dishing out warnings all over the place. Then, the picture came back, but it wasn't Buck Jones. It was another *Three Stooges*, so we all cheered and laughed again and Jebbers nearly fell off his seat with excitement. And then, just as it was getting started this broke down as well and nowt happened for ages except us booing and stamping and that. And then the lights went on and The Bull was stood on a chair at the front. He waved his arms about for us all to be quiet and then he shouted, 'There'll be no more pictures this afternoon . . .' Some lads at the back started booing but before it spread The Bull waved his arms and said, 'But as you go out yer'll all get a ticket to come with free next Saturday, and yer'll get a happle each as well.'

As soon as he said this there was a big cheer and a mad rush for the door where a couple of other chucker-outs were giving the apples and tickets away, and it didn't look as though Chinese Charlie was around either so it seemed as though me and Young Tush were going to get away with it. Anyway, we got to the doorway and as Jebbers got his ticket and his apple he said to these chucker-outs, 'It's a flipping twist. I'm not coming back here no more,' so one of the chucker-outs gave him a kick up the backside and told him not to be so cheeky. Jebbers ran off a few yards and then he turned round and shouted, 'You wait. I'll tell our kid about you and he'll get yer for that.' Then he trotted off eating his apple with one hand rubbing his backside with the other.

'Poor old Jebbers,' said Young Tush and then we got our tickets and apples and just as we were going out into the open air I said, 'Anyway, that misery Chinese Charlie didn't catch us, that's one thing.' And Young Tush said, 'No, it's a good job for 'im an' all else he might 'ave got a kick up the pants,' and then he shouted out, 'Oh' and grabbed his backside and then it got me as well before I could turn round and I yelled out an' all and then this voice said, 'Oh, it's a good job for me is it, well we'll soon see about that when you try to get in next week.' It was Chinese Charlie come from nowhere and looking at us through his glasses, but we didn't wait to listen to any more, we scooted sharpish, across to the other side of the road where we turned round and sang, 'Charlie is me darlin' ', a few times at the top of our voices until Chinese Charlie waved his fist and went inside. 'Well, that's got rid of him,' said Young Tush as we went off up their street. 'All we've got to do now is think of a way to get in next week.'

'Aw, that's easy, man. What we'll do is I'll get on your shoulders and we'll say we've just rode in from China and if he says owt I'll clunk him on the 'ead with this big mallet from our coal cellar.'

'Yer, man. Good idea,' said Young Tush. 'Just like *The Three Stooges.*'

# ALAN SILLITOE

# *A Time to Keep*

Martin drew the cloth from the kitchen table, folded it and laid it on a chair. After the anxious fuss of putting his brother and sister to bed he lifted his books from the cupboard and spread them over the bare wood, where they would stay till the heart-catching click of the gate-latch signalled his parents' return. Most of the books had been stolen. None had been read from end to end. When opened they reeked of damp from bookshop shelves. Or they stank from years of storage among plant pots and parlour soot.

He was staying in to see that the fire did not go out, and to keep the light on. He was staying up because he was older. When that unmistakable click of the gate-latch sounded he would set a kettle on the gas to make tea. Funny how thirsty they still were after being in the boozer all night. His two-hour dominion over the house would be finished, but as consolation he could give in to the relief of knowing that they had not after all been hit by a bus and killed.

He put a French grammar on to *Peveril of the Peak* and a Bible in Polish on top of that. The clock could be heard now that they were out and he'd extinguished the television. He sang a tune to its ticking under his breath, then went back to his books. He would start work next year and didn't know whether he wanted to or not. Things could go on like this forever as far as he was concerned. You got booted out of school though at fifteen, and that was that.

The certainty that one day he would be pushed into a job had hovered around him since he first realised as a child that his father went out every morning in order to earn money with which to feed them, pay the rent, get clothes, and keep a roof over their heads. His mother used these phrases, and they stabbed into him like fire. At that time work had nothing to do with him, but it soon would have, that place of pay and violence which his father detested – to judge by the look on his face when he came home every evening with his knapsack and tea can.

Under the dark space of the stairs he shovelled around for coal to bank up the dull fire – a pleasurable task, as long as the flames came back to life. A hole in the pan needed bigger lumps set over it so that cobbles and slack wouldn't spill on the mat between coal-heap and grate. They'd rather have a few pints of beer than buy a dustpan, he thought dispassionately.

He washed his hands in the scullery. He liked soap that was keen to the smell. Arranging his chair, he sat down again and lifted the cover of a beige leather-bound volume of French magazines. He read a sentence under the pictures: a bridge over the River Seine near Rouen. In other books he was able to put Portuguese or Italian phrases into English. When a word appealed to his sight, he manoeuvred through the alphabet of a dictionary to get at its meaning, though he never tried to learn a language properly. He handled books like a miser. In each one his name was written in capital letters, though there was no danger of their being stolen, because they were gold that could not be spent. The strange kind of hunger he felt in looking at them often fixed him into a hypnosis that stopped him using them properly.

If burglars came they'd nick the television, not books. They were stacked according to size, then sorted in their various languages. Excitement led him to range them from high at both ends, to small in the middle. He bracketed them between a tea-caddy and a box of his father's car tools so that none could escape. Then he spread them out again, like playing cards.

Summer was ending. It seemed as if it always was. He had a bike, but Friday night was too much of a treat to go out on it. He also thought it a squander of precious daylight on his parents' part that they should have been in the pub for an hour before it got dark. And yet, as soon as the outside walls and chimney pots were no longer clear, he swung the curtains decisively together, pushing away what little of the day was left. Once it was going, he wanted to be shut of it. He switched on glowing light that made the living-room a secret cave no one could get into.

His parents were used to his daft adoration of books, but for anyone beyond the family to witness his vital playthings would make him blush with shame. Aunts, cousins and uncles would mock him but what else could you expect? If it hadn't been that, they'd have teased him for something else. They had never actually seen his books, though they had been laughingly told about them by his parents. Books and the people he knew didn't belong together, and that was a fact.

He wondered what other eyes had slid across these pages. Their faces could be frightening, or happy. In any case, how had they felt about what they were reading? What houses had they lived in, and what sort of schools had they gone to? Did they like their furniture? He would rather have been any one of those people than himself. Maybe nobody had read the books. The thought made him feel desolate, though not for long. Books always took his mind off the world around. He lifted the picture album of France, and pondered on its travels between leaving the printers and reaching him.

A clatter of footsteps at the yard end, and the boisterous notes of a voice he did not at first recognise dragged him clear. Before the warning click of the gate-latch his dozen volumes were scooped off the table and stacked on the floor behind the far side of the dresser.

By the time the door opened the gas was lit and a full kettle set on it. He sat at the table looking through a car magazine as if he hadn't moved all evening. His cousin Raymond was first into the room. No stranger, after all. His mother and father breathed a strong smell of ale.

'He's the quickest lad I know at getting that kettle on the burnin' feathers!' his father said. 'A real marvel at it. I drove like a demon back from the Crown for my cup o' tea.'

Martin wondered whether he should take such praise as it was intended, or hate his father for imagining that he needed it, or despise him for thinking he could get round him in such a way. He was already taller than his father, and there were times when he couldn't believe it, and times when he didn't like it, though he knew he had to get used to it. So had his father, but he didn't seem bothered by such a thing. He decided to ignore the praise, though he *had* got the kettle on in record time.

'You brought him up right.' Raymond hung his jacket on the back of the door. 'He worn't drug up, like me.' He bumped into his aunt: 'Oops, duck, mind yer back, yer belly's in danger!'

Martin laughed, without knowing whether he wanted to or not. His father would put up with anything from Raymond, who had been to Approved School, Detention Centre and Borstal, though he was now an honest man of twenty-two, and able to charm anybody when he wanted. He did it so well that you were convinced he'd never get caught stealing again. He could also use a bullying, jocular self-confidence, having learned how to live rough, half-inch a thing or two, and die young if he must, without getting sent down every year for a Christmas box or birthday present. Another lesson well taken was that he must always look smart, talk clear and act quick, so that anyone who mattered would think he could be trusted. At Borstal he'd done boxing, because it seemed that both God and the Governor were on the side of those who stored the deadliest punch. He had developed one as fast as he could, and wasn't afraid to use it whenever necessary. He was loyal to his family, helping them with money and goods to the best of his ability and hard work. He was often heard to say that he couldn't go back to his old ways, for his mother's sake.

Martin wanted to be like his cousin, though sensing that he might never be so made him look up to him even more. He was certainly glad he'd got the books out of sight before he came in.

Raymond, with his bread and cheese, and cup of tea, was the first to sit down. Martin moved across the room, leaving the fire to the grown-ups. The yellow flames blazed for them alone, and for their talk that came from the big world of boozers that he was avid to enter. Raymond stretched out a leg, and expertly belched the words: 'Pardon me!' – at which they all laughed.

He held up his cup for more tea: 'I'll be off to Alfreton again in the morning. Help to build another mile o' that motorway. You know how it's done? I open my big gob wide. Somebody shovels tar and concrete in. Then I walk along, shitting out motorway and belching up signposts!'

'It'll soon be as far as Leeds, wain't it?' his father said.

Raymond turned censorious. 'Would be, if everybody got cracking. But they're too busy looting to get much done. The fields for miles on either side are laid waste by plundering navvies! Some of 'em sit around smoking and talking, and waiting for a turnip to show itself. As soon as it does, up it comes!'

He was a joker. They knew it wasn't true. No gaffer could afford to let you get away with not working full-tilt. But he *had* brought vegetables home. Ripping up a basketful was the work of a few minutes in the dusk.

Martin seemed born to listen. Maybe it went with collecting books. If he read them properly perhaps he'd start talking a bit more, and it might then be easier to know what other people were thinking.

'He don't say much,' Raymond said, 'our Martin don't, does he?'

But he did at school. Among his pals he was as bright as an Amazon parrot. If he tackled a book properly he might talk even less. Cut anybody's finger off who got too fresh. The teacher once stopped him bashing up another boy, and said if he caught him at it again he'd pull his arm off. He couldn't really be like Raymond, who'd once got chucked out of a school for hitting a teacher back.

'He'll be at work next year,' his mother nodded. 'It's looney to keep 'em till they're fifteen, big kids like him. Give him summat to do. *And* bring us some money in.'

'The bloody road tax is twenty-five quid now,' his father said bitterly, and Martin felt as if he were being blamed for it.

'I didn't have one for six months last year,' Raymond said. 'I stuck an old Guinness label on the windscreen. Nobody ever twigged.'

Martin knew it wasn't true.

'You never did!' his father said, who believed it.

'No, I tell a lie. It was only on for a fortnight. Then I got the wind up, and bought a real 'un.' He turned his grey eyes on to

Martin, as if embarrassed by somebody who didn't continually give themselves away in speech.

'Get our Martin a job wi' me on the motorway, though,' he advised. 'Settle his hash. Come home every night knackered.'

I expect I might, Martin thought. 'What would I do?'

'You'd have to get up early, for a start.'

That wouldn't bother him. Lots of people did it. 'What time's that, then?'

'Six.'

'He's dead to the wide at six.'

'I'm not, our mam.'

Raymond looked at the fire, as if he would have spat on it if it had been in his own home. 'I pass here in my car at half past. Pick you up tomorrow, if you like.'

'Will yer be fit for it?' his father wanted to know.

Martin, taking more tea and another slice of bread, didn't think he'd heard right. He often looked at the opening of a book, and when he understood every word, couldn't believe he'd read it properly, and then went back to make sure. 'Tomorrow?'

'Well, I didn't say owt about yesterday, did I?'

If Raymond said something, he meant it. He knew you must regret nothing, and he always kept promises. It helped his reputation of being a man who showed up in a crowd. So he promised something in a loud voice now and again in order to keep himself up to scratch. 'I'll stop my owd Triumph outside the Co-op. If you're there, I'll take you. If you aint, I'll just push on.'

'I'll be waiting,' Martin said.

He felt like one of those sailors in the olden days who, about to set off west, wasn't sure he'd ever get back again.

The sky was clear and cold. He saw it over the housetops, and above the façade of the bingo hall that he first went into as a cinema one Saturday afternoon nearly ten years ago.

The road was wet, and looked as clean as if a light shone on it. He buttoned the jacket over his shirt. You never wore a top coat to work unless you were one of the older men.

It was too early for traffic, making the road look different from when it was pounded by buses and lorries during the day. His mother had disturbed him from a hundred feet under the sand below the deepest part of the ocean when she had tried to wake him. She had to grab the clothes off him in the end.

Sandwiches bulged in his pocket. He enjoyed waiting, but his hands were cold. 'Never put your hands in your pockets when you're on the job,' Raymond had said. 'A lot of 'em do, but it don't look good.' He couldn't do it while waiting to go there, either. He wished he were setting off to work properly, and that he didn't have another year to do before he got real wages. There wasn't much point in starting work today, and then next year as well.

A postman went by on a bike. 'Morning, kid.'

'Morning.'

Raymond's car had rust along the bottom of the door as it swung open towards him. 'Get in.'

It sailed up Wollaton Road like an aeroplane, spun around the traffic island by the Crown, and went along Western Boulevard. 'Tired?'

'It's a treat, being up early.'

'Bring owt t'eat?'

'Yeh. Mam forgot some tea, though.'

'I've got a mashing.' He played the car with hands and feet as if on a big organ. 'Sugar, tea, and tinned milk – solid like a cannon ball. Enough for a battalion. Trust mam. She's old-fashioned, but she's a marvel all the same. You can stand a garden fork in *her* tea!'

Beyond the town there was a bit of cloud like a big white dog. Martin yawned.

'We like to start as soon as daylight hits,' Raymond went on. 'That's where the money is, in overtime. You don't mind getting up when you can mek money. I'd work all hours God sends, for money. Watch the tax, though. Bastards will skin yer dry. Dangerous work. Nearly got scooped up by a mechanical digger the other day. But it's money to be getting in your pocket, fartin' Martin! As soon as I know there's money for earning I'd dig that soil up wi' my fingernails. They don't need to tell *me* when to start sweating!'

Martin had a question. 'What do you do with it?'

'Wi' what?'

'The money you get.'

'Ah! Booze a bit – that's me. Treat everybody – now and

again. Save a lot, though. Gonna buy a house when I've got the deposit. Me and mam'll live in it. Not the other spongers, though. They wai'nt get a look in.'

His brothers and sisters had reputations as scroungers. Serve 'em right if Raymond dealt with them as they deserved.

The narrow lane was so rutted he thought they'd get stuck, the car swaying from side to side, sharp privet branches scraping the window. 'Fuckers should have cut that hedge down,' Raymond grumbled, seeing in his mirror another car grinding too closely behind.

As they topped the rise tears of mud lashed against the windscreen. When the wipers flushed over it Martin saw the vast clayey cutting between green banks. It was a man-made valley occupied by lorries, cranes, mechanical diggers. Those already moving seemed to be the ones that owned it. He was surprised at how few men there were, having expected to see them swarming all over the place.

Raymond drove parallel to the valley, and parked his car by a cluster of huts. He got out, and farted, then stretched his arms and legs. 'See that trailer?'

'Yes.'

'Well, I'm going to book myself in.'

The nearest wooden hut, full of tools, smelt as if it were made of still-growing trees. He expected to tread on leaves as he went in to have a look, but there was a crunch of gravel under his boots. His eyes were sore from little sleep. He yawned while trying to stretch his arms without being seen.

The sound of engines thudded from the canyon. Raw earth was being cleared. Soon it would be covered, and packed, and solidified, and paved to take traffic and huge lorries between London and Leeds. The men who did it knew what their work was for. They could see it as plain as a streak of paint across a piece of wood.

Raymond came back wearing a helmet and a livid pink jacket. 'Don't stand idle,' he called sharply, so that Martin didn't know whether he was joking or not. 'Let's get on that motor.'

The dumper truck swayed as it went down the track hewn in the incline. The narrow ledge frightened him, for the dumper might tumble any minute and take both of them to the bottom. Raymond fought with the wheel and gears, laughed and swore as he swung it zig zag along.

'If we don't get down in one piece I'll get the push,' he said. 'That's the sort of world we're living in, Martin. Owt happens to this dumper, and I get my cards. Don't matter about us, if we get killed. We'll get compo, but what good does that do yer? The bleeding gaffer wanted to know what *you* was doing here, so I told him you was the new mash-lad from Cresswell. Got so much on his plate he don't know whether he's coming or going. Looked a bit gone-out, burree din't say owt.'

He drove the dumper truck under the digger to take its load, then lumbered it back up the escarpment. Tipping it from above helped to heighten the embankment.

After two trips Martin decided to stay on top. He could watch the beetling dumpers doing their work from a distance, which was better than being down among them. He remembered a word from school that would describe the long deep scar: geology, geological. The layers of gravel and grit and clay were being sliced like a cake so that the motorway could be pushed through into Yorkshire.

In a while he sat down. It was a struggle to keep the eyes open when you weren't thinking about anything. The wind died, and the sun came out. He was dozing, then dreaming, but he never cut off from the distant punch and rumble of machinery, and occasional shouting. Diesel smoke wafted across. He opened his eyes so as not to lose contact with the sort of work he hoped to be getting paid for next year.

Raymond nudged him awake. 'You poor bugger! A bit too early in the morning, was it?'

'No, it worn't,' he snapped.

'You know why, though, don't you?' He had a can of hot tea and offered him the lid as a cup. 'Take this. I'll get some scoff.'

'Why?' The sweet strong tea went straight to the waking-up box behind his eyes.

'You stayed up too late. Can't go to work early if you don't get to bed on time. Not unless you're over eighteen, anyway. You'll 'ave to stop reading all them books. Send you blind.'

He'd heard that before – often. 'I'm not tired.'

Raymond rolled a fag. 'What about some snout, then?'

'No, thanks.'

He laughed. Smoke drifted from his open mouth. 'That's right: keep off fags. Don't booze, either, or go with women. Stick to yer books as long as you can.'

He went back to work.

Martin didn't know what to make of his cousin's advice, but he certainly wished he had one of the books that he'd stacked and shifted about on the table last night, even if it was only that Bible in Polish, or the Italian dictionary. When dumper trucks moved into the canyon again, and the first one came back loaded, they didn't interest him any more. He thought they might though if he sat at the wheel of one like Raymond.

An hour later he was so bored that he felt hungry.

Sitting high up and set apart gave him a picture-view. Everything on it moved so slowly that he wouldn't forget it as long as he lived.

Raymond's truck was easy to recognise. He saw clearly across the whole distance, and watched him go with his load up the far slope of the motorway. A wind blew from the sprawl of Ilkeston on the skyline, as if someone on its church top were wafting it over. With his vivid sight he saw Raymond's truck go behind a long low spoil bank, the helmet moving slowly. Then his body reappeared, and finally the truck again.

It manoeuvred into a clearing for about the twentieth time, always guided close to the precipice by another man. Then it tipped its load, and set off quickly towards the excavation for another.

He stared more closely, imagining he was Raymond sitting on the truck and working the levers, confidently steering it after four years experience, smelling petrol and soil and wondering how much he'd coin that day. He wouldn't mind working here, even if he did have to start by seeing to the men's tea and running their errands from one hut to another. A mash-lad was better than a school-kid.

The truck reversed towards the precipice at a normal and careful speed. At dusk they'd drive back to Nottingham. Maybe Raymond would call at home for a bite to eat before going to where he lived in the Meadows.

He could almost hear the engine speeding up. 'I'll get this

one over with,' Raymond might be saying, 'then I'll pack it in
and piss off out of it. Done enough for one day.' He sensed the
words going through his brain. He said them aloud, as if to
save his cousin the energy.

He couldn't say who was tired most: him, Raymond, or the
man whom Raymond's dumper truck suddenly knocked
flying over the precipice. The man had sauntered out of the
way as usual but then, for a reason which was hard to make out
(though he was sure there must have been one, since there was
always a reason – for everything) he leapt back against the
truck as if to dive underneath.

It wasn't easy to make out the exact point of collision. The
man's spade turned in the air, and Martin swore he heard the
clatter as its metal head caught the side of the truck.

The body rolled down the steep bank and smashed into a
mechanical digger. He watched Raymond jump from his seat.
Other men lined the top of the soil heap. Two or three,
Raymond clearly among them, started to scramble down.

The whole heart-side of Martin's body was dulled with
pain. It lasted a few seconds, then left him feeling cold, wind-
blown, and gritty at the eyes, which now seemed to lose their
vision. The sound of an ambulance came from far away as he
walked towards the huts. The flashing blue light of a police car
bobbed along the hedge-top.

Raymond was pale as he got into the car an hour after his
usual knocking-off time. He smoked a cigarette, something he
said he never did when driving. 'The pig-copper told me I'd
killed 'im on purpose,' he shouted above the engine as it roared
– and skidded – along the muddy lane. 'They said I must have
been larking about.'

'I didn't see yer, and I was watching.'

'A few others was as well, so I'm all right for witnesses. But
can you believe it? Killed 'im on purpose! One of the blokes I'd
known for weeks! Can you imagine him asking a thing like
that? Must be rotten to the bloody core. He just jumped in
front of my truck.'

Martin felt as if he was asking the only question in his life
that needed a proper answer: 'Why did he do it?'

After a half-minute's silence, which seemed so long that
Martin thought he'd never speak again, Raymond said: 'You

won't guess. Nobody on this earth would. I'll tell yer, though. He dropped his packet o' fags in front of my truck, and because he thought the wheels would crush 'em, he jumped to pick 'em up. The daft bastard didn't want to lose his fags. Would you believe it? Didn't think! Blokes who don't think deserve all they get. I'd a gen 'im a half of my own fags though, if only he'd left 'em alone.' He smiled on his possible generosity. 'Can't understand him doing a thing like that. I thought I knew him, but bogger me if I did.'

'He's dead now, though.'

'I know. The daft bleeder.'

Martin said he was sorry it had happened. He hated feeling the tears at his eyes as sharp as glass. 'Who was he?'

'An old chap, about forty-odd. Happy old chokker. He was allus singing, he was. You could tell from his mouth moving, but nobody ever *heard* him because of the engines. He didn't sing when he thought we could hear him. Funny bloke altogether. All my life I've been careful though, that's the best on it. I never wanted that to happen. I'm not a murderer, it don't matter what that copper tried to say. "I'm not a murderer, your honour! Honest, I'm not!" *That's* what I'll shout out in court, if it comes up.'

They got back to the lighted streets. Martin said nothing. He had nothing more to say. His cousin drove with one hand, and held his wrist tight when he reached across with the other. 'I'm glad you was with me, any road up, our Martin. I wouldn't have liked to come home on my own after that little lot. I'll drive you right to your door. Don't say owt to yer mam and dad, though.'

'Why?'

'Let me tell 'em, tomorrer.' He was on the edge of crying. Martin never thought he'd feel sorry for Raymond, but he did now. He also felt more equal than he'd ever done. There wasn't much to look up to. The big mauler was crushing his wrist. 'Aren't you going to the boozer with 'em tonight?'

He drew his hand off, to change gear. 'I think I'll get off home. Mam might go out and get me a bottle of ale from the beer-off.' He winked: 'If I ask her nice.'

Nothing could keep him down for long, though.

Martin wasn't as tired as he had been by the motorway.

When his parents drove off to the boozer he got his books out of the dresser, instead of going to the last house of the pictures as was usual for Saturday night.

The clear clean print was a sudden marvel to his eyes. He started to read the first page, then became so drawn into the book that he didn't even hear the click of the gate-latch when it sounded three hours later.

# ELIZABETH NORTH

# *Keeping Faith*

My own prurience was not matched by Celia's, I thought, as
we watched through curtain gaps the English mistress and the
Major making love on the sofa of his bungalow. In fact we
couldn't watch it all in detail because the sofa back was
towards the window. All we saw was actions like the time she
took her sweater off, the time she put her hands behind her
back and unhooked her bra. We saw the black bra on the floor
behind the sofa, the jersey hanging on the sofa back. Of him,
the Major, we saw that he still had his shirt on, though
unbuttoned by Miss Cartwright. What surprised me most was
the way she grabbed at the buttons, and when unbuttoned,
went at his chest like she was hungry for it. We had always
imagined that she would be the passive partner and the Major
was the predator.

There were three curtains at the window, drab and dusty
pink, and thus two gaps between them. Celia was the only
other one of the six of us who planned to watch who stayed to
see the project through. The others thought of reasons not to.
We'd found this old bench in the woods and wondered what to
do with it. That morning we'd put it up outside the Major's
bungalow, just under the window during morning break.
Celia at that time seemed the keenest of the lot to come out
here after supper and before bed-bell, creep through the crack-
ling autumn leaves, ignore the first frost and risk the history
mistress's Airedale dog. We called it nature watching; the
signal was at supper you would say to someone: 'Owls
tonight.' We could see the Major's bare leg coming off the end

of the sofa. But that wasn't right somehow. His feet were pointing to the ceiling; he must have been lying on his back. Miss Cartwright's toes were also visible, extended, pointing, with her ankles resting on the sofa arm. They were lying side by side and it may have been a squash. I may have missed him taking off his underpants, although his trousers were on the floor. 'I think he's got his underpants on still,' I said to Celia. 'I don't care,' said Celia, 'I'm getting down.'

'No don't.'

'You watch; I'm bored.' Which was a lie. You could detect lies in Celia so easily; she was so sincere normally and worried sick if she thought she hadn't been completely straight. You could spend hours with Celia while she talked in depth about slight deceptions she had practised in the matter of not having made clear her true feelings on any topic. Like – she would say: 'Oh dear – I told Miss Georgeson I hated maths, and that isn't really true; I mean I think I sometimes hate them, but on the whole I know they're worth doing and sometimes I can see the pleasure that other people get out of them. And is that really hating them when I can think like that about them? Perhaps I should tell Miss Georgeson. . .'

'Don't worry,' I'd say. 'She'll probably have forgotten. Unless it's on your conscience terribly.'

Celia had discussed her conscience more than ever since we were fourteen. It bugs her like hell, she says, but the rest of us have cheerfully discarded our voices of conscience and are bent on decadence and self-destruction over the years to come. We read this thing in the *Guardian* in the library, an interview with a young writer who said that he'd grown up in an environment of decadence and expected to witness decay throughout his life, in England that is; he couldn't speak for the rest of the world. In fact he thought it might be better to live in the Third World, to lose yourself as it were in a developing country; that is, if you liked development as opposed to decadence. But he liked decadence, he said, and felt at home in it. And what he liked about writing now was that you could write in detail about sex. We looked for his book in the library but of course it wasn't there. And anyhow we'd had a basinful of sex literature this term since Emma brought back *Knave* and other naughty knicker magazines she'd pinched from under her father's bed. They were confiscated incidentally, by Miss Georgeson; and we wished her pleasure from them most sincerely.

'Our sex experience is in any case vicarious,' said Maggie, 'that is, in term time, I mean.'

'It's very prurient I think,' said Celia, blushing, which she does quite easily.

'What's prurient?' several people asked.

'It means,' said Celia, 'it means, I think it means, but I'll look it up in the OED if you like, it means sort of wanting knowledge for the wrong reasons.'

'It's not so much knowledge,' I said, 'as actually living sex and blokes. We can get it in the holidays – we all know that.'

Well, actually, we couldn't all get it in the holidays. We all said we did but Maggie had had only one serious feel-up since last Easter, and Emma, although she boasts about a boy in the underground when she was staying with her father in Shepherds Bush, I think this was largely invented to keep her end up or her head above water.

In the summer term it's not so bad because boys from our nearest public school deign to play tennis matches with our school. But you have to be in the tennis team to get so much as a touch from any of them. You can, if you are first or second year, be a ball-boy. Lots of jokes about that function. But you aren't so interested in trouser bulges at that age. Fourth formers fare the worst; pubescent, ovulating wildly sometimes two or three times a month we think, we stand behind the boundary netting watching flashing hairy arms and legs. But that is something or nothing; it makes you randy and leaves you high-parched as Keats would say. We are deeply into Keats and sexual symbolism: berries, blood, pale flesh, etc. We have mentioned this phenomenon recently to Miss Cartwright. She said didn't we realise that sex in fact permeates everything in life and that we must learn to live with it. When we read D.H. Lawrence for A Levels, we might come to understand. 'Can't come too soon for me,' said Emma, who had this bravado to disguise her virginal innocence.

Sex, for Miss Cartwright, permeates in fact Tuesdays, Thursdays and Saturdays with Major Wadham, the man who looks after the grounds and lives in this woodland bungalow.

He is not in fact the gamekeeper but the thought of Lady
Chatterley and Mellors is not far from our minds.

This – this trip out to the woods – was Celia's idea to start
with and heavily backed up by Emma. But Emma turned back
at the cloakroom, her extremely spurious excuse being that
she had a premenstrual pain and might start any moment. We
suggested that she took precautions early, but she said no
because she was out of supplies and it meant going to surgery
to get them and signing on. And she didn't want to sign on this
time because she stood a good chance of being in the badminton team tomorrow, and, if she got in the team this time, then
maybe if they ever played the boys' school . . . well that could
be a good thing future-wise.

'Honestly,' said Celia in the cloakroom. 'Well, honestly.
You are so devious Em. You know you are mad about badminton in any case and very ambitious sportswise. Don't give
us this old toffee about having other motives for playing sport.
You know you're dying for your colours.'

'Nothing to be ashamed of,' I said. 'Sport will go on,
however decadent our society. It's just that being English we
shall never win an international match. Thus to me it seems
quite pointless to try and get in teams and things; it only delays
the final cataclysm. The only reason I need to keep fit is to be
hale and hearty at the barricades.'

So Emma didn't come. Nor did the others for various
weedy reasons. Celia and I slipped out, missed a confirmation
class (where you get coffee sometimes which is useful when
your caffeine level plummets) and went on through the cloak-
rooms, through a window and across the back drive in between the pine trees, feeling crisp leaves squidgy underneath
and smelling frost and also feeling cold. There was this old and
rather rotten bench which must have once been by the tennis
courts. But it is sound at each end where we stand to witness
what is going on inside the bungalow this Thursday.

Feeling as prurient as we'd ever felt and as decadent as we'd
ever hoped to feel we each put a foot to the bench. Then we
had to get a hand-hold somehow on the window ledge above
our heads. And then we had to pull ourselves up simultane-
ously so as not to tip the bench. 'One, two, three,' I whispered, and we were there, looking through the slightly parted

grubby curtains, and there were the backs of their two heads, the Major's blonde and curly, greasy but bald in the middle, and Miss Cartwright's straight, outdated bob.

The TV set was on; not colour; they were watching 'Softly Softly' and probably holding hands. Sometimes she put her head sideways on to the shoulder of his herringbone tweed jacket. That was rather moving really in a silly way. At that stage.

'I could have lent her some,' said Celia, whispering.

'Lent who what?'

'Emma. Some ST's.'

'Yeah – well like I said – it was a weak excuse. She's not due for days I happen to know. She comes on three days before me as a regular fact and I'm not due till tomorrow week, *si dieu le veut.*'

'How do you mean, *si dieu le veut?*'

'Well you never know, so close to the holidays.'

'I thought you said that Paul had never penetrated your vagina.'

'Yeah, but the way his sperm jets out at the speed of light – anything could happen if you don't leap out of the way.'

'But that would be a virgin birth!' said Celia.

'It happens, mate, it happens.'

'It happened,' Celia said. 'It happened once.'

Celia is, luckily for her, quite deeply into religious belief of a fairly conventional nature. Nothing eastern or droopy for Celia. Her father is a muscular Christian parson who fills his church to bursting every Sunday down in Sutton, Surrey.

We were on the bench, precariously, during this conversation, clutching the windowsill and pressing our budding breasts (Celia's are still budding – mine are a well-established 34 C cup and quite nice with it) against the same splintery wooden windowsill. And watching – not, as it happened, sexual delirium between the English teacher and the caretaker – but television, and not good television. Which you can get in this country, the only good thing we've got, my father says.

Celia, to do her credit, is the only one of us who has a possible solution to England's failing affluence. Or failed affluence. She is quite and deliriously convinced from time to time that there will be a second coming. This will be in Sutton,

Surrey. She looks at all new babies hopefully. She is quite sure
that it will be in her father's parish because she once dreamed
that it would be. She had this recurring dream where a woman
brings this child for one of the group christenings he has on the
second Sunday of each month, and he's holding it beside the
font, having summoned its batch of godparents from the body
of the church and got them to hold candles. When suddenly
this child, this man-child (Celia thinks not everyone's ready
for a girl Messiah) lets out a scream in Celia's dream, and the
whole congregation stiffen with this prickly feeling running
down their spines at this unearthly noise. And the sun comes
out around the church and shines through the stained glass
windows, and all the colours of the rainbow light the baby's
face and some strange radiance comes from, is emitted from,
this baby in its Babygro and matinée jacket held in its mother's
arms . . . and so on . . . saving us and all. . .

My father says, as far as the decadence of this great nation is
concerned, he hopes it will last his time; or better still that the
revolution will come next year to release him from paying my
school fees and more. My mother hates this attitude, goes mad
about it because, she says, it has made me feel uncommitted to
my education and generated feelings of guilt in my small heart
that I'm causing suffering in the family by having such a large
percentage of their income spent on me. In fact he paid for my
education out of capital ten years ago before capital gains tax
came in. It's only the extra since the fees went up which he has
to pay by cheque before they'll let you in to school each term.
Emma, lying as usual, says her father hasn't paid the fees for
several terms and she always expects to be turned back in the
front hall with her trunk. But they never do that, so it seems,
the theory being that however much is owing them they can
always get it in the end; so it's a good investment to keep
Emma on and add to her father's debt. Especially since they
think she may play badminton for England in 1982, *si dieu le
veut* that we survive that long.

Celia's father pays her fees quite regularly out of his incredibly small stipend. This being a church foundation school, he
probably gets a reduction, my father says. Fair's fair, my
father says. Maybe the reduction is only that he doesn't pay
each time the fees go up – about three times a term, the rumour

is. And we never have butter now and quite often hot chocolate instead of coffee. In the sixth form we shall brew our own
drinks from a kettle in the sixth form corridor, which will
make a welcome change from chewing caffeine pills when we
feel a touch lethargic. Celia's mother is amazingly economical
and makes tea from things she grows, which isn't bad. I've
been to stay there several times and got quite hooked on
dandelion tea. And Celia's father, between his Sunday ego-
trips, makes wine from stuff he gets from Boots, but makes it
strong or does something not according to the instructions. It
carries quite a kick, this vicar's wine. It makes him very
loving, as they say, towards Celia's mother and they go
upstairs. They never had any children after Celia, which she
much regrets. When they go upstairs Celia sits in the kitchen
praying that this time they will conceive. Not because she
minds not having siblings for herself, but because she thinks it
would be so nice for her mother whose maternal instincts
haven't been fulfilled enough. Not that Celia is missing much.
I have various brothers and, apart from bringing one up well
acquainted with the male physiology, there's not a lot to be
said for them.

My parents couldn't afford to send us all to posh schools. In
most families it would be the boys and not the girls that had
the goodies spent on them. In ours, because there's only one of
us, it's just the girl that gets the purgatory of confinement
within steep walls and pinewoods. The boys are at several
different comprehensives; my mother, being well up in her
rights of parental choice in education, did a consumer check on
all the comprehensives in the area and decided, after a lot of
revisiting and discussion with headmasters who must have
been bored out of their minds by her pestering, which school
would suit each boy. So all three of them go their different
ways each morning, wearing different coloured blazers and
catching different school buses. And haven't suffered from the
vandalising and orgies and pot-smoking which they can
indulge in freely and at will. And it is to my advantage that
they have friends upon whom I can work out my sexual
frustration each holiday. Paul is such a one, Paul of the
lightning sperm jet was my summer holiday beau, and well
may be my Christmas beau as well since it appears from letters

that he has stayed reasonably chaste and faithful since September.

A wobbly bench on a dark October night and cold in the feet and the hands all for the sake of seeing Miss Cartwright and the Major being as chaste as I hope Paul is being. 'Perhaps she's menstruating,' Celia said to start with. But then things changed. The news came on and the Major leaped up – still with his trousers on at that stage – and turned the picture off. We had to duck as he came back towards the window. Our hands would still have been visible had he looked, white knuckles clinging to the windowsill while the wind gets up in the tops of the pine trees and causes needles to drop on to the collars of our white school shirts and blows up our green school tunics in the uncivilised gaps between our kneesocks and our green school knickers.

Back on the sofa the Major wasted no time whatsoever. Off with his jacket and pullover and tie and Miss Cartwright stripped off her Marks and Spencers roll-neck navy blue sweater, and then we saw, as mentioned earlier, her hands release the catch of her black bra. But as to what was revealed by all this, our vision was limited to shoulder height and the clothes thrown off. And then to legs from the calf down. Then there was Miss Cartwright's lusty attack on the Major's chest; we could see a bit of this and it was a little hairy. As a boy he must have been quite smooth-chested, the thought of which gives me pause and makes me want to cross my legs, were it not for the delicate balance of the bench.

Celia has gone quiet. She had not said much since the end of 'Softly Softly'. Now she is quite silent. When you know someone as well as I know Celia, you can tell when she's bothered simply by the way she breathes, the way her head is held. It only needs a quick glance sideways to see she's off this whole idea and wishes she was in her dorm or back at home in the kitchen praying for a baby brother or sister, preferably a brother. And the idea hits me that this is what is troubling her. That this is like, a bit like going upstairs and watching her vicar father and her vicar's-wife-mother fucking on the vicarage double bed. And that is sacred; that is somehow, though I hate to say it, sacred. You see my mother and father don't fuck any more; I'm sure of it. I'm glad of it in a way because it means you can wander in and out of their bedroom and not catch them looking embarrassed or anything like that. I think it stopped last Christmas when I think my father may have fucked his secretary or someone. And my mother must have been offended; anyway she was tearful, red-eyed all those holidays, and at Christmas spoilt the turkey. Rather she pulled it out of the oven just before Christmas dinner to make the gravy and it slipped on to the floor. 'That's the last straw,' she said in her low and unhappy voice and ran upstairs and went to bed. The boys and I had to pick the turkey up and think of how to make gravy. It worked – sort of, but it wasn't much of a Christmas from then on.

So Celia going quiet is understandable. I used to think that having parents fucking was ridiculous, but since mine stopped, it seems that fucking at that age has some kind of awesome quality and I rather wish they'd start again. That mine would start again. The boys said they thought that once last term our parents came back from a party happy and pissed and there was *some* kind of vestigial noise coming out of the bedroom. *Rapprochement* possibly. But the atmosphere last holidays was not good to say the least.

But if Celia gets off the bench her end will tip up. 'Hang on, Celia,' I whisper, 'shut your eyes if you must, but I'm going to see this through.'

'All right.' She shuts her eyes, although there's nothing much to see so far except the legs and heads just jutting up and out from time to time. But the sofa moves. It's a funny old sofa, the colour of dust with what were once probably white flowers. No loose cover, just the upholstery. Messy, fucking with no loose cover I'd have thought.

My mother's voice is gutteral when she's fed up. She's been fed up on and off since last Christmas. I ought to write more regularly to cheer her up. I can think of funny things to tell her about school and the rules we break, but sometimes that upsets her. It would be funny to tell her this, about tonight, but that might not be tactful in her present situation. She is quite attractive for someone nearly forty. And my father is a dish to say the least. No wonder about the secretary; she probably tore at the buttons of his shirt at the office Christmas party like Miss Cartwright did to the Major just now. My father has an incredibly hairy chest, incidentally. It used to embarrass me when he left his top shirt buttons undone and hair sprang out. But he'd get hot if he didn't sometimes. And on holiday on beaches in Cornwall or Norfolk or Scotland or wherever we happen to pitch our tent, he gets admiring glances and it's quite rewarding to get vicarious pride on his behalf. He is a creep about some things, my father, but he is the best thing in the world to look at. And he knows it. And my mother knows it. Hopefully she will let him fuck her one day soon again.

The wind is blowing harder and our thighs are raw with it and cold and our fingers white with gripping, blue with cold. This dusty window gives a distorted image of the off-beige sofa on the off-pink carpet in the Major's lounge. Celia's eyes are shut.

The sofa moves – or is it the distortion of the poor glass of the windows? And then above the sofa back it is like the moon rising as the Major's bottom – just a segment of it – comes up into view and down again. A large white crescent piece of bottom.

'Celia,' I whisper, but don't repeat it when her eyes stay shut. Better, like leaving Em to carry out her silly lie about pre-menstrual pain, better leave sleeping dogs. Again the Major's buttocks up; then down. My eyes must stay wide open. I must not nudge Celia into watching. My eyes will stay wide open because I said I'd come and watch and I will. I can't stand people who say they'll do a thing and don't. Who promise they will carry out a thing right through and then fade out on it. I can't stand that. Can't stand it, really cannot.

# SID CHAPLIN

# *The Tramp*

Running down the lane at the end of Garden Street the boy checked himself at the fence and looked first at the faint pathway trodden through the wide expanse of meadow to the stile and then at the bull, quietly ruminating amongst the deep sweet grass by the pond in the far corner. Over the stile was the head of the pit-bank up which even now his father would be toiling; in the deep grass less than a hundred yards away was the bull who considered the field his kingdom and would assuredly rush him if he attempted to set foot on it. The only other alternative was a long meandering route by the Co-op and the old air-shaft – but that might lead him to miss his father. Gulping, he decided to run the gauntlet of the bull – black as night with smooth pelt under which the muscles rippled and with square-set head and slavering mouth. The horns he didn't dare to think about. Ducking under the rusty old cable stretched tightly between one post and another, he set foot on the bull's domain, deftly snatching up a ladybird on the way. Ladybirds were for luck, weren't they?

Halfway over he was aware without actually looking that the bull had raised his head and was curiously looking at him. It was hard not to look; harder still to walk easily as they'd told him, trying to concentrate on big patches of yellow buttercups scattered like bouquets and the clump of dickory-dock that spread out beyond and lasted all the way to the stile. In the end when it became too difficult to hold he cautiously stole a glance over his shoulder. And sure enough the bull with head down was raising first one hoof then another to the accompaniment of stentorian blowing. Even above the pounding within himself he imagined he could hear it; and for a moment he was frozen. Then he heard his father's voice: 'Walk away slowly, lad,' he was shouting. 'And for God's sake don't look.' His father was a hundred miles away. Beside him was a strange man. Even at that distance he could see his father's face. It was black with the pit and shining with sweat. Now he had taken off his cap and stood inside the meadow. Wave after wave of relief surged through him. Slowly he started walking. But his father was taking a diagonal path away from him. Nonplussed he held back. 'Make straight for the stile,' shouted his father. 'Slowly now. Slowly does it.' And then he was running, waving his cap in the air. 'Hup,' he shouted. 'Come an' get me.' He was shouting at the bull. Now he was shouting, running, waving his big red hankie. With all his heart the boy wished to run after his father, only the bull was there behind him, and with a deep sense of shame he realised that he feared the bull more than anything else in the world; that his fear of it was greater than his love for his father.

Where the dickory-docks were the stranger came running to meet him. There seemed an enormous gap between them. Ever afterwards he remembered the strange eerie silence of the field. All that existed was the pounding that went on inside him, the tall, tattered man striding towards him and the feel of the tall grass whipping against his legs – and far away the shouting of his father, taunting the bull as the tall stranger swept him up in his arms. Then in a flash he saw from his new point of vantage his father running like lightning with the bull close behind. Then he felt himself being pitched bodily over the fence and in a trice the stranger had vaulted lightly over beside him.

'It's all right, he's made it kidder,' panted the stranger. The father was waving from afar down the road, while the bull safely within the fence, stamped his baulked rage and frustration.

The father came toiling up the hill, mopping his brow and face.

'Mind, that was a bit of quick thinking,' said the stranger.

'Aye,' dismissed his father shortly. 'Mind, you're a little toy. How often have I told you?'

'I'm sorry, da,' said the boy.

'Never mind, he kept his head about him,' said the stranger. 'A chip off the old block.'

'As many brains as a shallot,' said his father. 'Can't handle a spade. Doesn't know one end of a hammer from another. God knows what we'll do with him.' To the boy's relief he turned his attention to the stranger again. 'God knows what we'd have done without you.'

'I'll tell you what,' said the stranger. 'He'd have kept on walkin', just as he was told.' His eyes were fixed on the boy's tightly clenched fist. 'What've you got in there, young 'un, if you don't mind me askin'?'

'I'll be bound it's something daft,' said the father. 'He goes around like a magpie, pickin' up all sorts of rubbish.'

For the first time since ducking under the fence, the boy became conscious of his tiny captive, and opened his fist.

'Well I'll be jiggered,' said the stranger. 'It's a ladybird.'

'What did I tell you!' said his father.

'Leave him alone,' said the stranger. 'Mebbe it'll bring me luck.' He picked up the little creature and set it on the back of his hand. It crawled about, flexing its wings. 'Look at it,' said the stranger. 'What did we used to say?' After a while he opened his eyes and chanted:

Two little dicky birds sat on a wall,
One called Peter and one called Paul;
Fly away Peter, fly away Paul,
Come back Peter, come back Paul.

With a flit of his gossamer wings the ladybird was gone. Then out of nowhere he appeared again and landed where he'd been before.

'There, little 'un, I can't go wrong today,' said the stranger, carefully placing the creature on a blade of grass. Rising from the grass he looked down at them. 'I'd better be on me way.' Despite the patches in his coat and trousers he stood there like a god. The boy felt a pang.

'Where you're makin' for?' asked his father.

'Barny and a decent kip for the night,' said the stranger.

'Come and have a bite to eat with us,' said the father. 'You'll feel better with a Yorkshire Pudding behind your ribs.'

The stranger shook his head. 'I wouldn't put on good nature,' he said. 'Besides, I've barely time to make it as it is.'

'You can say what you like, you're not leaving without a bite,' persisted his father. 'Now we're havin' no arguments.'

The stranger looked at his father. 'And I mean it,' repeated his father.

'I'd be glad of a bit of bread and cheese,' temporised the stranger. Then he paused. 'And a slice of onion with it, if you can spare one.'

'I reckon we can stretch as that far,' said his father. 'Maybe a bit further. Depends on what fettle the missus is in.'

The stranger looked sharply at him. 'Like that, is it?'

'No it's not,' said his father. 'Not if your thinking what I'm thinking.'

'It was only a thought,' said the stranger mildly. 'I've had a bit trouble that way myself.'

'Oh, ay,' said his father, encouragingly.

'Well, you know what it's like,' said the stranger. 'Finished my time just as war broke out. Got married and did my stint in the trenches. Came back and they set me on as an improver – then after a year and a month they sacked me.'

'A land fit for heroes,' said my father.

'There was all hell to pay,' said the stranger. 'So I lit out and she went back to her folk. I've looked high and low for a job.'

'It's a bloody mess and that's a fact,' said his father. 'What's your trade?'

'Fitter and turner,' said the stranger. 'But the truth is that I can't shake the war out of my system. Went through the Marne and the Somme.'

'Aeroplanes and tanks and observation balloons,' said the boy. 'Did you see them?'

'Mostly mud,' said the stranger, 'if you're talkin' about the Somme. You daresn't look up for watching your step on the duckboards. We lost more through drowning than bullets.'

'What about the dog fights?' said the boy. With his arms widely extended and making a humming noise he wheeled in a wing-dipping circle.

The stranger shook his head. 'We hadn't much time for looking at aeroplanes.'

'You run ahead and tell your Mam I'm coming,' said his

father. He turned to the stranger. 'Head full of trash,' he apologised. 'He's always reading.'

'Nobody knows what it smelled like,' said the stranger. 'Nobody.'

They came to the club at the bottom of the street. 'Just hang on a minute,' said his father. 'You can drink a pint, I'll bet?'

He disappeared past the doorkeeper into the noisy depths on the long bar.

George William Mattimore was sitting on his haunches beside the doorway. 'Sit down, old lad, and rest your weary bones a minute,' he said. The stranger tried to emulate him by sitting down on his hunkers pitman-fashion and collapsed on his backside. 'Sit on your heels an' prop thi backside against the wall,' said Matty. He took out a cigarette from a five Woodbine packet, tapped one end against the back of his hand, reversed it and tapped again. 'Come far this mornin?' he asked.

'I'm making it from Durham Workhouse to Barny,' he said. His eyes were eating up the Woodbine. 'There's a doss-house there that's well spoken of. I'm lookin' for a job.'

'They're scarcer than pitmen's wives with backsides decked with diamonds,' said Matty. 'Fancy a smoke?'

'Man, it's your last,' protested the stranger.

'What odds?' said Matty, breaking the Woodbine in half. Lighting the stranger's half and his own he blew out the match. 'I'm expecting a tuppenny multiplier to come off tomorrow.'

'That's lovely,' said the stranger, blowing out a ring which started narrow and broadened out to mingle with the shining diamond points of a million dust particles. The father emerged with a big dimpled glass in his hand. 'Forgot to ask you,' he said. 'Will a bitter be all right?' Gently, reverently, the stranger took off some of the froth which was brimming over the side and tasted it with his eyes closed. 'God bless you and keep you,' he said; only in a different way to Mister Willis when he gave the benediction at the Sunday School: but all the same he meant it.

'What mob were you in?' asked George William.

'Fusiliers,' said the stranger.

'Remember the Bull-ring?' asked Matty.

'I should,' said the stranger, and his face went dead.

They turned the corner. 'Happy huntin',' said a voice. When they looked it was Matty's face looking round the corner.

'Got up from his backside for that,' said his father to the stranger. 'Mind you're honoured.'

'Did you have a bull there?' asked the boy. 'A real, live bull, just like ours?'

'Oh, we had a bull all right,' said the stranger.

'I thought I told you to run and tell your Mam,' said his father impatiently.

He'd only half finished explaining to his mother, when the stranger and his father arrived.

'Now what?' said his mother dangerously in the voice that the boy knew so well.

'This is Mister Forsyth,' introduced his father. 'He's looking for a job.'

'Oh, is he?' she said.

'I've invited him in for a bite,' said his father, carefully placing the pint glass on the big dinner table, which was spread all ready.

'The dinner's hardly ready yet,' she snapped, 'and what there is'll hardly suffice for us.'

Snatching his cap the stranger moved to the door. 'Now look . . .' he began.

'Now just you sit down,' said his father, his voice dangerously level. Taking the cap he hung it behind the door. 'Butter him a couple of slices of bread,' he instructed the mother.

'I cannot stay long,' said the stranger. 'I've got to make the doss-house at Barny tonight.'

'Doss-house,' snorted the woman as she spread half a sheet of newspaper on the end of the little side table which stood by the window.

'What about a tablecloth?' demanded the husband.

'You must be joking,' she said and swept out into the scullery. The father took the glass and set it firmly on the little table.

'Howay, sit down,' he ordered.

'Sure?' said the stranger.

'Never fret,' said his father. 'Just sup up. You must be thirsty.'

'Well . . .' said the stranger hesitantly, then drank deeply. He sniffed appreciatively at the smell of roast and Yorkshire Pudding mingling. 'That's lovely,' he said, wiping his mouth with the back of his hand. It was hard to tell whether or not he was praising the taste of the beer or the lovely amalgam of Sunday dinner smells.

'I'm sorry,' said the father apologetically. 'Her bark's worse than her bite y'know. She's got a good heart in her belly, at the bottom of her.'

'Anybody can see that,' said the stranger.

'She's a good lass really,' said the father stoutly. There was something about the way he said it that made the boy sorry for his father.

'Just like our lass at home,' concurred the stranger heartily, and with that he got his eye fixed on Jenny, who had found her way over towards him by holding on first to the stool and then on to the table leg nearest the stranger. 'And who's this, like?' he asked.

'That's our little lass,' said the father. 'Bright as a button.'

'Let's see if we've got something for her,' suggested the stranger, his right hand diving into his jacket pocket. Bringing out a rattle made of interwoven green rushes he held it out to the child. 'Ta,' said the child as she grabbed it.

'She knows how to take what she wants,' said the stranger and held out his arms. 'How about a kiss, Jenny?'

The mother came briskly in and set down a plate of bread before the stranger. Then she snatched up the child. 'Our Jenny's not partial to strangers.'

'What's this?' said the father, his face darkening. 'Bread like house-ends. I shouldn't care if there was cheese to go with it.'

'It's just the way I like it,' said the stranger. 'Home-baked bread as well.' But even the boy could see that something was wrong – something about the way the stranger kept bolting every mouthful, the way he sluiced away every last particle with the beer.

'Is that all right?' said his father.

'It's grand,' said the stranger.

'Well if that's all,' said the woman, 'I'll get on with my cooking.'

'He'll need an onion,' said the husband. 'Give him a big 'un – one of our own. D'you like it with vinegar?'

'Just on its own,' said the stranger. Still grasping the child under her arm the woman departed, but not without a defiant lift of the head. They all waited. The woman brought in the onion, a knife, salt and pepper.

'I thank you,' said the stranger with an old-fashioned courtesy.

'Don't mention it,' said the woman.

The onion seemed to help down the bread and butter. In less than no time the stranger had finished. He stood up. For some reason he seemed embarrassed. 'Well, thanks, mister, thanks, mistress; you've been very kind. I'd best be going.' The man went.

'A fine carry-on,' said the woman. 'You and your tramps.'

'That man,' said his father, 'bled and died for you.'

How funny, the boy thought, the man was alive. How could he have bled and died?

'I don't care,' said the woman defiantly. 'Dirty stinkin' tramps – they're all alike. If they really wanted work they could find it.'

'That man's like me,' said his father. 'A time-served craftsman. He'd work his guts out if they'd let him.'

'It's a bonny good job I'm here to keep you straight,' said the woman, tossing her head. 'Anybody can pull the wool over your eyes – anybody. But not me; I sharp got his measure. I know the treatment to give his sort.'

The man stared at her, then went through to the scullery. Returning he threw an opened packet of margarine on the table. 'Like margarine, for instance,' he asked.

'That's right,' she said, giving him look for look. 'And I spread it on thick for him.'

'Oh, woman, woman,' said the father. 'Do you know what you've done?' And for a moment, while the question hung in the air, the boy shut his eyes, hoping his father wouldn't tell. Vaguely, though, he sensed the answer in what he owed to the stranger, he prayed for silence. He knew what her reaction would be. Punishment would be swift and sure.

'Of course I do,' she answered. 'Do you think I haven't got my wits about me? You've just got to look at him to know what he is. Dirty shiftless lot.'

'Ah, but we know better, don't we, old lad?' the father asked the boy.

The boy's heart pounded, worse than in the bull field. His mouth was dry and his tongue clove to the top of his mouth. He was looking down into the stranger's glass, deep and sour-smelling.

'Oh look da,' he cried, 'the man's gone away and left some beer. Shall I run and tell him?'

The father stared unseeingly at him. 'No, son, I shouldn't bother. That's only the dregs. It's not worth bothering about.' Wearily he unfastened his shirt buttons. 'God, but I'm tired,' he said. He dropped heavily on to the stool. 'He didn't want to come, you know,' he said. 'He had trouble with his own missus – that's why he left home.'

'I know, I know,' she said, unfastening his shirt buttons. 'I'm sorry I went on so much. But first the bairn fratching all morning, then you coming late –'

'It's all right,' he said. When the boy came back with the bath tin she had drawn the shirt over his head. The black was all over him, deeply set in his arms and knees, the knobs of his backbone shining where they'd rubbed against the low roof top. She filled his bath. 'That man's travelled, y'know,' he was murmuring.

'Your bath's ready,' she said.

'Ay,' he said, kneeling down before the tin. 'Up dale and down dale – there's a lot to be said for it. At least you can hear the birds singin'.'

The boy sat where the stranger had been. The smell of the beer was in his nostrils, sour and pungent. His face was clouded. The mother rumpled his hair. 'Stop worrying, Silly Billy,' she reassured him. 'He's not going to run away.'

'Ay,' said his father, smiling up through the soapsuds. 'I'll not leave you. I'm not the sort to do that. Anyway, who would I have to meet me?' The boy's heart suddenly lifted. The father wasn't leaving, after all. His father would keep his secret. Yet somehow he had disappointed his father. But beyond that he sensed a deeper hurt – and a hurt he would always remember. In some way, he felt, his mother had deeply hurt his father.

His mother was standing over his father with the laving tin full of cold tap water held at the ready – she had already washed his back. 'Come on Jack, get finished with it,' she said. 'Now!' said his father. His mother immediately tipped the water over his head and shoulders and in a trice the muck was sluiced away. Eyes closed, his father groped for the towel. He rubbed vigorously. 'It's a good job we've got bairns,' he said. 'By God it is.'

'You did your share,' she said. Her voice bubbling over with laughter. Then she departed into the scullery.

'I daresay,' said the father, 'I daresay I did,' watching her through the folds of the towel. Then he turned his attention to the boy. 'Howay, lad,' he said. 'Perk up. Dry my back for me. One way and another we've worked for our dinner today – you an' me.'

'Now,' said his mother, returning, 'what do you two think you're talkin' about?'

'Secrets,' said his father. 'Man's talk, that's all.'

She held up the pint glass distantly, wrinkling up her nose. 'The sooner this is washed out, the better,' she said. 'Then he can take it back to the doorkeeper.' The glass shone like crystal when she was finished with it. Every last trace of the sour-smelling beer had gone by the time the boy took it back. But the face of the tramp stayed with the boy forever.

# DAVID POWNALL

# *First Words*

I speak as the boy's mother which is what I've been asked to do. If you say it will help him somehow, then I'll have a go. It is a strange thing to be asked – my Kevin being so different from myself in every way imaginable – but I'm going to try and be clear about the whole business because I do care about him, even though I could never get close to the person I still call my son. That boy was just a bolt out of the blue and there isn't much you can do about those.

Parents have a tremendous effect on their children. I don't think anyone in their right mind could argue with that. What Kevin ever got from me I don't know, except perhaps his colouring. Certainly not his mind or any of his ideas. They have nothing at all to do with me. Also I could never teach him anything because as soon as he started talking it was obvious that he thought it was his job to teach *me*.

I was born and brought up in Lancaster. I don't live there now, thank God. Give me this place any time. There's more life in a city and people are more easy-going. I went to an ordinary primary school then a secondary modern, not being too smart, and left when I was sixteen. My Dad worked in a timber yard and my Mum worked in a shoe factory putting buckles on sandals and punching lace-holes in brogues. All this part of my life was very straight-forward and just like anyone else's. You can guess what it was like so I won't bother to go into that.

By the time that summer came round and I went to the Appleby Horse Fair with Yvonne I had left school (I couldn't get out soon enough, I'd been bored rotten for years), and I had a job as a cashier in a café. And I suppose I wasn't bad-looking by then, having filled out and got rid of a lot of skin trouble which had been worrying me since I was twelve.

Yvonne was going around with a man who ran a riding school just outside the town and he was going to the Appleby Horse Fair to buy some ponies. On the way in his car he told us about the tricks that the gypsies get up to to sell their horses, and how he was going to have to watch out for them. He had a friend who had bought a horse up there a few years ago and as soon as the man had got the animal home, it had started coughing fit to die. After a while he got hold of the gypsy who had sold it to him and complained, so the gypsy bought it back from him for thirty pounds less than he had sold it for.

It was an old trick and he should have known better, Yvonne's friend said. The horse had been fed chopped straw straight after the sale, and after a couple of hours it had got stuck in the horse's windpipe. There was nothing else the matter with it and the gypsy was thirty pounds better off. After a bucket of water the horse was as right as rain.

When we got to the fair we started drinking in all the pubs. They were full of gypsies who were flush with money after they'd made sales. I can see them now riding up, two on a pony, with fistfuls of notes. The pubs were open all day and by twelve o'clock a lot of them were drunk which is the state Yvonne's friend had got into pretty quickly. After a while it was plain that Yvonne and her boyfriend didn't want me around. I think they went off somewhere in the car to be frank. She was like that. Not that I minded. I could take care of myself, so I thought.

One of the pubs, the one they left me in when they slipped off, got very noisy and a fight started, so I left it and went for a walk down by the river. It was a fine day and the water was very clear. I enjoyed the quiet and didn't mind being alone. A few of the gypsy lads had made a few passes at me and played around, showing off, but nothing serious. But no one followed me. I wasn't even disappointed, says she.

He was drying himself with his trousers and shirt. I could see the wet marks on the rocks where he'd come up out of the pool. At his feet there was a fish, quite a big one. It was such a surprise. It wasn't that I was shocked because I'd seen all that before, but I'd never seen anyone at a distance with no clothes on and it does change things. He didn't see me while he was drying himself, and I stood there and watched him put his wet shirt and trousers back on (why hadn't he just jumped in with the lot on I asked myself?). Then he came along the river bank towards me with the fish in his hands, his fingers stuck in its gills.

I had to start giggling. I couldn't help it. He looked so serious striding along. I've always been a bit of a giggler. I know what I'm going to turn into when I'm fifty odd. I'll be one of those stout women in coach parties who never stop giggling and drive everybody mad. My grandma was like that. You could hear her a mile away when she got going.

Anyway he stopped. What was I giggling about? he asked. He had a long, dark face and very good teeth. Not like my Kevin at all to look at. For a moment I thought he was angry and then he smiled. That was it. I have never seen a man smile like that again. You've never seen a man smile like he did. Women can do it, some women (not me mind you).

He told me that he'd been tickling trout. That started me off again.

When he asked me if I would like to have a drink with him I could hardly refuse, having laughed at him. He bought me something to eat and we chatted about this and that. Then we went up to the fair which is held on a little country road where the gypsies gallop the horses up and down shouting and whistling to put them through their paces. You can buy anything there from six white matched horses for a circus act, to a kid's pony. The gypsies take no notice of the crowd and charge straight at them on the horses, but they never run into anybody. There was a young lad riding a big brown horse with a bristly chin and he came down the hill at a terrific speed and I thought he was going to run straight into us.

That was when the trout-tickler put his arm round me. He had to. I was frightened.

It was a hot day. I'd had plenty to drink. He was nice. We wandered off into the nearby fields. We sat down and started talking, but then we both went quiet. After a while I thought we'd run out of things to say. You know what I mean. You tend to panic in a situation like that, especially if you fancy the person. So I asked him where he came from and he just said Britain.

That's not enough, I said back. Whereabouts in Britain? That started him off. All over, upwards and downwards, inwards and outwards, Britain.

It didn't make any real sense to me. He wasn't just a Briton. Even if he was a wanderer there was somewhere he could put his finger on and say, I come from here. But he wouldn't have it. I teased him, but he wouldn't change his mind, so I left it. The long and the short of it is that we had a bit of a frolic just after.

He walked me back to the pub where I'd last seen Yvonne and her boyfriend. We had a drink then he said he must be going. I must say I didn't expect him to ask to see me again and I was dead right. He didn't. It would have been pointless asking him for his address, because all he would have said is Britain. Off he went and I haven't seen him from that day to this.

Kevin, as you've guessed after all that build-up, came nine months later, bang on time, full moon, the lot. I had a lot of trouble with Mum and Dad, Mum especially as she was quite prim and proper in a very silly way and worried about the neighbours and all that – which I didn't give a damn about to be honest. What happened to me while I was pregnant that was interesting had nothing to do with all the gossip and my terrible plight as Mum kept saying it was, but it was about dreaming. They say that everyone dreams, but I never had until then, not once. When I went to sleep that was it. Nothing. I never even moved. You could cover me up at night and I'd be in exactly the same position the next morning and I never saw anything or heard anything like a dream until Kevin quickened in me.

It was upsetting at the time because things weren't exactly perfect at home, and I was trying to find a place of my own to live so I could get away from Mum who had become a right old whiner. When I came down in the morning I had her to face, starting up like a factory siren, and on top of that I got quite bad with queasiness. Put the memories of the dreams on my plate with the rest and you'll have some idea what it was like. I tried to talk to my Dad about it, but he always shut me up and said the less dreaming I did in my position the better.

Now you'll want to know what the dreams were about. Natural enough considering I've been going on about them for long enough. Well, I can't tell you. I've not the foggiest notion. There were no recognisable people in the dreams. No places. No one said anything. Every sound was either a hiss or a bang or a weird bubbling noise. I couldn't make head nor tail of them. They swam, full of colour, full of heat. My head was teeming. I used to wake up with headaches especially after the ones which were all black and heaving. My eyes used to be out of focus for a good five minutes after I woke up.

When Kevin was born the dreams stopped.

By then I'd moved away from home, sick of Mum's hysterics and Dad's sulking. I'd decided to make a go of it on my own. It was a struggle and I think I made a mistake by not getting right out of old Lancaster, dump that it is, altogether. But I stuck it out for Kevin's sake so he could have his grandma and grandad near to make up for not having a dad.

He was a very demanding, very difficult child.

When he started to talk it was a lot of gibberish like all babies, but his had a pattern to it from early on. He was making up his own words for things, and when I tried to teach him the proper word he used to fly into a rage and go blue in the face. Then, when I was sitting quiet and letting him know that I thought he'd been naughty he'd come over and get round me, climbing up on my lap. After a minute he'd start up again, pointing to whatever it was and using his word. I had him looked at by the health visitor to find out if his hearing was all right. She gave him a test and said his hearing was better than a dog.

It goes without saying that potty-training him was impossible. His word for that was KWANDOS, or something like that. Whenever I heard him saying KWANDOS I was behind him with it in a flash. He'd sit there for half an hour, doing nothing, then once I let him get up he'd creep over to the cupboard where the gas meter was and do it in there.

I did love him though. I do love him. I'll stick to saying that no matter how it looks. It may seem odd that I can't have anything to do with him (won't, some would say), nor do I ever want to see him again until he's sorted out and something that I can understand, but that's the only way I can cope with being his mother. And that I still am, oh yes, definitely.

He had to find out that he couldn't have all his own way with his language because he couldn't speak to any person but himself. He had to change and accept English so I don't see why that ability should be dead in him now. He has to change like we all do.

He was a beautiful child. As I said, not like his father in his colouring, but nearer me, blondie. That little boy shone, bad as he was. His hair was so bright and his body so straight that I used to love bathing him (when I could get him into the water).

There were only the two of us in that house. Sometimes it felt like an army I was living with. He fought me on every issue. I could feel it. No matter what it was he wouldn't do as he was told, in fact he'd do just the opposite if he could. Then he started wandering off and dodging school. Three or four times a week he just disappeared and I spent hours traipsing the streets looking for him, worried to death in case he'd been knocked down by a car.

Then they found him sleeping under the dust-covers on one of the billiard tables in the Freemasons Lodge. The cleaning woman found him curled up with all the balls in his arms. And he'd wet himself all over the baize. You should have heard the earful that I got off the police for that.

Why? I asked him once. Why do you do these things? Tell me about my Dad, he said, not even bothering to answer my question.

I walked away from that one. What could I have told the child?

It was his idea as much as mine that I send him away. You can disbelieve that if you like, but it's true. He could see me going to pieces and he knew that I'd never really get interested in the things he was interested in, or speak his kind of language. But you must remember that he'd never done anything serious enough to merit approved school or Borstal. All he did was to wander off and be a nuisance in such a way that people were forced to wonder whether he was right in the head or not. That is not criminal.

When he was thirteen we agreed together that he should be looked at by the authorities and they gave him a number of examinations at the Horsefall Hospital. After the last examination they came round to the house for his things and said that he'd asked if he could stay. I had to give my approval and sign a form. I did this and then packed my own things and left that house and I have never been back since.

A lot of this you know, of course.

Yes, I will abide by any decision that the board takes about Kevin's future. I know you are all professional people trying to do a difficult job, and I don't want to put obstacles in your way. No, I don't want to see him and I don't think he's asked for me, has he? I thought not. When he's more like the rest of us, that will be the time for that. You must never tell him where I live without my permission. Yes, you can give him my love. But do it very carefully.

# ALAN BLEASDALE

# *Ba Ba Blacksheep*

It was the Easter holidays. I had three crusty cobs filled with slices of cold meat, collected from the grocery shop where my mother worked, and I was going to eat them on the bench near my grandmother's flat on the new estate. I was eleven. It was nineteen-fifty-seven.

At that time I ran everywhere. It was my hobby. I ran across the main road and galloped up the hill away from the traffic lights at Page Moss, past the rows of terraced houses, heading for the roundabout at Woolfall.

In the Thirties, before the roundabout was built, boys on motorbikes, flushed from a fortnight in the Isle of Man, would try to emulate the 'TT' riders on this downward stretch of road into Liverpool. The roundabout was built after the first boy splintered against the Off Licence wall of the Eagle and Child, the alehouse at the bottom of the hill. That boy was my Uncle Ben's son, an only child, chasing his manhood but never finding it. Seventeen.

My Uncle Ben used to drink in The Eagle. As if in memory. I would sometimes see him on summer Sunday afternoons, conducting the playing of 'pitch and toss' outside, or laughing at the Salvation Army Band whining on the disused tram tracks. He owned two of the new betting shops in Kirkby and a sweets and tobacconist on the block opposite The Eagle.

The houses stopped for about two hundred yards of waste land and then started again in a different form; lower and tighter together, their clenched profiles linked by identically proportioned gardens, stapled with the occasional block of flats.

My mother said there had once been trees and fields on the hill until the estate was built, and when I was no more than a baby she had taken me there often. She told me I had chased the sheep that grazed there and she had taught me 'Ba Ba Blacksheep' but I couldn't ever remember the hill without the barrack of houses.

I reached the benches and sat on the only one that still had a backrest. All the others were broken, except for two that had been delicately dug up and stolen complete. I opened my white paper bag with 'Maxwells Family Grocer' written on the side and ate my dinner while I waited for my grandmother to arrive.

My mother's mother, she had dragged twelve children through the dockland life of Liverpool with a heavy hand, the Catholic Faith, carbolic soap and a husband who never took the cure. Alone now, she rose early on mornings that promised well and took the bus to the city with the clerks and shop girls, returning at times to the Dingle where she was born, or going down to the riverside to sit among the other pensioners and the pigeons and bus conductors. In reality, memory being her only surroundings.

The ten-past-one bus came up the hill from Page Moss, swinging wide at the roundabout, making angles out of curves, but not bringing my grandmother. The day was too fine; I knew she would wait till her pass ran out with the next bus in half an hour.

As the bus approached the stop and the queue twitched, two boys smaller than me ran from the back of Woolfall School and climbed on to the locked gates a few yards further up the road.

They rode the gates like cowboys but they were villains and gangsters already. Their rings, made out of melted down half crowns, flashed on their fingers in the sunlight; their hands held cigarettes. No half-hidden drags and splutters but proud lungfuls. Ten years old and able to smoke. The world take note and watch out.

When the queue sank into the bus and the wheels rolled forward, the boys jumped down from the gates and ran alongside, screaming into the lower deck singular words they had seen and heard rumours about in the playground toilets. Not content, they reached out for the handrail and swung on to the platform, spitting practised lengths into the bus. Figures moved, a man stood, an old woman swore back at them, and the bus conductor came swinging down the passageway to aim a boot at the nearest boy. They both jumped off the bus laughing, satisfied at a job well done.

And then they turned round and saw me. The one with the broken front tooth did all the talking. The other just stood at his side, looking at me as I held on to my bag and edged slowly away from them on the bench.

'Wha' y'waitin' for?'

'Christmas.'

Smack.

'Oow!'

'Oh a friggin' comedian. *Wha' y'waitin' for?*'

'Me gran.'

'That's right, I know already,' he said, as if the secrets of the universe were secretly all his. 'I've seen y'before. You're the kid with the Rockefeller Granma.'

'The wha'?'

'You heard. Everyone knows about her. She's loaded. Got a fortune under her bed in silver sixpences, an' keeps her pound notes in the back of her piano.'

'She hasn't got a piano,' I said but it made no difference to his belief.

'Gorra key t'get in there, have yer? Course y'have.' He wiped his nose on his sleeve and came nearer to me as I bumped into the wooden arm of the bench.

'No.'

'Give us it.'

'I haven't got one an' if you hit me I'll get me dad on to you. He was a boxer.'

'What was y'mam then – a friggin' poodle?' he said and laughed so his companion laughed, showing more broken teeth.

'We'll go halves with yer,' the spokesman said as he stood up and saw another bus, this time coming down the hill. 'Honest.' He pointed at the bus and the two of them ran towards the roadway. I watched them cling on to the handrail of the bus and swing around the roundabouts and down to Page Moss.

I moved back to the centre of the bench and waited, but when the next bus came from the city my grandmother was not on it. Her free pass ran out at two o'clock and no more buses came till after then. I sat there wondering what to do next.

Many times, during the holidays, I had waited and watched, eaten my lunch and sat on the bench, following an adopted ritual for which I would later acknowledge there was no need. I could have arrived while she broke eggs into the tiny frying pan or brushed the ashes from her blackened grate; perhaps bringing the coal up the steps as I came, carrying the bucket lopsided, coal dust down the side of my right leg. I could have done all these things, but instead I had always waited, made an audience, saw her sturdy entrance, her grey hair and creased smile and all the lines that life left. Had I waited too for this day when she would not come?

I stayed for the next bus and then I ran home. Halfway down the hill the two boys were walking back up and they chased me for some distance shouting a mixture of threats and bribery, but they stopped at the boundaries of the old estate. I had made it safely into our kind of Mexico.

My mother was returning to work, her lunch break over. I caught her at the pathway adjacent to the derelict church, walking through the prize nettles which overhung the low slab wall. I told her what had happened and as we talked, the bus that I had waited for without hope returned to the city.

'Go back again,' she said.

'She won't be there.'

'I know,' she said.

She always feared the worst. In dictionaries, definitions of 'pessimism' should include my mother's name and particulars. Insecure, perhaps unaware of her talents, never even knowing her now fading beauty, my mother had become trapped within the locked door of family life. Her own mother had both held and strengthened her, and then she had built her dominion around my father and me. Her life had been an empty one. She said so often.

The funeral cars weaved through the churchyard and stopped. My grandmother was carried into church through the back door, dressed and coated in wood and varnish. For the first time I realised that mortality was not just an ugly rumour.

She had not favoured friends and we were not many in that high arched church, concrete and brick like the area it served. Draped and sagging in black, we lined the first two pews as the twelve o'clock Mass dragged on. The priest, heavy jowled, unshaven, probably only seeming human in the masked closeness of the Confessional as he mumbled his easy forgiveness and penance, stooped awkwardly to spray water on the casket. When it was over, she was lifted by my uncles and carried down the aisle past the few grey faces, praying for time or lost causes, pretending they weren't in some sort of queue.

The tea was at our house. I stood in the backroom with my cousin Barry and compared pimples. We talked of football and ate heartily what the others just picked at in the parlour, their knees together under sandwiches and cake, tea with two sugars. Not a close family, now broken by the years; meeting more in distance than in occasion.

I was called in to take the plates away and hear my mother talk of me as though I was not there. I saw my father, a good man, sparse with words, listening to Uncle Ben, waiting for him to stop so he could go away and save what he had to say for someone worth speaking to. Uncle Ben laughed and then coughed agonisingly, the whole room seeming to stop and watch, considering the possibilities of another funeral. He carried heavy the years of social drinking and secret assignations over illegal betting slips, and his face was heavy with loose flesh, indented at the eyeholes, wet with sweat. As he stood, his stomach seemed to lie in folds before him, while his rear end provided some sort of state of balance.

'Hello, Johnny,' he said as he held his cup up to his moustache, his little finger held at half-mast in a travesty of manners, ash and dandruff congregating on his jacket. He dropped his Woodbine into the dregs of the tea and gave me the cup with a conspiratorial wink. I held my breath and moved away, immune.

'He wanted the key,' my father said when the last taxi had

gone; the vestiges of family departed, the black ties tucked away till the next time.

On other days my mother, to whom defence was the first ambition, would perhaps have struggled more with the implications of this move. Now though, tired and at loss, knowing her mother's absence to be a state of permanence and not just a distance up the hill, she only asked if he had given it to him.

'Yes,' my father said. 'Until five o'clock. He wants to get the television set he gave her. He said he'd bring it straight back then, at five. The key's as much his as ours now. Or the council's.'

'He looks ill himself,' she said, peering into the tea leaves at the bottom of the cup.

It was half-past six and my shadow was ahead of me as I ran. All the shops were shut except the corner one that never seemed to shut. I went past our church without making the sign of the cross and raced up the road to The Eagle.

At the entrance to the bar, by where they kept the sawdust in canvas bags, I saw the man who managed Uncle Ben's sweet shop, a thin nervous character with stained teeth and shares in hair oil companies. He was, I thought, very shifty because he kept his weighing scales hidden behind jars of sweets. He stood now as if in need of an accomplice before entering the bar.

'Hey!' he said. 'Have y'seen y'Uncle Ben?'

'No, I was going to ask you that,' I said.

'He was supposed t'meet me here at six o'clock.'

He looked at his watch as he walked up and down past me, blowing on his hands as though it was a cold day.

'I've got eighty-five quid here in me pocket. One of the Rooney brothers asked me f'a light there before, I couldn't keep the match still . . .'

He wasn't really talking to me. I just happened to be there, that's all.

'I'm goin' up t'me Gr . . .' I stopped. I wasn't goin' to see me gran ever again. He was still walking around as I went away.

Outside the small block of flats where my gran had lived was an old van lined with thick strips of rust and the name

'Herbies Mobile Veg' thinly painted over in white. Uncle Ben was at the back door of the van with two wooden boxes, like small packing cases. Lace curtains at several of the windows in the flats were pulled apart and grey ancient faces could be seen dully peering out.

I waited and hid in the telephone kiosk across the road, holding the flex that dangled from the hollow machine. When I jumped up I could see the top of my head in the cracked mirror.

Uncle Ben locked the door and went up the narrow steps to the second floor. There was a sound of breaking glass from the school on the corner and the two boys who had chased me on the day my gran never came back, walked cockily across the grass and jumped over the wall. They strolled straight past me and went over to the van, kicked the tyres, picked at the paintwork, looked through the windows and then tried to force open the back door.

'Give y' a hand, mister?' the talkative one said when Uncle Ben came back, struggling down the steps with the television set. 'Go on, be well worth it to yer; better than Pickfords we are, fact that, always removin' things aren't we, Joey?'

'Remove y'selves then,' Uncle Ben said. 'Go on, go an' play in the traffic.'

'Try an' make us, jelly-belly.'

'You stay there an' say that again, sonny,' Uncle Ben said, bent double as he placed the television on the pavement.

'Wha're you goin' to do – chase us? Couldn't catch a cold in a chest clinic, you.'

He couldn't neither. By the time he'd turned around and gathered strength and steam, they were dancing up the hill shoutin' 'Billy Bunter's dad' and 'Bimbo the Elephant' at him. When they got to Woolfall shops at the far end of the road they stopped briefly before, quite suddenly, the boy who rarely spoke walked into the roadway and roared at the top of his voice, 'Robber, robber! We know what y'doin', we know what y'doin'!'

So did I. I watched him as four times he went in and out of the flats. To unlock the door of his van he had to put everything on the floor and I saw him bend, unlock, lift, lock and go back again. It was like a ceremony, an act of worship.

Finally, I followed him into the flats; heard his heavy foot-
fall, his steel-tipped heels above me on the stone steps, the
sound of the borrowed key in the lock. I climbed up the steps
till my head was level with the door mat. The door was open
so I carried on up the stairs to the landing. My toes touched the
mat, my intentions unclear till I heard a noise behind me and
turned in time to see the flap of the letterbox in the door
opposite, slowly shutting.

I quickly stepped forward through the open door for the last
time, meeting the constant smell of mothballs, the painted
crucifixion, the hollow statue of the Virgin Mary and a picture
of a dead Pope, his arms outstretched and edged in blue, his
hands held up as if in self-defence, his eyes looking slightly
crossed.

I could hear my uncle pounding about in the bedroom,
moving furniture that wasn't used to action or built for
movement. And neither was he. He started to cough; a con-
vulsive ache whining within his body, finding a way out. I
heard him sit down heavily on the bed and curse again.

If he had moved from the bed I would have heard him in
time to put the statue back on the hall table. I lifted it up gently
and quietly turned it over but I knew from the second I picked
it up that nothing had been taken from inside the hollow shell
because it still weighed far heavier than any plaster of Paris
Virgin Mary had a right to weigh. 'Silver sovereigns,' my
grandmother once said to me. 'Keep y'money in silver, never
mind your pieces of paper.' That was my grandmother's
hobby, collecting silver sovereigns.

He finally came through the bedroom doorway, not seeing
me at first, carrying three sweet jars awkwardly. He turned
into the hallway and stopped. Surprise is hidden well when
you're fifty-five years old and seen everything from Burma to
bankruptcy; when you know that whatever might cry out
loses its percentage; that refusal to admit defeat is almost
victory.

'Hello, Johnny,' he said. 'I suppose y'dad wants the key?'
'It's in me pocket,' he said. 'Take it.' He indicated his jacket
pocket without the bulge of loose money.

I went up to him and took it out. Pieces of tobacco leaf stuck
to my fingers in his pocket. For the first time I was frightened

and I pulled quickly away from him as soon as I had hold of the key. Even now, all these years later, whenever I come into a stale room the morning after a party and look at the fallen bottles and swollen ashtrays, I can smell my Uncle Ben and see him standing there, smiling grotesquely and holding three sweet jars full of silver sixpences.

I stood in front of the Virgin's Statue and looked down at my feet.

'I've just about finished now,' he said. 'You can see yourself out, lad, can't you?'

'Yes.'

'Is there anything you want?'

'My gran said I could have her statue when she . . . y'know . . . when . . .'

'Very pretty too it is,' he said as his foot dragged the door open. 'I'd give you a hand with it except I have t'have the van back pretty sharpish.'

'It's all right,' I said. 'It's really quite light.'

I know that if one of his hands had been free, he would have slipped me a grubby few bob and patted me on the head. At the doorway he half-turned still out of breath.

'Once I had a son just like you,' he said.

As he went down the stairs, his pockets jangled.

# BARRY HINES

# *Another Jimmy Dance*

They got off the bus and walked towards the Ground. Other spectators, joining the road from the side streets, made something of a crowd and the traffic had to slow down because of people crossing and stepping without warning off the pavements. Ian pulled his dad's sleeve and pointed ahead.

'Look, dad, you can see the floodlights. Do you think they'll put them on?'

Ronnie looked up at the sky. There were two layers of cloud; dark ones travelling fast under a wash of paler grey. When a mass of dark ones came over, it rained until the wind had blown them away.

'They will unless it clears up. It'll be dark by half-time at this rate.'

He took out his handkerchief and wiped the front of his spectacles without taking them off.

'I could do with some windscreen wipers for these.'

'Did you play in your glasses when you used to play football, dad?'

'No, I didn't need them when I was a lad. I didn't start to wear them until after I'd got married.'

A gang of boys ran past. Dozens of them, down both pavements and in the road. They shouted the name of the home team and banged on the roofs of cars as they passed them. Most of them were wearing scarves, some on their wrists and belts, and as they ran the scarves streamed out like pennants. Ronnie took Ian's hand and pulled him close until they had gone.

'Bloody hooligans.'

But Ian was thrilled by the episode and his face was flushed as he watched them run away towards the Ground.

'What are they running for, dad?'

'Cos they're daft, that's why.'

'Can I have a scarf, dad?'

They walked on and Ian had to ask again before Ronnie answered.

'We'll see how you get on.'

'What do you mean?'

'Well, you might not like it. You might not want to come again.'

'Course I'll like it!' He was indignant at his father's lack of confidence in him.

'It's not like 'Match of the Day', this, you know. This is Fourth Division, not First.'

As they approached the Ground they could hear the music from the tannoys inside. They crossed the road and Ian pointed to a group of people standing around a man in a white overall.

'What's them pamphlets they're buying, dad?'

'What pamphlets?'

'Them, look.'

Ronnie looked, then laughed.

'They're programmes. They tell you the teams.'

'Can we have one?'

Ronnie bought a programme and checked his change.

'Ten p. They used to be sixpence when we used to come. I mean sixpence in old money, not new.'

He opened the programme to find the teams. Ian stood on his toes so that he could see, too.

'There he is, look.'

Ronnie pointed to a name on the visitors team list; number 10. Dance.

'Who will you shout for, dad, now that he plays for them?'

'I don't know as I'll be shouting for anybody. I can hardly call myself a Town supporter now. I haven't been for years.'

He looked down the Home team in the programme and shook his head.

'I don't know any of these players now. They're all new 'uns to me.'

He gave the programme to Ian. There was no queue at the turnstile and they went straight in. The mechanism of the gate was stiff and when Ronnie had clicked by he had to pull the bar to help Ian through it.

'It's rusty through lack of use, that's the trouble with it.'

Ronnie asked Ian if he wanted to go to the toilet. He didn't, so they walked up the steps at the back of the Spion Kop. When they reached the top and Ian looked down into the Ground and saw the freshly rolled pitch with the nets up, the fresh white markings and the red corner flags, he smiled shyly at the splendour of it all.

'It's the first real football ground I've ever seen, dad.'

'It's a pity they haven't got a real football team to go with it any more. Where do you want to stand?'

'Let's go nearer to the pitch.'

They walked down the terracing towards the back of the goal and Ronnie chose a barrier a few steps up from the wall. There was no one else on the barrier. There was no one else within five yards of them and there were large spaces on the Kop and on the other sections of the Ground.

Ronnie rested his arms on the barrier which was mottled with rust and Ian ran down the steps to look over the wall at the pitch. Some of the steps were cracked and crumbling at the edges and grass and ragwort were growing in their angles. Ian ran back up to the barrier and gave Ronnie the programme to save.

'It's a better pitch than that one in the rec, dad.'

'You should have seen it when I was a lad, Ian . . .'

He paused and looked round the Ground, remembering it all.

' . . . when Jimmy Dance was playing and we won the Cup, it used to be packed. We'd have had to come in an hour before the kick off to get where we are now.'

Ian was looking at his watch.

'How long does it last, dad?'

'90 minutes. It'll finish about quarter to five.'

'Do you think we'll get back in time for 'Doctor Who'?'

Before Ronnie had time to answer, the Town ran down the

tunnel on to the pitch. There was some desultory cheering and clapping which echoed round the roof of the stand and emphasized even more the sparsity of the crowd. They ran to the other end of the pitch and warmed up busily, shooting and passing and doing loosening exercises.

Then the Visitors came out to ritual abuse and moved to the end where Ronnie and Ian were standing. Ronnie found Jimmy Dance and his smile was like the sun coming out. Dance flicked a ball up and kept it off the ground with his feet, thighs and head. Ronnie bent down and pointed him out to Ian.

'Which one?'

'Him out there, look, on the edge of the penalty area.'

'Do you mean that fat 'un?'

Ronnie straightened up, his smile gone.

'That's not fat. He's always been well-built has Jimmy.'

The goalkeeper placed his cap and gloves behind one of the posts then spat on his hands and pranced along the goal-line ready to receive the first practice shot. Dance volleyed his ball straight past him, high into the net. Ronnie nudged Ian with his hip and grinned.

'See that?'

'He's going bald, dad, like you.'

Ronnie clipped him across the back of the head with his programme.

'What do you mean, bald? He's not bald. It's because he's fair that's all.' Then, 'Bald or not, I wish he was still playing for the Town. I might come a bit more often then.'

The captains tossed up. The teams changed ends and the referee started the game. Ian went back down to the wall and stood near two boys of his own age who soon lost interest and started to chase each other around an empty crash barrier.

Play was brisk and earnest. The players ran hard and moved the ball quickly. But their skill was not up to the pace they were playing at and passes kept going to the other team. Ronnie couldn't stop watching Jimmy Dance even when the ball was nowhere near him and he was just standing about waiting for it.

It was ten years since he had been transferred, but Ronnie still saw him in the Town's colours. And although he had now played for four other clubs in a steadily declining career through the Divisions, for Ronnie he would always be a Town player. He had played for England when he played for the Town. He had scored both goals the year the Town had won the Cup. Ronnie had been there to see him do it. He had gone down on Friday after work with his mates. They had got drunk and roamed Soho all night. And next day the Town had won the Cup. So they got drunk again, got locked up for the night, and when he finally arrived home he went straight to bed and stayed there for two days. It was the best time he had ever had in his life.

He had told Ian about it when they were having their dinners and watching 'Football Focus'. Ian said he had heard it before and wanted to listen to what the commentator said. His wife said she had heard it a thousand times already.

Dance took a pass, evaded a tackle and held the ball, waiting for someone to move into space before releasing it.

'Watch, Ian!'

But Ian had his back to the pitch and was watching a group of Town supporters singing and swaying with their scarves held horizontally above their heads. Ronnie glanced round to see what he was looking at, then called him back up to the barrier to stand with him.

'I've brought you to watch the football, not them silly buggers,' he said.

'Don't you want the Town to win, dad? I do.'

The Town scored first when Dance was dispossessed, leaving the Town striker a clear run at goal. He took it on and shot it low past the goalkeeper as he advanced to narrow the angle. Ian jumped and clapped and cheered like the gang of lads behind him. Ronnie shook his head slowly and looked serious.

'Terrible defensive play, that. There was no cover at all.'

Ian started to pull at Ronnie's coat.

'Dad.'

'What?'

'I want to wee.'

Ronnie looked away and swore softly.

'I can't help it.'

'I asked you if you wanted to go before we came in.'

'I know, but I didn't want to go then, did I?'

Ronnie led him back up the Kop and out through one of the exits. While he was waiting for Ian a second shout went up and Ian ran out of the toilet zipping up his jeans.

'What are they shouting for, dad?'

'The Town have scored again, I would imagine.'

'It's not fair. We've missed it.'

'Well, if we'd have asked them nice, they might have held the game till we got back.'

Ian looked up at him.

'Would they?'

He had missed the sarcasm completely and his innocence made Ronnie feel ashamed of himself as he led him back up the steps to their place.

At half-time Ronnie bought an orange drink and a packet of crisps for Ian and a cup of tea for himself. He explained to Ian how to read the half-time scores of the other games by matching up the letters on the terrace wall with the teams in the programme. Then he showed him their programme number and told him to listen carefully for the lucky draw.

'I once came to the Town for a trial you know, Ian.'

'Did you play here?'

'No, they've got a training ground out at Thorncliffe.'

'What position did you play?'

'Half back. They don't even call it that now. They call it midfield . . .'

'Listen, dad!'

It was the tannoy announcing the lucky draw. The prize was two stand tickets for the next home game. They listened for the winning number. It wasn't theirs. They were thousands out.

'Thank God we didn't win,' Ronnie said and he turned back to the team page and checked the rest of the half-time scores.

'They don't even set the teams out properly in the programmes any more. There aren't any real positions these days. Everybody just seems to play anywhere now.'

'Did you play well, dad?'

Ronnie finished his tea and volleyed the plastic cup down the steps.

'I wasn't on long enough to play well. They kept taking players off and bringing new ones on. There were hundreds there.'

He lit a cigarette and flicked the match down after the cup.

'Still, it was a good thing, really. There's no security in football. Too much luck involved.'

The teams walked back on to the pitch to a few cheers and boos and the game re-started. The Visitors attacked vigorously but with little wit or imagination and the Town appeared content to defend their two goal lead. They played one forward in an attacking position and left him to salvage a succession of long, high clearances aimed in his general direction. It was a graceless affair.

Once, Dance slipped his marker and chipped the ball over a defender for one of his team mates to run on to and shoot. Ronnie couldn't help himself.

'Well played, Jimmy!'

Ian was surprised and embarrassed at his father shouting like that. Especially as they were standing on their own and everybody could tell who it was. The next time Dance controlled the ball it was taken off him by a Town defender who cleared it upfield.

'Well played, Jimmy!' One of the boys behind Ronnie and Ian shouted. Ronnie turned on them, furious.

'What do you lot know about it? You've never seen a decent team down here.'

'It's not our fault that we weren't born last century, mister.'

The boys laughed and Ronnie turned back to the game, pale and trembling with anger.

'Ignorant sods. They've no idea. They never saw Jimmy when he was at his best. He scored thirty-six goals one season. We followed them everywhere that year. Me and the lads.'

'He's too slow though now, dad. He's too old.'

'Is he heck too slow. It's the others that's playing too fast, that's the trouble.'

Twenty minutes into the second-half, Bamforth scored his second goal for the Town and five minutes later the Visitors' trainer came out of the dugout and held up a board with number 10 on it. Dance's number. The ball went out of play and Dance walked off. He touched hands with his substitute who sprinted on to the pitch looking conspicuous in his clean white shorts and socks. Ronnie shook his head slowly.

'Bloody ridiculous. He's the only player on the park with any skill.'

'I bet he's off to draw his pension!' One of the boys shouted as Dance walked up the tunnel. The others laughed. Ronnie turned on them again.

'You'll never see a better player down here.'

'You what? I've seen better players in 'Dad's Army'.'

They laughed again and Ronnie turned round, too miserable to argue.

'What's the point?' he said and looked at his watch.

'Do you want to go, Ian? There's not long left now.'

Ian was surprised and indignant at the question.

'Do I heck! It's great. They might score again.'

They didn't, but Bamforth shot against the crossbar and the boys chanted Bam-forth! Bam-forth! with Ian chanting with them.

At the end of the match, Ian had to watch all the players and the officials leave the pitch before he would go and as they walked down the steps to the gate, he pointed to the legs of a boy in front of them.

'Look, dad, I'm going to write all the Town's players names on my jeans like him.'

Ronnie looked at the pale jeans with the names felt-tipped all over them.

'You'll have to see what you mother says about that.'

'Bamforth's a good player isn't he, dad? I wonder how many goals he's scored now?'

He stopped to look in the programme while Ronnie, unaware of this, carried on. When he realised that Ian was no longer with him he looked back but he could not see him amongst the crowd that had converged at the gate. Then a gap appeared and Ronnie saw him standing there, reading the programme, oblivious of the bustle around him. Angrily, Ronnie went back and grabbed him by the arm.

'What are you trying to do, Ian, get lost? I'll not bring you again if you don't behave yourself.'

Ian shook the hand off and tears came to his eyes.

'What do you mean, behave myself? I haven't done owt yet.'

Ronnie took his hand roughly and they left the Ground and

crossed the road. As soon as they reached the pavement, Ian pulled his hand away and they walked down the road without speaking. It was dark now. The shop windows were lit and the street lamps and car headlights were on. The floodlights inside the Ground had disguised how dark it really was.

When they reached the bus stop there was a queue and after they had been standing there for a while it started to rain again. Ronnie pulled up the hood of Ian's anorak and zipped it to the top, then he took the boy's hand and pulled him close to keep him warm. Ian did not shrug away this time, but stood still and let his father hold him. There was a different kind of silence between them now.

Ian looked up. 'Dance's a good player isn't he, dad? They were daft taking him off. Him who came on was rubbish.'

Ronnie looked down at the little face in the hood.

'That Bamforth's not a bad lad either. He's definitely got the makings. I reckon they might have another Jimmy Dance there if they look after him.'

'Can we come again, dad?'

'If you like. You'll not need me to bring you much longer, though. You'll soon be coming with your own mates.'

'I'm going to save up and buy a scarf and a bobble hat and two rosettes like them lads were wearing.'

They didn't have time to say any more because the bus arrived just then and they had to concentrate on keeping their place as the queue pushed forward.

# VALERIE GEORGESON

## *Sophie's Blues*

At first, she felt nothing . . . the music that had danced wildly
through the child's body continued to invade the quiet garden
from across the fields, but Sophie had stopped dancing. She
glared at the wall which had got so thoughtlessly in her way,
and rubbed her elbow. Then, surprise gave way to anger.
Screaming and yelling, she beat her fists upon it to punish it for
the dreadful thing it had done, tears flying from her face like
poisoned arrows. Her din surpassed even the amplified music
of the pop concert and brought her mother dashing from the
kitchen.

'What's up with you?' Sophie's mother stared at the belli-
gerent child who was rubbing her elbow and scowling.

'I banged me elbow on the wall,' she mumbled. 'What'd it
want to get in me way for?' She glared at the unresponsive
brick.

'How'd you manage to do that?'

'I was dancin'.'

'What? In the garden? Ye daft fool!'

Sophie's hands left her elbow and turned into fists in her
eyes as the tears flowed. Her mother melted and took her in
her arms, consoling her.

'There, there,' she said. 'Rub it better.'

'Now I've hurt meself, can I go to the pop festival to cheer
meself up?'

'You cunning devil . . . no. You can't. It's high time little
girls of eight were in bed.'

'I'll cry meself to sleep,' Sophie warned.

'You'll do no such thing.'

'What was all that about?' Her father shouted from his study.

'She banged her funny bone.'

'Can she not learn to suffer in silence?' Sophie's father, cottonwool in his ears, turned back to his book.

Sophie, deeply offended, pursed her lips tightly and flung her mother's arm from her, refusing to speak till her mother was brushing her shock of yellow hair and trying in vain to make it lie down flat.

'I won't be able to sleep anyway . . . because of the noise.'

Her mother sighed. 'They're only here for one night,' Sophie added.

'Thank God.'

'They'll be gone in the morning . . .'

'You're not going.' She gave up her child's hair in despair and Sophie shook her head like a dog after grooming.

'I haven't said goodnight to me owl.' The mother watched her flounce off to the window in her nightie and throw up the sash. The music crashed into the room. The mother winced but the child thrilled to the rhythms dancing across to her over the trees and breathed deep of the darkening air. The floodlights made interesting patterns in the sky.

'I can't hear me owl,' Sophie shouted over her shoulder.

'I should just think you can't,' answered her mother.

'It's there, though.'

'How d'you know?'

'It's always there. I've been watchin' it; every night.' The light shape of a creature rising from the trees darkened into an owl against the floodlights.

'There it is,' Sophie pointed excitedly.

'It's only little,' said her mother deprecatingly.

'It's its proper size,' Sophie snapped back. 'I'm only little.'

'Yes,' said her mother. 'I know.' She gazed into the big, round eyes, darkened with indignation in her pale face and halo of pale hair that was the bane of her life, and wondered just what went on in that strange child's head. She reached for a doll as for an anchor and put it in Sophie's arms; but the child threw it back at her.

'I don't like dolls. Daft things dolls.'

'Most little girls like dolls . . . your aunty Cath gave you that.'

'I like live things . . . toads and gerbils and . . . owls. Dolls are daft.'

'You can't take gerbils and toads to bed with you.'

'Can I take me owl?'

'What? No. Of course you can't. Dirty thing like that! Anyway, it wouldn't like it.'

'No.' Sophie stared at the darkened window and imagined the owl twit twooing about, catching mice for its supper. She hoped it would get a lot, not caring about the mice. Served them right . . . they ate things too.

'Come on to bed,' said her mother pulling down the sash. Then, as she tucked her daughter in she asked: 'Would you like a story?'

'No.'

'All right.' She kissed the child goodnight, lingered awhile looking at her pale face and the tightly shut eyes, then crept out of her room.

Sophie's eyes sprang open. She ran to the window, hurling it up and searching frantically for the shape of wings over the treetops. She must say goodnight. There was no sign of the bird but the dancing noises stirred her imagination. Rushing to her dressing table Sophie knelt and resting her cheeks on her fists stared into her own large, grey eyes. As she stared they got bigger and bigger and rounder and rounder. The room, on the edge of her vision, trembled out of focus. Her breath deepened and the range of her thought touched the trees beyond the garden, far into the darkness of the night. A loud squeak on the window pane and a flutter of feathers told her she had been visited. Quietly Sophie pulled the window down and went to bed, crying herself to sleep as she had promised she would.

Sophie's eyes opened slowly, wary of the silence, and scanned the room without moving her head. She followed the pink light down to where it hid under her bed and up to where it melted into the ceiling, cowering in the corners of her room, creeping round her where she lay in bed. Flinging back the bedclothes she leapt to the window and threw it wide, freeing the air that had been trapped with her in her room through the night and breathing in the gentle light of dawn. The concert was over. The people had gone, crashing their gears through the night, searching the road with their bright headlights or drifting aimlessly through the country roads back to the town. But perhaps there would be someone left to tell her what it was like. Sophie tore off her nightie and arranged a dress and knickers haphazardly about her body, forgetting her shoes and coming back for them when the soles of her feet touched a sharp stone and hurt her. Her parents snored deeply after their disturbed night. Sophie raced over the lawn before the dragon should wake and take her back to its lair, and sought the comparatively safe shadows of the wood beyond their garden.

She slowed as she reached the dark places in the middle, searching the undergrowth for shadows that should have fled with the night, watching the light as it filtered through the leaves of the trees, glancing at the odd root, a squirrel that stared at her as at some strange thing, then scarpered up a tree trunk, a bird twittering warnings of her coming. Sophie smiled and spreading her arms wide to touch the bark of the trees as she passed, skipped out of the wood into the fields. Here the intensity of light made everything suddenly twice as real as it should be. It caught Sophie's breath and she stood for a moment, watching the tall grass wave at the edge of the wood, the sudden green of the turf, then, at the top of the hill, the sharp outline of a black woman, huddled in a blanket, staring out in front of her. And, between them, on the ground, lay Sophie's owl.

The shriek of rage caused the black head to turn abruptly and the woman stared at the scene before her. A white child, howling, screaming abuse at her and pouring her body over something in the grass.

After a while Sophie looked up and met the red eyes, saw the tear on the black cheek, and paused. 'Are you crying for my owl?' she demanded.

The black eyebrows raised. 'Owl . . .' The woman's voice was low and tired. She did not try to curb Sophie's temperament; did not care. Uncertain, Sophie stared then dropped her eyes again to the creature at her knees.

'You killed him.'

'I didn't kill him.'

'Somebody did then.'

'It wasn't me.' They stared again. 'Show me,' said the woman.

Sophie picked up the little owl and brought it to her. Black fingers searched through the feathers, gently spreading the wings, stroking the head. The movements comforted Sophie. There was a black, searing mark across the breast of the bird where the tawny feathers were singed.

'See,' said the woman, showing Sophie. 'He must've flown into an electric wire. Maybe one of ours for the floodlights.'

'It's your fault,' said Sophie.

'Why is it my fault?'

'It must be somebody's fault.'

'Must it?'

Sophie sniffed and took the bird back, hugging it to her chest.

'Little girl . . .'

'I'm not a little girl.'

'Oh, what are you then?'

'I'm a person.'

'Ah.' The black woman's tired eyes brightened. 'What's your name then, person?'

'Sophie. Why? What's yours?'

'Joan.'

'Hallo.'

'Hallo. Was that your owl, Sophie?'

Sophie, gripped by sudden grief, could not answer. She nodded. The woman looked away, respectful of the child's emotion, not trying to offer comfort.

'I didn't buy him,' the strangled voice explained. 'I loved him. He loved me.' The tired, black face creased in sudden pain and when the eyes opened again there were tears in them. 'And now somebody's took him from me,' Sophie said, biting her lip, staring at the ground, her body taut, like a wire singing in silent grief. Joan wiped away her tears and looked at the child.

'What are you going to do about it?' she asked.

Sophie's angry eyes darted up to meet the black ones. 'What CAN I do?'

Joan shrugged. 'You can cry,' she said.

'My dad says you should suffer in silence,' Sophie paused, 'especially when he wants to read his book.'

'Grown-ups tend to think like that,' said Joan. 'I'm not sure they're right though.' Sophie's look questioned her. Joan thought. 'Well . . . we ought to bury him . . . don't you think so?'

Sophie nodded. 'A proper funeral, with dirges and everything.' She grew excited at the prospect.

'Yes.' Joan nodded in growing approval. 'Let's hold a funeral with . . . dirges and everything.'

And Sophie's eyes widened as Joan brought a guitar out from under her blanket. 'You collect a lot of small stones to build a cairn. I'll write him a special song . . . dirge.' Joan took a notebook and pencil from her jeans pocket and Sophie watched from the corner of her eye while she gathered stones and Joan scribbled and twanged intermittently on her guitar.

'You must've written one by now,' said Sophie.

'Nearly.' Joan tried a tune on her guitar, humming softly to herself.

'Will I be able to join in?' Sophie asked.

'Sure. If you learn fast.' Joan didn't look at her and Sophie watched while she finished scribbling and crossing out. Then the black face turned to her.

'Are you ready?' Sophie nodded. 'Good. Fetch the owl.' Sophie went back for the owl. The early sun had warmed its body and the feathers felt almost alive, but its eyes were fast shut and the scorch mark on its chest stung Sophie's eyes with new tears. She sobbed, and kissed it, then laid it gently in the little hollow Joan had made with her hands in the grass. And when Joan took her hands away the grass sprang back to receive him, half covering the tawny feathers.

The black face and the white watched the stems snap back one after another. Then Joan picked up a stone and began to build a circle round the owl. Sophie built on top of it then Joan, then Sophie, then Joan until there was only one brown feathered patch left and as Sophie laid the last stone, she howled, while tears rolled down Joan's cheeks. Then Joan took up her guitar and began singing:

\*　　　\*　　　\*

This thing is now dead
This living thing
There is nothing left between us . . .
A pair of night owls we . . .
Flying in the dark . . .
Poles apart
So different
Yet magnetised . . . by love.

Tell the world . . .
Don't suffer in silence
Hang it out for all to see . . .
Dance and shout
Dance and shout
Don't suffer quietly.
Don't suffer quietly.

Flying down the planes of light
Night owls together
Caught by the energy of light
Blinded by brightness
Too much love
There was too much love between us
We had to die
We had to die
In a flash of inspiration.

Tell the world . . .
Don't suffer in silence
Hang it out for all to see . . .
Dance and shout
Dance and shout
Don't suffer quietly.
Don't suffer quietly.

Sophie watched the black face, listened to the black voice,
soft and low, sad, beautiful, then the child's heart soared as the
dark voice reached out of the chorus, higher and higher, until
it danced and shouted on the mountain tops and she thought
the dark sound must have snow on it when it came down

again. Then she knew that the owl had to die, but at least it had flown, as Joan said, on the planes of light. She also knew that she, Sophie, would never suffer in silence again, no matter what her dad said. Joan's voice went on playing games with the sounds her fingers made on the strings and Sophie danced and howled round and round the cairn, until at last the voice stopped and the fingers dropped from the strings and Sophie flopped down on the grass beside her friend. They lay feeling the sun on their skins and thinking of the cold bird under the stones.

'Did you know my owl?' Sophie asked

'Not personally,' answered Joan.

'Oh, I thought you did.'

'No. You can still be sorry about something that's died though, can't you?'

'Yes,' Sophie nodded. 'Anyway, he can't have suffered much, can he?'

'Perhaps not.'

'Are you a singer, then?'

'Yes.'

'Were you a singer at the pop concert last night?'

'Yes.'

'Do you think I'd be a good singer?'

'No.'

'Oh.'

'You might be a good dancer though . . . or an animal trainer . . .'

Sophie's eyes brightened.

'Did you have a stage last night, for the concert?'

'Yeah. Sure we did.'

'Is it still there?'

'Might be. It's over the other side of the field if it is.'

'I think we should do the song again, on the stage, don't you?'

'No, I don't.'

'Why not?' Irritation sharpened Sophie's eyes. Joan looked at her and smiled, then raised her hand to the pale cheek and stroked it.

'Hey . . . listen. That bird's dead. Right?'

'Right.'

'And we're alive . . . huh?' Sophie nodded. 'So we've got to get on living now . . . It's done . . . dead and buried.'

'Yes.' Sophie nodded and looked back seriously into the woman's eyes. 'We've got to go on living,' she said.

'Right.' The hand dropped.

'I'm hungry.' Sophie realised suddenly that she had had nothing to eat that day.

'So'm I,' Joan laughed.

'Would you like to come home with me for breakfast?' Sophie was all excitement, longing to drag her strange new friend home with her.

'I don't think so, person . . . I don't think your parents would entirely appreciate seeing me so early in the morning and all.'

Sophie's face dropped. She couldn't deny it. Her father would put on his pained look and her mother would smile too much, then tell her off afterwards.

'Anyway,' said Joan with decision, 'it's time I was on my way . . .'

Sophie watched her gather up her guitar and her blanket and waited until she turned to her again. Joan looked at the solemn, pale face and the strange eyes. 'Thank you,' she said. 'Thank you very much, person.' Joan watched the question pass across the child's face and vanish as she shrugged her shoulders and answered: 'That's all right.'

They smiled. Then Joan turned and strode off over the hill towards the main road. Sophie picked a stone from the top of the cairn and threw it in the air, catching it as it fell, then throwing it up higher and higher. She started singing as she skipped home:

> Tell the world . . .
> Don't suffer in silence
> Hang it out for all to see . . .
> Dance and shout
> Dance and shout
> Don't suffer quietly.
> Don't suffer quietly.

And as her voice came down it had snow on it too.

# BILL NAUGHTON

# *Tom's Sister*

One rainy Tuesday morning, when I was nearly sixteen, I put on my Sunday suit, and set off for the Royal Navy recruiting office in Moncrieff Street, Bolton. My mother had been crying when I kissed her goodbye and her tears nearly set me off, so that I had to keep swallowing little hard lumps in my throat as I walked along the wet streets, amongst the folk hurrying to the cotton mills before the quarter-to-eight buzzer went.

The recruiting officer, a grey-haired man in a blue overcoat, made out a railway pass for me to go to Manchester, where I would be given a medical examination. I went there and was examined with eight more fellows, all older than myself. They all failed early on, except another chap and myself. I passed everything so it seemed, but the doctor kept listening to my heart. I was very nervous at the time and I could hear it pounding away. Then he said to me: 'You'd better come back in a year's time, sonny, when you've calmed down.'

I felt ashamed of myself for having failed. I kept trying to think what I'd tell my mates. I wandered round Manchester a bit. I was hungry but I hadn't the courage to go in anywhere for a cup of tea since I'd never been in a café in my life, except once at a funeral. But then, feeling full of misery, I went home.

I'd no job to go back to, since I'd given up my job in the weaving shed to join the navy. It wasn't easy to get work at the time, because the mills were doing badly. But a man called Tommy Cheadle told me where to go.

'Go to the Hilton Mercerising Company,' he said. 'It's out in the wilds, but there's sure to be a job because Abraham

Hilton is always sacking somebody. If they like the look of your face they'll let you work night and day. But don't tell 'em you're a Catholic – he goes in for Wesleyans, and he's a local preacher.'

I went there, and I didn't say anything about being a Catholic or anything else, and I got a job. It was shift work and I had to clock in by six o'clock next morning. I was very excited and happy. Nobody I knew worked there and it was like making a new start in life.

I was up at half-past four next morning, and went off to work through the dark streets just after five – my mother kissing me goodbye and crying a bit. But I liked the streets at that hour. You were almost alone and you didn't have to pass groups of mill girls who would suddenly burst out laughing and who made going to the factory a bit of a trial.

The mercerising and dyeing shop was a very big high steamy sort of place with a wet concrete floor and eight heavy roller machines on which smoothed-out bundles of cotton yarn were placed, immersed in liquid caustic, stretched and pressed, and came off the machine as mercerised cotton, known as lisle.

It was my job to learn how to run one of these machines, straighten out the dry yarn, strip the machine of the finished yarn, and feed it again. The foreman was a man called Albert, and he was known as Ta-ta. He was about forty-eight with dark blue eyes, a quiet manner and very nice full smile.

The lads all made fun of him. Not to his face, but within his hearing. They liked to come out with dirty talk in front of him just to see how he would shake his head. We all went for our one break of the shift at half-past eight and we used to take our clogs off to ease our feet, because most of us had little burns on our toes where the drops of caustic had got through our clog tops. We used to tear strips off our shirt-laps and bind them round our feet to protect them. This meant that we were often late getting back to our machines, for we only had half an hour break. Albert used to come up about a quarter past nine and take his watch out of his waistcoat pocket and look at it and say: 'What time did you come to breakfast, lads?' He would get us bits of cloth for our feet, do little jobs for us on the machines and try to make life easier for us. He was the one who came around two o'clock just before we were finishing and asked us if we'd like to work the double shift. That meant working on till ten o'clock at night. But we got a free lunch, and free tea, and overtime. Nobody ever refused. But he didn't seem to like to ask us.

At that time I was almost as bad as the others in thinking of Albert as an old ta-ta. But when I look back I see Albert in all his goodness, and I remember him more than anyone else, except Tom's sister. I'll never forget her.

Tom worked on the machine next to mine. We used to stand shoulder to shoulder at the sorting poles dividing the wet finished hanks into noddles, and preparing the new dry ones for the machine, loosening the yarn and putting it on large scoops known as shovels, which were used to get the yarn over the steel rollers.

Tom was not really my sort of mate. I always like lads you could have a nice little chat with about life and girls and things like that. But Tom would never listen properly. In the middle of something you were telling him, his clown's face, with its long nose and freckles, would suddenly burst into a smile and he would say something that showed he hadn't heard one thing you had said.

'Hey, hearken them spadgers, Bill,' he said to me one summer evening. 'Ee, I wish I were a little sparrow. You could have plenty of fun, you know. Perch on a house-ledging, see, an' pretend to fall off. Drop like a stone, with folk watching bog-eyed with pity, then as you got near the ground, open up your wings, and fly off!' Then he looked at me and said: 'Has it never crossed your mind, Bill, that you'd like to be a gull or a swallow?'

'If I were flying high,' I said, 'I'd be frightened of fallin'!'

'I damn well wish I'd never asked thee,' said Tom.

The dyers and bleachers all went home about six o'clock, and Albert would stay on until about seven.

After that we eight machine lads had the place to ourselves, apart from Dirty Ernie, who worked the whizz. Our quota of work was laid out for the evening – a machine did eight pounds of yarn every five minutes – so that we couldn't do any dodging.

As soon as we lads got the place to ourselves we used to start

singing at the tops of our voices. Between songs Ernie would
look up from the whizz, let his false teeth down, and call out:
'Anybody like to kiss me?' We used to yell things at him,
which he seemed to like. Then he would sing 'The German
Clockmaker' or some other dirty song.

But about nine o'clock in the evening we all seemed to grow
a bit tired and we'd stop singing. It was usually about then I
could get Tom to talk in a sensible sort of way, about life and
himself, and not so much about birds.

One evening, about half past nine – we'd been on since six in
the morning, so we weren't too chirpy – we were making up
feeds we'd like to eat, when Tom suddenly looked serious and
said: 'What I'd like thee to taste, Bill, would be one of our
Mary's hot apple pies.'

The way he said it caught my interest, for his usual rough
voice became gentle, 'Your whose?' I asked, thinking over his
words.

'Our Mary's,' he said, 'my sister.'

'Ee, Tom,' I said, 'I never knew you had one.'

'I never liked bringing her up,' he said. 'Not in this place
with all that dirty talk going on. Would you bring a sister of
yours up with a chap like Dirty Ernie around?'

'No, I wouldn't,' I said.

The way Tom spoke about Mary got me very interested in
her. She was nearly seventeen and she worked in a chemist's
shop.

'When her's going off to work of a morning,' Tom told me,
'our Mary is nicer dressed than any wench is on a Sermons
Sunday. She wears a tailor-made navy blue costume –'

'A what?' I said. I'd heard him, but I wanted to hear him
again.

'A tailor-made navy blue costume,' said Tom. 'She wears a
white blouse. She has a silver brooch where it fastens at her
neck-hole. And when it's raining she wears a posh raincoat
over the top with a tight belt. But if tha's got the idea in thy
head that our Mary's swank – get it out! It's just that she knows
how to look nice without swanking.'

I found the one thing I looked forward to every morning
was Tom talking about Mary in the evening. Some evenings
he would go on for half an hour or more about her, and other

evenings he wouldn't mention her. If Dirty Ernie was singing he wouldn't mention her, and if one of the other lads came up he would shut up at once about her. I got that I couldn't stop thinking about Mary.

I couldn't get the weekends over fast enough, until Monday evening came and Tom would tell me all that Mary had been up to. In time I got that I could ask little questions about her, but I hadn't to be forward in them.

'What colour of hair has she? I've never took much notice. I know it's full of glints when she's just washed it. Sometimes she lets me dry it for her and many a time I've brushed it for her. It comes through your fingers just like silk.' And Tom's hands moved as though they were stroking silk. In between our chats we had to run to our machines. In a way I liked the interruptions, because it became a bit too much just to listen. I liked to run away for a minute and think of her. Then one evening Tom suddenly gave me a shock.

'I was talking about you to our Mary last night, Bill,' he said. 'An' she began asking me all about you, what you looked like an' that. So I told her. And what do you think she said to me?'

It had made me feel a bit sick just hearing him tell me about Mary talking about me. But I was able to say: 'What did she say, Tom?'

Tom looked up from straightening the hanks of yarn. 'She said: "Will you put me a good word in with Bill?" '

I could hardly believe it. I'd never known any wish in all my life come true, and here was one I'd never dared hope for – given to me without any prayers or anything. I wanted to do something for Tom. I felt very happy.

But a minute later, as I was sorting out the wet yarn I saw my hands. The fingers were all shrunk and shiny from the caustic water. In the gloss of the smoothing pole I imagined my face, pale and pimply. Then I thought of my Sunday suit hanging up behind the bedroom door at home – the sleeves short, the seat shiny, the jacket tight. I knew I didn't have a chance with Mary. I felt very miserable.

But in bed that night I saw it all in a new light. Out of my overtime I'd be able to order one of those fifty shilling suits, made-to-measure. My mother would help me to get a new pair of shoes. And if I rubbed my hands with olive oil and sugar they'd come up nice.

I told my mother next morning. 'I've been thinkin' I could do with a new suit, Mam.'

She nodded. 'Yes, you could,' she said. 'It would be nice.'

'But I don't want one from the Scotsman, Mam,' I said. 'His only fit where they touch. I'd like a proper cash-down suit. Will you give me something towards it?'

'A pound,' she said, 'or maybe thirty shillings.'

I gave her a kiss. 'Thanks, Mam,' I said, 'I'll get measured next Saturday afternoon.' I took my snap-basket and I had a good look at myself in the big overmantel mirror. I wasn't so bad after all.

Tom began to talk about Mary again that evening. 'Our Mary was goin' to a dance last Saturday night,' he said, 'an' there were only her and me in the house. She was giving herself a bit of a bath at the back kitchen sink, and I was in the front place dozin' in front of the fire. I must have dozed off, because when I woke up, there she was standin' in front of me. She'd this black silky frock on, an' her hair done up an' everything. "How do I look Tom?" she says. "Not too bad," I says, "I wish old Bill were here to see you." "Yes, I wish he was," she says. Tha'd have fell in love with her, Bill. I nearly did, an' I'm her brother! She'd some perfume on, you see, and smelt just like one of these posh women you sometimes sit next to on the tram.'

We ran to our machines and back again to the pole, straightening out the hanks of yarn.

'She puts her best coat on over her shoulders an' sits beside me. The next thing I hears a car come chugging up the street an' stop outside our front door. "Who's that?" I says, as this chap in the car blows his horn. "Don't you go to that door," says our Mary, an' blow me if she'd budge. She wouldn't answer the door for a honk. I could hardly abide it, hearin' that engine runnin', an' the petrol wastin'. Then he must have got out because there's a knock on the door. "Gimme a kiss, Mary, afore you go," I says. Just out of devilment she gave me a kiss on the end of my conk, an' do you know, Bill, it never stopped ticklin' all night long!'

A few days later Tom was laid off work with the flu. Whilst

he was away I got my new suit. It was a real beauty, broad in the shoulder and made me look older and bigger. Some nights, before going to bed, I would try it on. I used to put a white piece of tissue paper across my chest to make it look like a posh shirt, then, holding a candle in either hand, I'd stare at myself in the looking-glass in the bedroom. I used to practise new smiles and serious expressions, and I'd say in a posh voice: 'I'm very pleased to meet you, Mary. Tom has told me about you.'

It was one Monday that Tom came back to work. As soon as I saw him the one thought on my mind was Mary. I wanted to go and ask him about her at once. But I had to go all through the day, working beside him on the machines, and listening to talk I had no interest in, hoping all the time he'd let slip some word about her, until evening came. There was the usual singing bout, and after this the quiet period, during which you could only hear the whirring clank of the machines and the lads' clogs as they ran to feed them.

About nine o'clock I was getting desperate over Mary, and Tom hadn't spoken of her. I daren't mention her because I knew he didn't like me to bring up her name, and I might spoil my chances with her if I did. I gave Tom a cigarette, lit it for him, and chatted more warmly than ever; went silent, tried everything but still he did not bring up Mary.

When it was going up to ten o'clock, with the time to talk about her going less and less, and every tactic of mine to draw him out had failed, I could stand the strain no longer, and, trying to sound at ease, I said: 'Oh, Tom, how's your Mary going on?'

I'd timed it for just before the machine needed changing, so that there'd be a few seconds break.

'Our who?' said Tom.

'You know,' I said, 'your sister Mary.'

Tom took the fag-end out of his mouth, dropped it on the wet concrete floor, put his clog-iron on it, and said to me: 'I've got no sister.'

I couldn't properly make out the meaning of what he had said. It was so unexpected that it didn't make sense at first. But almost at once I was able to sense that something you always meet up with is the truth.

'You what — Tom?' I said.

'I've got no sister,' said Tom.

For a second I didn't know what to say or do. I was ashamed for fear I should give away all it meant to me. My machine grunted and went quiet, the cogs rolling over at ease, and I ran to it and began to strip the wet finished yarn from the rollers, and then I ran round and fed it with the shovels of new yarn. I mustn't have been as quick as usual, or perhaps my mind wasn't on my work, because when the steel rollers began to turn, I still had my hands on the yarn, smoothing it out. I saw my hand carried along to where the big rollers joined together, and I suddenly snatched it away as I felt a tight close nip. I saw the yarn being pulled round and heard the groaning of the strands as the tension was put on, and the yarn was flattened between the rollers. Another half second, I thought, and my hand would have been crunched in amongst that lot. But even that thought didn't bring me round properly. All the grinding and groaning of the rollers seemed to be going on inside a haze, whilst close and near, just under my shirt, a keen sick pain was fastening itself to me.

I went back to the sorting pole and began to sort out the yarn. Tom's shoulder was close to mine, and I heard him say: 'I've got me Dad an' four brothers. An' a right mucky gang they are, with no woman around. I've no mother, no sister.' He stopped sorting the yarn, and turned his face to me. 'I don't know what came over me to keep talkin' away like that about our Mary. It wasn't cod, Bill —' That tender tone in Tom's voice was more than I could stand, and this time I didn't let him finish but I burst out singing 'The German Clockmaker', singing it as loud as I could. Dirty Ernie looked up from the whizz: 'Hey, mate,' he yelled, 'you're in good fettle tonight. Have you had your birdseed?' And I yelled back at him: 'Aye, I have that an' all!'

# JAN WEBSTER

# *Rose Would be a Lovely Name for It*

Annette Bassie, sixteen, of 112, Cumberland Place, Chennock, an overspill estate of the outer London suburbs, walked carefully along the grass verge on her six-inch cork wedgies, avoiding the dog excrement and thinking of little babies in yellow stretch jumpsuits with Snoopy on them.

She saw this particular little baby, hers, being held up by Damon, who would be wearing a denim two-piece and an Afro hairdo and shiny white clumpy wedgies which Annette really fancied at the moment. There would be a struggle, getting Damon to buy the wedgies, but she had nearly eight months to work on him to get him used to the idea. Anyway . . . Damon would be holding up the baby, who would be laughing and dimpling like in the adverts for baby powder and she would be standing nearby with a proud smile and maybe a yellow dress with those sort of cap sleeves. Hair up or down? She couldn't quite decide but up would maybe look more in keeping with having a baby.

A him, would it be, then? She didn't mind if it was a her because Jackie Prince's little Theresa Jayne was ever so sweet, with little soft padded hands and long lashes and curly hair and you could dress little girls up ever so nice . . .

There, she'd done it. Stepped in a dog's woopsie because she hadn't been thinking of where she was going. She sat down on the grass verge, removing the shoe and cleaning it on the grass, aggrieved out of all proportion to the incident and the tears running down her face so fast she couldn't stop them. She put up the back of her hand and all that bloody mascara that they'd said was waterproof came away on her skin.

'I'm afraid so, Annette,' Dr Ramsay had said, shaking his head at her. 'Didn't they teach you about contraception at school?' She had been too weary to explain to him what Damon had said about it being all right if he took his thing away in time, and, anyway, they hadn't done it all that often and it hadn't made sense to take the Pill *every* day when she and Damon might go quite a long time without him taking her up the fields or her Mum being out and nothing good on the telly.

He had quite a kind face, Dr Ramsay, but his trousers smelled and there was a brown line along his lower lip from smoking. She'd nearly said, 'What business is it of yours?' but she'd been feeling too dizzy. He'd started asking about whether she'd told her mother and sending up a social worker and she'd begun to cry because the social worker would be Mrs Berry and her mother thought Mrs Berry was a cow and had told her so to her face.

'We'll sort something out,' Dr Ramsay had said, vaguely, patting her on the back. 'And then you get yourself down to that birth control clinic and take proper precautions. You hear me?'

She'd nodded, and come out, and it hadn't been bad, walking along the grass in the middle of the morning, seeing mums putting sausages and Surf and Mother's Pride loaves and tins of peas and frozen crinkle-cut chips and Six Selected Iced Fancies into those wire baskets under the prams and little kids with green iced lollies dribbling down their fronts running in and out of the shops and touching the mongrel dogs tied to pram handles.

'Do you take this woman . . . ?' She stopped crying as the picture popped up in her mind of her and Damon getting married. She was all enveloped in white, all over, like in fine Terylene net curtains only it was her wedding veil, from whence her face peeped out, rosy and beautiful as the dawn. The girl of his dreams. Memories are made of this. Make it a wedding to remember. Only Damon stayed thin and angular and even in the picture she couldn't get him out of those lowslung denims, so tight at the crotch it was a wonder, her mum said, it didn't ruin his prospects, and that white tee shirt with Billy Bremner on it because his dad came from Leeds.

She got up, a little groggily, knowing it wasn't going to be like that. If she went down the supermarket, Damon might be bringing in the wire trollies or unloading a van and she could get speaking to him. She didn't like seeing him in the long white overall. It made him look too small and young. But she felt very desperate. 'In view of your case history,' Dr Ramsay had said, 'we might be able to arrange for you to abort this child. Good gracious, lassie, you are no' much more than a child yourself.'

She looked inside the supermarket and just past a display of chocolate digestive biscuits on unrepeatable offer she saw Damon putting bottles of malt vinegar on the shelves. She grabbed a wire basket and walked up to him.

'Congratulations,' she said. 'You are going to become a dad.'

His face was a study. It went as white as his overall.

'Not here,' he hissed.

'Gotta be here,' she said, relentlessly. 'I'm supposed to be having an operation to get rid of it.'

'Oh, Jesus,' said Damon. He dropped a quart bottle of malt vinegar and it hit the supermarket floor with a resounding thwack, breaking and sending the brown liquid over an unbelievably large area of floor.

'Bloody go,' he said to Annette, as the supervisor bore down on the scene with tch-tch written all over her body. Annette backed away from the vinegary tide. She went outside and peered over a placard offering marmalade at drastic reduction. She saw Damon laboriously wipe up and then fetch a mop and bucket to wash the floor. It was going to take too long, he would never be finished, so she walked away. She had had no breakfast that morning and she felt suddenly and ravenously hungry; she could eat beefburgers and chips and beans but when she got home it had to be toast. She ate two slices and drank two mugs of milky tea with a lot of sugar in it. She looked at the paper from Sunday and a girl with no clothes on: 'Aeron is going places. A part in a new werewolf film and that of a sexy waitress in the TV series "Dr Banks, Superstar", are rewards for this uplifting view of her very vital statistics.'

The front door banged and Mrs Bassie returned from her morning cleaning job. The woman she worked for, who had three teenage daughters, had given her some worn clothes which she bore in on a note of minor triumph in two bulging paper carriers.

'Get us a cup of tea, Annette,' she begged. She threw off her coat, saying, 'I'm buggered, so I am.'

'You been down the Labour?' Mrs Bassie demanded, gulping down the tea Annette put before her.

'Yeh,' Annette lied.

'Nothing doing?'

'No, nothing doing.' Feeling the need to convince, Annette added, 'There was a job at the baker's but I said I couldn't do it for my eczema.'

Her mother looked at her suspiciously, then began pulling out the cast-off clothing. Annette fingered it mutinously. The girls who had worn these went to a fee-paying school and sat O levels. Her mother sometimes mimicked the way they said, 'Hellow' to her, patronisingly, as she tidied up their rooms. They had a sauna in the garden and went to France for their holidays. She hated the feeling of gentility that came from their clothes. 'I'm not wearing any of that rubbish,' she told her mother.

Mrs Bassie tried on a short-sleeved jumper in apple green that stretched perilously across her generous bosom.

'This is all right,' she approved. Annette looked at her detachedly. She was all wrong, her mother, the way she looked. Those big boobs, the long, knobbly-kneed legs in the youthful wedgies, the peroxide hair, were meant for a younger face. Her mother's face was wrinkled, anxious, lived-in, middle-aged. She wished she didn't have to tell her mother about the baby, what with her older brother being in the open prison for a fire he had never done and little Tone stealing and going through this phase of not wanting to go to school and Dad having fallen off the ladder and being dead quite a long while.

'Mum,' said Annette, fearfully.

'Just a minute,' said Mrs Bassie. She rose and switched on the television at full volume. Then she brought out an elderly Hoover and switched it on also, placing it as near the inside television walls as possible.

'I met that black cow down the bus-stop,' Mrs Bassie

shouted. 'I told her I'd been down the Council about that bloody industrial sewing machine and she turned round and said she never had one. It went till half-past two this morning *and* he had his bongos out. I never slept a wink.'

'But she's out next door,' Annette protested.

'He isn't,' said Mrs Bassie. 'He don't put his nose out till it's time to go down the betting shop.' She grew tired of the self-created din and switched off both machines. 'It's like living in the middle of the bloody jungle,' she complained. 'And on Sunday she'll be down the mission hall in that lemon tulle hat crying out that Jesus saves. He won't save her if I get hold of her by that coconut matting she calls hair.'

'Mum,' said Annette, 'I'm going to have a little baby.'

'Decent people,' said Mrs Bassie, continuing her harangue, 'decent people don't have a chance.'

'Mum,' repeated Annette, 'I said, I've been down the doctor and I'm going to have a little baby.'

Mrs Bassie sat down suddenly, gripping the edge of the Formica-topped table.

'Eh?' she said.

'They're sending Mrs Berry down and I might have to have an abortion. Because of my case history.'

'Oh God,' said Mrs Bassie, gulping for air. 'Didn't they learn you nothing about that at school?'

'I was off with the rheumatic fever,' said Annette. 'I only picked up bits from the other girls.'

'I thought you knew,' said Mrs Bassie, bewilderedly.

'Knew what, Mum?'

'How to stop it.'

'Don't cry, Mum.' Mrs Bassie was weeping, as someone used to it, soundlessly and efficiently, putting big, rough hands up to dash away the tears. 'I could have it,' said Annette. 'Me and Damon could get married and get a council house and have it.'

'He's a bloody little runt,' said Mrs Bassie, a shade more hopefully. 'What age is he? Fifteen? Sixteen?'

'He's sixteen next week,' said Annette. 'I mean, he's working, he gets eighteen quid a week.'

'You'll never get a place,' said Mrs Bassie.

'Could we live here?'

'It wouldn't be allowed. We'd be overcrowded.'

'I could sleep with you and Damon with Tone. For a bit.'

Her mother shook her head, but a little more kindly.

'You randy little bitch,' she said, almost fondly. 'What you want? Boy or girl?'

'I think girl, really,' said Annette, smiling for the first time that day. Her hair, dyed blonde like her mother's, peaked out in front of her pale face, like a cap. She put skinny arms over her flat little bosom.

'You can dress 'em up nice,' said Mrs Bassie.

'I thought Rose would be a nice name for it,' said Annette, boldly. 'Rose Yvonne.'

'You thought if it's a boy?' demanded her mother, sharply.

'Dean or Larry.'

Mrs Bassie considered these and did not dismiss them out of hand. 'We could get your cousin Marilyn's pram and cot,' she said, 'and you get second-hand things down the clinic that are ever so new-looking.'

Annette decided she would not remind her mother what Dr Ramsay had said about getting an abortion. She had already decided to go ahead and have the baby. It hadn't been something she had thought out, carefully, the way she thought out what she would wear to a dance, for example. It was just a foregone conclusion. She could see the baby as plain as she could see the nose on her mother's face. Rose Yvonne or Dean. In a big cream pram. With a wire basket underneath and a dog tied to the handle.

She snivelled a little, worrying about Mrs Berry coming up to see her mum. She said, 'I thought of getting it a yellow jumpsuit, with that Snoopy dog on it. Jackie had one for her Theresa Jayne, only it was a apple on it.'

'A apple?'

'Instead of a Snoopy.'

'Yellow does for boy or girl.'

'Yeh. That's what I thought.'

'She can't be allowed to have it,' said Dr Ramsay.

'He must have a leaky bladder,' thought Caroline Berry. Some doctors, the kind who liked their patients, got ropeylooking as they got older. But he had a reputation for good diagnosing, this one, and the solid matrons going through The Change sat out the long minutes in his surgery for the chance of a reassuring word with him, just as the nervy young ones took the Valium prescriptions from his hand with the faith of votaries taking the Sacramental wafer. Last of a dying breed, he was. A doctor who gave himself. He gave her a piercing, aware look and said crisply, 'Well?'

'You tell me, doctor.'

'She could probably scrape through on the physical side, with great care, perhaps in hospital. But she's a hysterical child, she's been in care, her mother's been through too much. The skids are under the whole family.'

'Right.'

·'You'll take care of it.'

'Yes.'

'Up to three months, it's only tissue, isn't it?' Caroline thought. Have we a right to bring babies into the world who will be neglected, perhaps battered, who will have the Big Hand against them right from the start? No, we haven't, she thought, but a persistent other voice was putting up other arguments, saying stridently, who was she to decide? Was life, no matter how tragic or brutal, not a precious gift they had no right to withhold? As if there are any easy answers, thought Caroline, wearily. I wish I didn't have to keep facing them. I wish I didn't have to take responsibility. Mrs Bassie will insult me again. I wish I didn't have to see her. I'll see anybody but her. Dr Ramsay's cool, dedicated face came back to her. She'd promised him she'd take care of it. She wouldn't have any lunch. Just a cup of coffee, and then she'd go.

Annette went down the big block at the end of the estate where Damon lived and waited for him by the brick wall that among other graffiti had a slogan saying 'Send the Pope to the Moon'. At six-thirty he emerged from the flat entrance and she could see at once there had been trouble. One eye was a puffy red and he had been crying.

'Was it your dad?' she asked.

'He bloody thumped me,' said Damon, beginning to weep again. 'Said I could get out and never come back. I ain't going back there, never.'

'Oh, Gawd,' said Annette. 'And I was hoping your mum would give us a room.'

'She never said a bleeding thing,' said Damon. 'Just sat there.'

'What we gonna do?'

'Go up to your mum's.'

Annette said, red-faced, 'I don't want to go up there just yet. She's had the social worker in there today. She'll want me to have the operation now, if I know anything.'

'Maybe you should.'

'Don't want to.'

'Where can we go?' he demanded, desperately.

'Anywhere,' she said, blankly. She began to move away as though in a dream.

He was still overwrought. Across the street stood a clapped-out old banger of a car, rust enveloping its radiator and bumpers.

'We'll take our Syd's car,' Damon decided. 'He can't drive it till he gets his licence back.'

'Will it go?' asked Annette doubtfully. She got in. After a few doubtful wheezes, the car moved forward, Damon drove it carefully round the estate then along a quiet road leading to countryside.

'You'll get in ever such trouble,' said Annette, but she was quite enjoying it. Damon had his tongue out and was concentrating on his steering. He had been up before the court for taking cars before, but what they didn't understand was that he just *knew* how to drive them, it was second-nature to him. They drove past a golf club and then they went driving past small farms and riding stables and smallholdings. It was a sunny evening, cool, fresh and invigorating.

'It's like an adventure,' said Annette. Damon looked ever so small, like a little boy driving the dodgems at the fair. Grave doubts arose in her mind about the possibility of getting him into a denim two-piece or of him sanctioning an Afro hairstyle or looking remotely *father*-like. She gave a troubled sigh.

'I know a place,' said Damon suddenly, 'where we could go and they wouldn't find us.'

'Where?'

'It's just up here. You go along this sort of road that's been made by lorry wheels and there's a sort of wood. Nobody would see us. We could make a fire.'

He looked at her and her spirits rose at his intense, excited expression. He was going to take care of her. It was possible he really loved her. The car would be like a little house. All their own. Maybe they would never have to go back and she would never have to know the outcome of the discussion, if that was the word, between her mother and Mrs Berry.

Damon swung the car up the rutted track and into the edge of the lightly-wooded area. All around were fields and there was only one sign of habitation, a white farmhouse with broken-down out-buildings, lying several fields away.

'I could go down there, after dark,' said Damon, 'and pick us up something to eat.'

'How do you mean?'

'Potatoes, fruit. Might even be able to get into the house and get milk and bread and stuff.'

She drew up her shoulders in scandalised delight. 'They might get you, Damon.'

'Nah.' He smiled at her, the bruise from his father's fist coming up blue and purple under his eye. She put out her hand and touched it. 'Is it bad?'

'Nah.' He caught her hand and they held each other close. It was all right for them to make love because the baby had happened anyway and couldn't happen again. Annette had some fruit pastilles in her jacket pocket and they smoked the last four of Damon's cigarettes. The evening deepened in gradual layers of blue until it was quite dark, but there was a moon and shapes remained clear and unalarming. They moved into the back seat of the car where it was warmer and huddled together, talking and planning.

Some of the things Damon planned, like going to Ireland or America, Annette knew to be impractical. What would they do for money?

'We can sleep in the car,' she argued. 'It can be our house like. Even when the baby comes. And during the day we can go out and work and get some money.'

'I can't drive it about no more,' said Damon. 'I ain't got a licence, you know.'

'But if we stayed here.'

'How'd we get to work?'

'Maybe there's a country bus.'

He acknowledged this possibility. After that, they gave up planning because their brains were getting tired. Annette persuaded Damon against going to the farm and instead they exchanged reminiscences of their childhood.

'What was the very best Christmas you could ever remember?' she demanded.

'In the home,' Damon answered. He had told her about it before, but she liked to hear and he liked to talk about it. 'Time me mum left me dad and he went into hospital with his nerves. We had turkey and plum pudding and trifle *twice over*. And in the morning after breakfast, we all went to church.

'I had new clothes from the skin out. Shoes and everything. We never had no cast-off clothes there. The house-mother took us into the shop and we got everything new. And then after dinner with paper hats and those things you blow and they curl out we had a rest and then the superintendent dressed up as Father Christmas and gave each child a toy. They were good toys, too, nothing rubbishy. I got a football game 'cos it was what I asked for. They tried to give you what you asked for. I could hardly believe it. It was great.'

'Yeh,' Annette gave a dreamy sigh. 'I think I would have liked being in a home for Christmas.'

'Nah,' he said, smiling at her affectionately. 'You wouldn't have liked all them baths and things. And they wasn't like your own mum and dad, know what I mean? They was nice, and they taught you to talk proper but you couldn't tell them to sod off, like you could your old man.'

'They never hit you, did they?' asked Annette. 'My turn now, Damon, to tell about my best Christmas. It was when I got a proper ballet frock for dancing in, in the school concert. Miss Baines was going to make me one at the school but me mum got this lovely flare-free net in a beautiful pink colour and she went up Mrs Andrews, the dressmaker, and got her to make it proper.

'And when I got up Christmas morning, it was lying at the bottom of my bed, and there was a pair of them silver dancing slippers in my size.'

She held him very tight, as though he was this marvellous

memory, and shivering with recollected pleasure she said, 'Me and the boys all clubbed together and we went down Woolworth's after Christmas and we bought my mum a locket to go round her neck saying "To the best mum in the world". She liked it ever so much. It'll be nice when it's Christmas with the baby, Dame. We can get a little tree and put a star on it and cut out things from milk-bottle tops.'

'A real tree,' he said.

'Yeh, they're best. Not one of them silver, made ones.'

'I'm frightened about you having the baby. Maybe they won't let you.'

'Don't be frightened,' she said, with a tremendous feeling of tenderness welling up inside her, so that she could not resist pulling his head down to her bosom and cradling it, almost though he were the baby. 'It'll be all right. I love you, Damon. This car is our little house and we are safe here. They can't get at me here.'

The moon sailed behind a cloud and the landscape became mysterious, undefined. Damon's breathing became regular and with his head on her shoulder he went into a deep, dreamless sleep. Annette pushed her face into his hair, liking his human animal smell. Soon she, too, was sleeping, curled into a foetus-like ball on the back seat of the rusty car.

'Their lives are two-dimensional, cardboard cutouts,' said Caroline Berry to her husband, Simon, pouring him more warm red wine. 'They have no cultural heritage now, just the telly. They *had* something when they lived in the East End, even if it was just "Knees Up Mother Brown" in the pub on a Saturday night or hop-picking every year in Kent. Now they're just overspill — annoying rubbish to be packed into concrete boxes. All the individuality's been knocked out of them. Bloody bureaucracy has knocked them sideways.'

Simon sighed. He gave the impression of only half-listening. He *was* only half-listening. Caroline felt that these days he was getting farther and farther away from contact, like a swimmer setting out across the ocean. *O Simon, don't leave me*. She didn't know how to make him turn back. She kept on talking. She had had a terrible interview with Mrs Bassie, who had thrown a half-empty Coke tin at her, and then Annette had disappeared altogether and Dr Ramsay had accused her, unjustly, of being clumsy.

'Come to bed,' said Simon, peremptorily, after the meal. Their bed-sitter was large, airy, with a nice Habitat bedspread Caroline liked and Soutine and Bonnard prints they'd brought back from the Museum of Modern Art in Paris.

Simon's desk, piled with his philosophy books and novels in the original French and German, stood by the window and the branches of a sycamore tree waved through the glass in friendly fashion. When he got his Ph.D. he would be happier, released, not beholden, galvanised. It couldn't be easy for him just now. Caroline stroked his hair with a delicate touch.

He caught her wrist.

'How do you know,' he demanded, 'that up there their lives aren't fuller, happier than ours?'

'They haven't read Thomas Mann,' she teased.

'They've never heard of Wittgenstein.'

'They think Mahler's that wrestler with the hood over his head and slits for the eyes.'

'And that Hockney's some kind of cheap wine.'

They laughed and he held her close and began to make complicated love to her, kissing her here and there, till she panted a little and said, 'Now, darling, now.' But he lay back, flicking his wrists back on the pillow, groaning and saying, 'It's no bloody good, I can't.'

'It'll be all right,' she soothed.

'No, Caro. We both know it won't.' He got up abruptly, zipping on his jeans, lighting a Gauloise, striding up and down the room, slim-hipped and agitated.

'Simon. Please! Please let's talk about it.'

He turned an angry, tortured mask of a face towards her.

'I don't want to talk! Something's wrong –'

'You don't love me any more –'

'And all you can say is let's talk about it.'

He sat down beside her. 'Caro, are you aware how much you talk? How sensible, how pragmatic you are! It's like making love to your old head mistress in the junior school.'

She gave a cry of pain and he said contritely, 'No, I don't mean that –'

'You aren't attracted to me! Why don't you say it?'

'Because it's not true. But –' He paused.

'No. Go on. You must say it.'

'I don't want to upset you.'

'Please,' she insisted, stonily.

'Well. Do you ever feel that what we have is – is a sterile thing? We've put these restraints, the restraints of marriage, on ourselves, and marriage turns out to be a tense, watching relationship in a single room. No babies. You taking the Pill and getting bloated –'

'And keeping you.' Her venom was deadly.

'Yes,' he admitted. 'Keeping me. A process of rational emasculation.' He rose. 'I'm getting out, Caro. Let's call it a day.'

She rose and buttoned up her dress. She could feel her nipples, still hard and engorged from caresses and her vagina, wet and slippery. A terrible primal need to throw herself on his mercy, to plead that he should take her, give her a child, fill her womb, overcame her, and with it, as always, the weary realisation that there were too many children in the world, not enough rooms to hold them. Too many careless Bassies, that the Simons and Carolines had to make up for. But at that moment, she would not have cared. She wanted him to come to her and the situation was that they could no longer make it together: that they had held each other once too often. World was not rational. World was mouth and breast and womb and penis: world was skin and hair and semen. And world was the starving children of Ethiopia, who every night paraded before her mind's eyes when she said her formless prayers: big-bellied, hollow-eyed, inhabitants of the hell made by those who would not take the Pill, adopt the coil, remember the sheath. Who would not think. Who had not been to university or entered the world of books and words and theories and principles.

Simon came out from the kitchenette where he had put the kettle on.

'I'll make the coffee,' he said, in his normal voice.

'You *can* go, you know,' she said, tonelessly.

He went over to her. Held her briefly, by the arms.

'It's temporary, of course,' he said, shrugging. 'But it worries a man.'

'I know.'
'Be patient.'
'Of course.'
'I'm sorry.'
'So am I.'

'What made you think you'd get away with it?'

Mrs Bassie took a long swig of tea, lit a cigarette and took a deep inhalation of smoke. She looked at Annette with genuine curiosity.

'We was going to stay there,' cried Annette, defiantly. 'We was going to stay there and sleep in the car.'

'Don't be so bloody daft.'

'I know couples what have done that. I've read it in the papers. When they couldn't get a house.'

'Then they had no more bloody sense than you have. Daft gits! You must have known Damon's dad would go down the cop-shop. You must have known Syd wouldn't stand for having his car took.'

'Rotten old car,' said Annette, sulkily. 'He never drove it, did he? And Damon drives good. He just knows how to handle a car and nobody never showed him.'

'And he knows how to pinch things, too.'

'Prove it!'

'I don't have to prove it!' Mrs Bassie gave a laugh that was almost merry. 'Seven cartons of soft pink toilet paper and a crate of malt vinegar, under his bed. Didn't take the cops long, did it? They'll put him away this time and a good job, too.'

'He might get probation.'

'Not a chance. He's in breach of his last probation order.'

Annette pleated the knee of her dress between her fingers.

'When they hear about the baby, they might let him off.'

'And that's another thing. You can't have it.'

Annette said nothing at all. After a brief interval, long slow tears slid down her face and plopped on to her hands and knees.

'Did she say it? Mrs Berry?'

'Yeh. I flung Coke tin at her, didn't I? Doesn't alter what she said. It would be bad for your mental and physical health if you went ahead and had it.'

'Sounds as though you've swallowed a bleeding dictionary,' said Annette. 'If I want to have it, I should be allowed to. Nobody should be allowed to stop it.'

'And who's going to bleeding keep it?' demanded Mrs Bassie. 'How am I ever going to save up for Majorca, if you keep on falling with a kid?'

'It'll be all right, Annette,' said Caroline Berry, soothingly. She had driven the girl to the hospital because Mrs Bassie had refused to go with her. She had left Simon asleep in bed. Last night, they had been to a party and she had met a marvellous man from the London School of Economics. She had gone to bed with him in an upstairs room. She did not know if Simon knew.

Annette was very pale and a crop of little spots freckled her chin. Her dyed hair peaked out in front, so that she looked like a seedy, groggy chicken straight from the shell.

They sat in the hospital ante-room. Annette with her overnight bag on her knee.

'There'll be other babies. When you're older. When you've had time to grow up yourself and to know whether Damon is the right person to share your life with.'

'He is.'

They looked at each other. At least, Caroline thought, we've established some kind of rapport. She even felt a sort of surprised respect for the girl.

'You have to be sure.'

'Can you ever be that sure?'

The consultant came towards them beckoning to Caroline. He was very pink, an unattractive man with a thin mouth and very little hair.

'A word with you, Mrs Berry.' Caroline entered his room. She had her notes with her and gave him the information he required. It came to her that he rather fancied her, that he was posturing, half-flirting, trying to register with her. She permitted herself a grim half-smile.

'I must make a move, Mr Williamson. My day is hectic.'

'Come and have a drink with Iris and me. We're open house Sundays.'

'That would be nice.'

She thought, a little wildly, blue eyes can look *hot*.

They went back along the corridor together to the ante-room. The chair that Annette had been sitting on was empty.

Caroline went all over the building, looking for her. She looked in her own car, thinking Annette might have taken refuge there.

She spoke to the janitor at the door. Yes, he said wheezily, a thin girl with blonde hair had walked out ten minutes ago. Quite casually. Nothing to make him suspicious.

Caroline began to laugh, shakily. She thought: If anyone says a word to me, I'll cry. Then she thought, forcefully: Let her go. If they ask me to chase her up, I'll refuse. The hell with them. I'm going home to Simon and I'm stopping taking the Pill.

She rode triumphantly home in the car, a little hysterical, but chiefly happy. So there, she thought. So there, world, so there.

# LEONARD BARRAS

# *On Behalf of the Nation's Cats*

It was because of the cat's impending birthday that Uncle Hal raised the subject of Darkness Preservation. 'A month come Thursday,' he said, 'if it turns out fine, will be Wolf's fifth birthday.'

'Fancy!' said my old Aunt Emma. She was assiduously mending my underwear.

'We should consider something auspicious,' said Uncle Hal.

'There are thirteen holes in this bairn's flannelette vest,' said my old Aunt Emma.

The cat was called Wolf because Uncle Hal had always wanted a parrot. The cat resented this and used to sit on the mantelpiece staring malevolently down at him.

'The lad loves that cat, Emma,' he said. 'So do I, mind you.' But I knew he had been disappointed when I had failed to teach the cat to fetch sticks out of the pit pond, like Mrs Proudboot's Pomeranian bitch. 'Darkness Preservation,' he added. 'Something felicitous. Or auspicious.'

'It's time for the bairn's cod liver oil,' said my old Aunt Emma. 'Where are you, hinny?'

I was under the table, counting my cigarette cards.

'British Double Winter Time,' said Uncle Hal. 'The country cannot go on without it.'

'I thought you said Darkness Preservation.'

'I did.'

'Well, then.'

'It's the same thing,' Uncle Hal testily explained. What he aimed to do, he said, was to work for the reversal of Willett's

Daylight Saving Act, so that the clocks would always be put back instead of forward, thus preserving the hours of darkness for cat lovers. He was a lifelong Marxist and neo-Hegelian, he acknowledged, but he was also a cat-lover. 'I think you're sitting on my propelling pencil, Emma,' he said. 'I'm going to write to the Press advocating Darkness Preservation.'

'I thought you said British Double Winter Time,' said my old Aunt Emma.

'I did, I did! I'll need my bicycle.' He blew on the pencil, which was still warm. 'And I'll need some writing paper, shan't I?'

'I'm not sitting on the writing paper,' said my old Aunt Emma.

The cat was sitting on the writing paper, which was on the mantelpiece. 'Move over, Wolf,' said Uncle Hal. 'Good cat!'

The cat extended a swift paw and scratched his hand. 'Oo, you bugger!' said Uncle Hal.

The sign outside the barber's shop read: 'First Class Saloon. Moustaches by appointment. Proprietor S. Elphinstook. / Head Office, Nonconformists' Argus. Editor S. Elphinstook.' Uncle Hal propped his bicycle against the wall and we went inside. Seppy Elphinstook was cutting the hair of Herbert Mangle, the Wallsend poet, who was declaiming his 'Ode to the Two Ginger Barmaids at the Old Dun Cow':

> Oh, ginger barmaids at the Old Dun Cow,
> For both of you my passion comes in gusts;
> If I had but two heads I'd lay them now
> One each upon your great engulfing busts!

'A bit near the knuckle, that,' said Uncle Hal.

'That's what I'm telling him,' said Seppy Elphinstook. He removed the enfolding cloth from Herbert Mangle and flourished it at Uncle Hal.

Herbert Mangle said such censoriousness merely underlined Wordsworth's theme that England was a fen of stagnant waters. 'If you like,' he offered, 'I can recite my "Verse Dedicated to Your Unbenign Cat".'

Uncle Hal said perhaps another time, if the wind dropped. He hadn't come for a haircut, he added. He acknowledged the inordinate length of his hair, but that was dictated by economic hardship flowing from the Wall Street collapse. No, it was in Seppy Elphinstook's capacity as editor that he was visiting him. He had a letter for publication.

It was his eleventh letter to the Nonconformists' Argus, all pleading for Darkness Preservation, otherwise British Double Winter Time, and all signed 'Mrs Valerie Greenhawk', because, owing to his massive shyness, he could never bring himself to reveal his true identity.

'What about the Town Council?' asked Herbert Mangle.

'Now there's a stagnant fen,' said Seppy Elphinstook.

'No, no,' said Herbert Mangle. 'I was thinking of opportunities to stand as a councillor, thus promoting the interests of the Cat Lovers' Charter.'

But Uncle Hal had already declined such invitations because of his peculiarly oppressive diffidence, even though he had been urged to stand for the Council by a group of men fervently supporting Darkness Preservation.

'Mind you, it must be admitted,' said Herbert Mangle, 'that these men had a vested interest in Darkness Preservation. They were burglars. Are you sure you wouldn't like to hear my "Verse Dedicated to Your Unbenign Cat"?'

Uncle Hal said he would rather not. He had promised my old Aunt Emma he would collect some elastic for my underpants. 'Night after night she sits,' he said, 'endlessly filling up the holes in this lad's flannelette vest.' It wasn't an atmosphere conducive to revolutionary ardour. He didn't suppose that when Lenin was plotting the Bolshevik insurgence, he had Krupskaya sitting opposite him, rambling on about a juvenile's drawers.

'Or what about the pole attendant?' asked Seppy Elphinstook. 'They're advertising for a pole attendant at the Fire Station.'

Uncle Hal was aware of this. It seemed a job well within his range and it might give him the chance to influence council officials in the matter of Darkness Preservation. The Town Clerk, he knew, liked to drop in at the Fire Station to see the fire engine being rubbed down.

'Come on, lad,' he said.

As I perched on his crossbar and we pedalled off, the voice of Herbert Mangle was floating through the shop doorway:

> O cat! – must we suppose thy sphinx-like face
> Masks mordant thoughts about the human race?

The next night, I asked Uncle Hal if I might take the cat for a walk, but he was busy drawing up a petition and failed to hear me.

'Have you had your cod liver oil?' my old Aunt Emma asked.

'It's a petition, Emma,' said Uncle Hal. 'To Ramsay Mac-Donald.'

'Ee!' said my old Aunt Emma.

'Mrs Proudboot takes her Pomeranian bitch for a walk,' I said.

'You must drink your cod liver oil,' said my old Aunt Emma. She regularly forced cod liver oil into me because of my left knee, permanently weakened after I had been kicked by a cow during a football match behind the pit heap.

'Why can't the cat have pups,' I asked, 'like Mrs Proud-boot's Pomeranian bitch?'

'You're not to talk about things like that,' she said.

'After all, he's Prime Minister, Emma,' said Uncle Hal. 'He's a purported Socialist. Not that he conforms to any kind of Hegelian philosophy as modified by Karl Marx.'

'Fancy!' said my old Aunt Emma.

'Wolf! Wolf!' I cried. 'Where are you, Wolf?'

But the cat was under the sideboard, staring moodily out.

'Notwithstanding,' said Uncle Hal, 'what did Immanuel Kant say? "If everybody did as I do, would the world be better and happier?" On the basis of this celebrated Kantian Text, I'm asking Ramsay MacDonald to accept my petition on behalf of the nation's cats. I then expect him either to introduce a Bill forthwith, bringing forward proposals for British Double Winter Time, or face the country.'

'I thought you said Darkness Preservation,' said my old Aunt Emma.

'I did.'

'Well, then . . .'

'Never mind!' said Uncle Hal. 'Where are you, lad?'

He bent to look under the table, expecting to find me there with my cigarette cards. 'I'm here, Uncle Hal,' I said, from behind him. He straightened up sharply and caught his head on the table. 'Oo you bugger!' he said.

'You've bumped your head, Uncle Hal,' I said.

'Of course I've bumped my head,' he said. 'I know when I've bumped my head, don't I? I want you to put your sandshoes on and slip around to the Post Office with this petition. Have you a three-halfpenny stamp, Emma?'

'Can I take Wolf?' I asked.

'There should be one in the tea caddy,' said my old Aunt Emma.

'He hasn't got a lead,' I said. 'Mrs Proudboot's Pomeranian bitch has got a lead.'

'Be very careful with this,' said Uncle Hal. I stuffed the petition into the top of my trousers.

'You'd better have some cod liver oil,' said my old Aunt Emma. 'The nights are pulling in.'

'I don't like it, Auntie Emma,' I said.

'Certainly you like it. Look the cat likes it.'

But the cat had dashed into the scullery.

As it happened, I failed to reach the Post Office. On my way there, I joined in a football match in the backlane, jammed the petition into my vest for safety and forgot about it. It slipped through one of the numerous holes in that garment, lodged in my underpants and was all but boiled with the next week's washing. My old Aunt Emma retrieved it, severely lacerated, and deemed it wise to throw it in the fire, unknown to Uncle Hal. 'Waste not, want not,' she murmured, returning the stamp to the tea caddy.

'Auntie Emma,' I said.

'Yes, hinny?'

'Uncle Hal called the cat Wolf because he'd always wanted a parrot.'

'That's right.'

'Why?'

'Pardon?'

'Wolf's a dog's name.'

'You may be right, hinny.'

'He couldn't call a parrot Wolf.'

'That's right.'

'Even if we had a parrot.'

'No.'

'So the dog would have to be called Wolf, if that was what he wanted to call the cat – if it was because he'd always wanted a dog, not a parrot.'

'That's right.'

'I see.' It had been puzzling me for some time.

Several nights later, we were listening to the Boyd Neel Strings on the National Programme when Stuart Hibberd broke in to announce that the Prime Minister had sought an audience with His Majesty the King, with a view to dissolving Parliament.

'A General Election!' Uncle Hal shouted. 'I've forced Ramsay MacDonald's hand, Emma!'

'Fancy!' said my old Aunt Emma.

'The cat's gone into the gas meter cupboard, Auntie Emma,' I said. 'Is he going to have pups?'

'I shall tackle both candidates,' said Uncle Hal. 'I intend to find out where they stand on British Double Winter Time.'

'Mrs Proudboot's Pomeranian bitch had pups in the pantry,' I said.

My old Aunt Emma said they were all alike.

'What?' said Uncle Hal.

'Political parties,' said my old Aunt Emma. 'They don't care. Say anything.'

'May I play football in the backyard?' I asked. 'May I have a slice of jam?'

'That's ignorant comment, woman!' Uncle Hal shouted. 'You've got to discriminate.'

'Put your cap on, then,' my old Aunt Emma told me. 'You heard what the wireless said. It's been snowing in America.'

Uncle Hal said that no doubt Maggie Bondfield, the Labour candidate, would be holding her meetings in the Free Thinkers' Ping Pong hut. 'I'll be there to ask a question,' he said.

'I can't head the ball with my cap on,' I said.

'I'm going into the scullery,' said Uncle Hal.

My old Aunt Emma crammed my hat on to my head. 'You had kippers for dinner,' she said. 'You can't have jam on top of kippers.'

As I went out, Uncle Hal was in the scullery, rehearsing his question with his head in the sink, to simulate the faulty accoustics of the Free Thinkers' Ping Pong hut. 'Will the candidate say whether she is in favour of Darkness Preservation?' he called. 'How's that, Emma? May I further add a brief summary of the Hegelian doctrine? Affirmation gives rise to negation and the two results in a synthesis, the negation of the negation. Oo, you bugger!' He had lifted his head swiftly and caught it on the tap.

The platform of the Free Thinkers' Ping Pong hut was draped with Labour Party favours. Gazing around the audience of four, Herbert Mangle remarked that there was no doubt the British were the most politically aware nation in Europe.

'Mind you, social priorities,' said Seppy Elphinstook. 'Newcastle United are playing a cup-tie this afternoon.'

Uncle Hal was patently palpitating. He was screwing himself up to ask his question and his abysmal bashfulness had taken possession of him, just as it had in the matter of the pole attendant's job at the Fire Station. He had recanted on his bid for that exotic appointment because he was too shy to submit to medical examination by the lady doctor and withdrew his application, pleading toothache and religious scruples.

The chairman and Maggie Bondfield linked arms. There was a short silence during which they both realised they didn't know 'The Red Flag'. After a pause, Maggie Bondfield launched into 'The Marseillaise' at the same moment as the chairman, who was the Sunday School superintendent, began 'Rock of Ages'. The audience remained seated, gazing fixedly ahead.

An hour later, the candidate limped to her peroration, Seppy Elphinstook clapped tepidly and the chairman rose to say that before rushing off to another mass meeting in the Boilermakers' Emporium, Miss Bondfield was prepared to answer questions.

'Go on, then!' Herbert Mangle urged.

Uncle Hal leapt to his feet, quivering with fright, and shouted, 'Mrs Valerie Greenhawk!'

'What?' said Maggie Bondfield.

'Miss -say -will -favour -Bondfield -whether -she -is -of -in -Darkness-Preservation?' Uncle Hal gabbled.

Maggie Bondfield said, 'Will you repeat the question, please?'

Uncle Hal lost his head, shouted, 'Excuse me – toothache!' and dashed out.

That night, he told my old Aunt Emma they were all alike.

'What?' said my old Aunt Emma.

'Politicians,' said Uncle Hal. 'Say anything.'

'That's what I said,' said my old Aunt Emma.

Uncle Hal eased her off Bernard Shaw's *Guide to Socialism and Capitalism*. 'They don't care,' he said. 'Look at Maggie Bondfield.'

'It had five, Uncle Hal,' I said.

'Did she answer my question?'

'Mrs Proudboot's Pomeranian bitch,' I said. 'It had five pups.'

'If it comes to that,' Uncle Hal said, 'what about Ramsay MacDonald? He never answered my letter.'

'Fancy!' said my old Aunt Emma.

Uncle Hal said he had made up his mind. He would stand for Parliament himself. He would be the Revolutionary Darkness Preservation candidate.

'I thought you said British Double Winter Time,' said my old Aunt Emma.

'I did, I did!' said Uncle Hal.

'I don't think we want a dog in the house,' said my old Aunt Emma. 'What would the cat say?'

'How many times must I tell you, woman?' Uncle Hal demanded. 'It's the same thing!'

'The cat can't carry the paper from the corner shop,' I said, 'like Mrs Proudboot's Pomeranian bitch.'

'I shall sit on the cross-benches,' said Uncle Hal.

'What about your toothache?' my old Aunt Emma asked.

'I'm not going into that!' Uncle Hal shouted. 'Where have you hung my bicycle?'

But his chronic cowardice reasserted itself, conquering his blaze of indignation, and he loosened his bicycle chain, ensuring that it came off before we reached the Town Hall with his nomination papers. He and I were fiddling with it outside the Dun Cow when a woman came up and adjusted it for us.

'I have to see the Town Clerk,' Uncle Hal explained. 'Darkness Preservation.'

'I beg your pardon?' the woman said.

'British Double Winter Time.'

'Is that so?'

'It's the same thing,' said Uncle Hal.

'We've got a cat,' I said. 'It's his birthday next week.'

'Splendid,' said the woman.

'My Auntie Emma doesn't want him to have pups.'

'Of course not,' said the woman. She handed the bicycle back to Uncle Hal.

'Very kind,' he said. 'I would have managed, only I have toothache.'

'The Town Hall's over there.'

'I know, I know!' said Uncle Hal.

In any case, we were a fortnight late with the nomination papers, the Town Clerk told us. Besides which, where was Uncle Hal's deposit? He excused himself and hurried down to the Fire Station, where the Fire Chief had promised to let him clang the bell. Uncle Hal put me on his crossbar and pedalled furiously back home. It was disgraceful, he said. He would have appealed to the House of Lords, but for his religious scruples. As we entered the backdoor, my old Aunt Emma greeted us with the news that the cat had run away from home.

The cat had run away before, but had always returned for Sunday dinner. On the Tuesday night, after Uncle Hal, Herbert Mangle and Seppy Elphinstook had for five days roamed the lanes and allotments, uselessly calling, 'Wolf! Wolf', I sat, inconsolable, on my old Aunt Emma's knee.

'The cat'll come home, hinny,' she said. 'Won't he, Uncle Hal?'

'He didn't like cod liver oil,' I sobbed.

'You may be right,' said Uncle Hal. 'Either that or the Boyd Neel Strings.'

'Cats are always running away,' said my old Aunt Emma. 'Would you like a slice of jam?'

I shook my head.

'Of course they're always running away,' said Uncle Hal. 'It's what Hegel called a triadic process endlessly repeating itself in the universe.'

'And if he doesn't come back,' said my old Aunt Emma, 'd'you know what we'll do? We'll get one of the pups from Mrs Proudboot's Pomeranian bitch.'

'Really?' I said.

'Promise,' said my old Aunt Emma. 'Say goodnight to Uncle Hal.'

I dried my eyes. 'I think I might have a slice of jam,' I said.

With the cat's defection, Uncle Hal lost his avidity for Darkness Preservation. On election day, he voted, after a fearful struggle with his Marxist conscience, for Irene Ward, the Conservative candidate. 'After all, Emma,' he said, 'the woman did mend my bicycle.'

# PETER TINNISWOOD

# *I Likes Screech, I Does*

It was Bonfire Night.

We lived in Cardiff.

My dad worked on the docks.

We were bored, Spike Lewis, Soapy Rodgers and me.

Soapy's as black as the ace of spades. His dad comes from
Antigua. That's in the West Indies. I read about it once.

We'd mitched the day off school.

Well, when you're fifteen what else is there to do?

A rocket exploded in the sky at the back of the Mountstuart
pub.

It sent out spangles of silver and gold.

'I hates Bonfire Night, I does,' said Spike Lewis.

'Why?' I said.

'Because there's too many bastards enjoying theirselves.
Dads with nippers letting off roman candles. Mams making
welsh cakes special. It's all a load of crap, mun.'

He put up both his nicotine-stained thumbs and smiled.

'Everything's a load of crap. Right?' he said.

And he cackled.

I never did like that cackle.

It was like a rattlesnake on them crappy cowboy films you
sees on HTV.

'Right then,' said Spike Lewis. 'What'll we do now, boys?'

We were kicking a can around on the open ground behind
the New Sea Lock.

'Don't know,' said Soapy Rodgers. 'Have a fag, is it?'

'Why not?' I said, so we lit a Sweet Afton and passed it round.

It was cold.

It was growing dark, too.

Oystercatchers piped out on the mudflats. A cormorant flew low towards Steepholm.

I likes birds, me.

When I gets the chance, I reads about them in books.

'I wouldn't half fancy a pint of Brain's Dark,' said Spike Lewis. 'Go in the New Sea Lock and see if Danny'll serve us one, is it?'

'Cor blimey, Charlie,' I said. 'My dad'd bloody murder me, if he caught me drinking beer.'

Spike Lewis cackled again.

'Mine couldn't give a monkey's,' he said.

He couldn't neither.

Well, I don't suppose you bothers with things like that when you've still got eighteen months to go in Bristol nick.

'Let's have a boat trip,' said Soapy Rodgers.

'Don't be a dum dum all your life,' said Spike Lewis. 'The Campbell steamers has stopped running a good three months by now.'

'I don't mean that,' said Soapy Rodgers. 'I knows where there's a rowing boat, see. We can nick it and go for a trip in the bay.'

Spike Lewis looked at me.

I looked at him.

I paused.

I knew what I should say.

I didn't though.

'Why not?' I said, so we had a good spit and set off to find the boat.

It was round the back of the Pier Head we found it. Close by the new Maritime Museum.

It wasn't a rowing boat in the accepted sense of the word. It was more like a bloody great whaler only the stern – that's the back of the boat, see – was sort of curved in on itself.

I thinks they call it a coble.

I read about it once in a book.

Still, it don't matter a monkey's one way or the other, if the truth be known.

It was tied to an iron ring by a bit of rope.

We untied it and tried to drag it to the water's edge.

It wouldn't budge.

'What'll we do now, boys?' said Soapy Rodgers. 'Go back to the New Sea Lock, is it?'

'Don't be bleeding daft,' said Spike Lewis. 'If a job's worth nicking, it's worth nicking proper.'

We heaved, and we tugged. We cursed, and we sweated, and after half an hour or so we got it into the water.

We was knackered by then, so we lit another Sweet Afton.

'The wind's getting up,' said Soapy Rodgers. 'Let's go to the Marl and let off a couple of rockets.'

Spike Lewis cackled.

'Losing your bottle, is it, Soapy?' he said.

'No,' said Soapy Rodgers. 'No, Spike. It's just that I nicked these two rockets off my sister, see. Be a sin to see them go to waste, right?'

'Bleeding rockets,' said Spike Lewis. 'What a load of crap.'

He looked down at the boat, and he kicked it with the toe of his boot.

'I names this boat the *SS Daitanic*,' he said. 'God bless all what sails in her.'

I laughed.

But I felt a flutter in my guts, and my cheeks started to twitch.

It was pitch dark by now.

You could see lights twinkling on the derricks of a tanker sitting high in the dry dock. You could see the lights glowing in the back room of the Red House across the other side of the bay.

They sort of shimmered on the water.

The wind was rattling things.

It began to rain.

A tug boat heaved itself out of the lock gates and blew this long mournful note on its siren.

Dead sad.

'I thinks I got a touch of diarrhoea coming on,' said Soapy Rodgers.

'Come on,' said Spike Lewis. 'Push.'

So we climbed into the boat, pushed off and the tide began to carry us out into the bay.

It went quick, too.

The water skidded along the hull of the boat.

The bow rose high.

'You know what we could do with now?' said Spike Lewis.

'No,' I said. 'What?'

'A pair of oars.'

'Cor blimey, Charlie, hasn't we got no oars?' I said.

'No,' said Spike Lewis. 'I just looked.'

He cackled.

'Smashing, eh?' he said.

In the pitchy darkness I could see the whites of Soapy's eyes.

I couldn't see his teeth.

Well, I don't suppose he was grinning if the truth be known.

I wasn't.

I was shit scared.

By now we could feel the rush of water coming down from the Taff, and the boat began to rock.

'Sit still,' snapped Soapy Rodgers.

'I am sitting still,' I shouted.

But I wasn't.

I was shivering like hell, if the truth be known.

The tide snatched us up quicker.

I saw a bonfire and fireworks being let off on the muddy beach outside the Red House pub.

It was a party for the nippers.

My mam and dad took me there once.

I wished I was there now.

I wished I was anywhere else, but on this boat.

We passed the point where the River Ely flows into the bay, and the wind began to billow and blow.

Behind us there was a bloody big bonfire on Caerphilly mountain and rockets speared into the sky.

It reminded me of this hymn of the blokie what asks God for a spear of gold and arrows of desire and things like that.

I likes singing hymns, me.

There's something religious about it, I thinks.

'Smashing crack, this, eh?' said Spike Lewis.

Soapy Rodgers jumped.

'What's that?' he said.

'I says it's a belting boat trip,' said Spike Lewis.

Soapy Rodgers said nothing.

He just rolled his eyes.

The waves began to roll us, too.

The bow was high and the water hit under it with a smack and threw spray all over us.

Three gulls wheeled and mewed above us.

'Way hay,' screamed Spike Lewis at the top of his voice. 'Way hayeeeeee.'

His voice echoed, and the wind snatched it and threw it in ribbons round my ears, and it was then I knew for certain what I'd always suspected – he was a bleeding nutter, Spike Lewis.

Course he was. He was right off his beanpole.

I'd never have mitched off school today but for him.

I'd never have been had up for nicking lead down Bute Terrace.

I'd never have seen my dad's tears and the long, slow look of pain in my mam's eyes.

'This is the bleeding life,' screamed Spike Lewis, and he stood up in the bow and raised his arms to the heavens.

'Sit down, you madman, you'll have the bloody boat over,' shouted Soapy Rodgers. 'Sit down, mun.'

Spike Lewis turned.

Very slowly.

'Scared, is it, Soapy?' he said.

Soapy Rodgers didn't answer.

'Lost your bottle, is it, Soapy?' he said, and this time there was barbs of anger in his voice.

Very softly Soapy Rodgers began to cry.

It was a soapy sort of cry. Like as though you was slowly squeezing out a pair of soapy football knicks into a tin drum.

'He's scared. Cor blimey, he's bleeding scared,' screamed Spike Lewis.

And he began to laugh, and he began to rock the boat with his two hands tight to the gunwhales or whatever they calls the bleeding things.

And, by God, the boat didn't half rock.

It pitched and tossed, too.

And Spike Lewis began to cackle like a maniac as he turned his face to the wind and let it whip through his spikey hair.

We were well out into the estuary now.

There was fireworks sparking over Penarth.

The wind howled and the waves roared, and it was biting cold.

'Spike,' I shouted.

He turned.

'What?' he said.

'Turn back, is it?' I said.

He crawled along the bottom of the boat towards me.

Well, it was so rough he couldn't have kept his balance. He'd have been bleeding overboard, if he'd stood up.

He hauled himself up alongside me, and he put his ear close to my mouth.

'What's that you said, my old sweetheart?' he said.

I paused.

I knew what I should say.

I didn't though.

It was what I should have said the night we broke into that house down Cathedral Road.

It was what I should have said that Saturday afternoon before we ripped the bog apart on the train to Bristol City.

It was what I should have said before we smashed into the headmaster's study and set alight to the books on his shelves.

Smashing books, they was.

He'd lent me a couple.

I'd enjoyed them, too.

My mam had hummed happily round the house when she'd seen me reading them.

'Sling them in the Taff, is it?' Spike Lewis had said.

'Right,' I'd said.

I had, too.

Two books with leather binding that felt nice and smelled nice.

Now with the boat plunging and plummeting and the spray scuttering over our backs I knew what I should say.

'What's that you was saying?' said Spike Lewis, and his fingers dug into my arm. 'What's that you was saying, my old buttie boy?'

'Nothing, Spike,' I said. 'Nothing.'

He tossed back his head, and he roared with laughter.

'We'll show them,' he screamed. 'We'll show the bastards.'

And snickering and cackling he clawed his way back to the front of the boat, and Soapy Rodgers lay on the boards and slowly puked his ring up.

I looked down on him and saw the water slopping round his thighs.

It was a good nine or ten inches deep.

'Oh good God almighty,' I whispered to myself. 'Why didn't I say it? Why didn't I say Turn Back?'

And then I heard the roar.

It was a different roar from the roar of the wind.

It was a crashing roar. It echoed and thundered and rumbled.

It was an angry roar.

It was a malicious roar.

Malicious.

I learned that word from this book the English teacher lent me.

It was a book about monsters and things like that and fairy bints with golden hair and snow white skin.

Well, this teacher was an old blokie, mind.

He was about fifty or sixty and he lent me books all the time.

He lent me a book by this blokie called Shalimar.

It was a book about the sea and Chinese pirates and tea clippers and brigantines and engineers called McGregor and first mates with drunken captains locked in their cabins fighting typhoons and things like that.

And then I recognised what this roar was.

I'd read it in this book wrote by this blokie called Shalimar.

It was the roar of waves pounding against rocks.

I looked up quickly.

The moon had come up and there was stars, too.

And in the moonlight I saw it.

I saw the great cliffs of Steepholm Island and the waves crashing against them.

And the tide was sending us racing towards them.

'Soapy,' I yelled. 'Soapy.'

He didn't move.

'Soapy, you black bastard,' I bawled.

I kicked him.

I pounded him on the back with my fists.

I took him by the scruff of his neck and dragged him to his knees.

'Soapy, you black bastard,' I bawled again. 'Look.'

I yanked his head round with one hand. I pointed with the other.

I pointed to the high cliffs of Steepholm Island looming nearer and nearer and the waves spewing up them in fountains of white and roaring and gurgling and crashing and booming.

I pointed to Spike Lewis, head hunched into his shoulders, gripping the front of the boat, staring straight ahead at the great soaring cliffs and cackling and cackling.

He turned, and he saw us cowering together, clutching each other, shivering.

'Way hay,' he screamed. 'Way hayeeee, boys, we'll knock the living shits out of them, eh? We'll bloody show them.'

And he stood up, and he stretched out his arms wide to the cliffs, and he howled at the top of his voice:

'Out of the way, you bastards. Out of the way, if you don't want doing in.'

Then I remembered this story what this blokie, Shalimar, had wrote.

It was about this barquentine what the tide was tearing towards the rocks.

The captain was drunk in his cabin, and the first mate, what had got a cleft in his chin, was fighting this bloody great Lascar, what was frozen to the wheel with panic, and suddenly this cabin boy, what come from a farm in Devon, smashed open this locker and he took out . . .

'The rockets,' I yelled to Soapy.

'What?' he said.

And his voice was all hollow.

'The rockets, you black bastard. Where've you put the bleeding things?'

He gawped at me, and his mouth fell open.

He looked like that nigger money box what my mam give me when I was a nipper.

'The rockets,' I cried at the top of my voice.

I ripped at the buttons on his jacket.

They all come off dead easy in my hands.

Well, I bet they don't have much call for sewing on buttons in Antigua.

I ripped at his pullie and I felt the rockets nestling against his chest.

I wrenched them out.

My hands was so cold I could hardly hold them.

My fingers was so numb I could hardly take the matches out of the box I had in my trousers pockets.

Thank God, I'd been smoking since the age of eight.

Well, if I hadn't, I wouldn't have been carrying matches at the age of fifteen, would I?

I tried to light them, but the box was sodden, and the wind wouldn't allow no flames to grip.

The cliffs came nearer and nearer, and the roar got louder and louder and more louder still.

I began to sob.

I bloody did.

I began to sob like a babe.

I grabbed Soapy by the collar and pulled his jacket over his head.

'What you doing, butt?' he said in his hollow voice.

I crouched inside the tent I'd made of his jacket.

There was only one match left.

Light, you bastard, light.

I scratched and I scratched against the box.

'Light, you bastard,' I bellowed.

It did.

Just for an instant.

But in that moment I rammed the blue touch paper of the rocket against it, and it glowed dully and then flared into life.

I shoved Soapy away and the paper sputtered and sparked.

At that moment Spike Lewis turned round.

He saw me with the rocket held out in my outstretched hand.

He opened his mouth to shout, but before any sound came from his mouth, the rocket shrieked from my hand and hit him slap in the face.

It blew up in a cloud of sparks and gold and silver spangles, and Spike Lewis screeched.

My God, I'll never forget that screech.

It was worse by far than the thunder and the roar of the waves against the cliffs.

The whole of his head seemed to go up in flames, and his coat began to burn.

He looked like the guy they'd had on the bonfire outside the Red House when my dad and my mam took me there as a nipper.

I couldn't move.

I froze solid.

And all of a sudden something very strange happened.

Soapy dragged himself to his feet and stumbled to where Spike Lewis lay spread-eagled over the bow.

He crouched over him for a moment, and by God, I thought he was going to pray or do something religious.

But, no, he took the rocket he'd snatched from my hand, and he held it into the flames coming from Spike Lewis's jacket, and he lit it, and he held it high above his head, and it curved off into the sky and it exploded in a festoon of red and green and yellow.

If the truth be known I don't remember much else.

I do remember they hauled us aboard the tug, and this blokie what smelled of wintergreen ointment poured rum through my teeth.

Some blokie in a white uniform wheeled me in a trolley along a corridor.

My mam looked down on me as I lay in bed, and for the first time in three years there was no pain in her eyes.

About a week or so later me and Soapy Rodgers took a bus to Chepstow.

Well, besides the race track they've got a hospital for burns there.

They'd bunged Spike Lewis in it.

He'd lost the sight of his eyes and his face was a bit of a mess, too.

We stopped off in a pub and had a pint or two of screech.

That's what we calls rough cider in Cardiff. Screech.

Nice name. Nice sound.

When we got to the hospital gates, I took hold of Soapy Rodgers by the sleeve and I stopped him.

'What is it, my old butt?' he said.

I paused.

I knew what I had to say.

A heron flapped slowly overhead.

A magpie cackled.

What a cackle.

'Well?' said Soapy Rodgers. 'What is it?'

I looked him straight in the eyes, and I said:

'Turn back, is it?'

He looked at me for a moment, and then this great slow smile came to his great black face.

'Sure,' he said. 'Sure we will, you white bastard.'

We turned back and before we caught the bus back to Cardiff we had another couple of pints of screech.

I likes screech, I does.

If you drinks enough, it makes you forget.

# JIM ANDREW

# *A Box to Keep the Screws In*

It was a two cigarette job. Every job Uncle John Temple Byrnie ever did at the workbench in his coal cellar, he'd get his shop set out – everything he needed in the way of materials laid ready to hand; then before he'd pick up his first tool, he'd light up a cigarette. Have five minutes, as he put it, while he weighed up 'the ins and outs and the malefications'.

The five minutes was often nearer fifteen. It was generally reckoned that Uncle John Temple Byrnie could get a whole fresh cigarette's worth of satisfaction out of the butt that any other man would throw away. He would smoke a cigarette down until it was just a crumble of ash and yellowed collar of moist paper holding a last smouldering ember of precious tobacco, small as a wart against his blister-proof lower lip – a lip like the rest of him; wind and weather chapped, cracked and healed and cracked and healed again into a natural, invulnerable armour of baked and frozen tissue.

So you'll see when Uncle John Temple Byrnie needed a second cigarette before starting a job, he must have found himself really up against it. Malefications! You could bet the job was a job and a half – a real poser. From my perch near the coal shoot, I watched in an agony of suspense. Could it possibly be that Uncle John Temple Byrnie had come across a job he wouldn't tackle? At that time a grown man and a workbench added up to a near omnipotent combination for me and the possibility that there might be some jobs that combination couldn't tackle alarmed me. Filled me with a fearful apprehension similar to the apprehension that comes with the first doubts in the existence of a cosy, Sunday School Almighty.

But I was too young to have experience of those doubts then and as it happened, I needn't have had any doubts in Uncle John Temple Byrnie. The second cigarette smoked through as only he could smoke it, I caught my breath as he picked up a piece of hardwood in his big, red hands. He looked at it for a long minute. Perhaps he was having second thoughts. Perhaps he was going to put off the job until another day. Almost he put the wood back down on the bench. Would he? Wouldn't he? I decided that if I held my breath long enough, he wouldn't. I held it and he didn't. Still holding the first piece of wood in one hand, he picked up a second piece of wood in the other. I let go my bated breath and my bursting lungs got back to work, sucking the air audibly in grateful sighs that matched the laboured breathing of Uncle John Temple Byrnie – a sign of great concentration – as he held the two pieces of wood together and matched them with his eye.

I settled myself more comfortably in my corner by the coal shoot.

'What are you making, Uncle John Temple?'

Uncle John Temple Byrnie was a big, quiet, simple man but he had a great sense of mystery.

'Na'then, we'll have to wait and see,' he said. He took a square and a stub of pencil from the drawer of his bench, sucked the pencil point and began to plot an elaborate dovetail on the first piece of wood.

I always loved to watch him working at his bench, but on that day in particular I was especially glad to watch. An hour before, I had arrived home from school to find my grandmother's house, where I lived, a gloomy place of whispers. Mysterious aunts in black cotton stockings, who usually visited singly on rare market days, or presided grimly at Sunday teas in tiny over-furnished cottages a best behaviour bus ride away – these aunts now sat in a body in the kitchen, gloved hands scrabbling on the ebony handles of their huge umbrellas, reeking camphor and discussing adult secrets with my grandmother in phrases beyond my young comprehension.

A curt word from grandmother had ordered me to occupy myself and I quit the house to wander the streets, scuffing my shoes up and down the pavements in the never-never time before tea when other children stayed indoors. Yes, I had been especially glad that day to see the light in the cellar window of Uncle John Temple Byrnie's and to find him busy at his bench, at such an unusual time of day – a time when he was normally at his real work at the quarry. Perhaps I wondered about this and perhaps I asked. But if I did I cannot remember. In any case, as I said, Uncle John Temple Byrnie was a man with a great sense of mystery. If I did ask him why he was home instead of at work, I know full well what he would have said – as he must have said a million times to a million babbling queries of mine. Just: 'Na'then, that would be telling.'

The dovetails had been cut and the two pieces of wood joined; two more pieces dovetailed and joined and the four joined together to make the skeleton of a box, before my belly insisted that I went back home to Gran's.

'Tarra then, Uncle John Temple, I'm off for my tea,' I said. 'I'll see you after.'

'If I'm not here, I'll be gone out,' he said. He began to measure up a piece of wood for the bottom of the box. I slid from my place by the coal shoot and went home.

The aunts had surrendered their huge umbrellas to the stand in my grandmother's dark, narrow hall. They had removed their gloves and sipped delicately but copiously from the best china teacups and nibbled at fancy cakes from Custy's confectionery shop, sucking the last traces of cream daintily from their old fingers.

For me it was bread and dripping, standing at the stove in the scullery. 'And where've you been all this time?' Gran wanted to know. Huh! – first send you off from under their feet, then create 'cause you're not back the minute they want you.

'I've been round at my Uncle John Temple's,' I said, finishing my bread and dripping. 'Is there a fancy cake for me?'

'No, there isn't. If you wanted a cake you should've been in sooner. I had an errand for you to do taking a note to Mr Osbolbee at the church. I had to send young Morrison from next door – and he had your cake.'

'And another thing,' she added, 'you're not to go bothering your Uncle John Temple – not tonight, you're not.'

'Why?' I asked. 'He doesn't mind.'

'Never you mind whether he minds or whether he doesn't mind. You do as I tell you. You're not to go round there tonight, that's all. So think on now!'

'Can I go round tomorrow then?'

'No.'

'Can I go round the day after tomorrow then?'

'No.'

'No – nor the day after that – nor any day till I tell you.'

'Can I have another cup of tea?'

'No.'

'Can I have my train set out?'

'No. If you want to play then go outside and think on what I've said.'

I didn't want my train set out anyway, not with all my aunties sitting round depressing you. Sitting round like old sniffing parrots when they weren't yaketty-yaking. All right for them – they can sup as much tea as they want. Not just one measly cuppa for them. Only the rotten smallest cup in the house too. Old parrots. Yaketty-yak.

In spite of my Gran's warning, once she was letting me out of prison I was straight back round to my Uncle John Temple's. The skeleton of a box now had a bottom and while I watched, he cut and hinged a lid, driving the screws home with slow precision.

'Gran said I hadn't to come round here tonight,' I said. 'You won't tell her will you?'

'I won't let on.'

'She says I'm not to go bothering you.'

'You don't bother me.'

'That's what I told her, but she don't listen.'

Uncle John Temple began sandpapering and polishing the box. The bottom of my foot began to itch and I tried to scratch it with my other toe through the thick sole of my shoe.

'Is my Auntie Gracey home yet.'

'No,' Uncle John Temple said.

'Will she be coming home soon?' I asked.

'Na'then, that'd be tel . . .' he began. He paused. His hands lay still. Draught from the open window blew his piece of sandpaper to the floor.

'She won't be coming back,' he said. He picked up the piece of sandpaper and resumed his work.

Back home, the old parrot-aunts were still parroting and it was a quick swill for me before being packed off straight to bed.

'Where've you been getting your breeks covered in coal?' Gran demanded as she peeled me in front of the sink.

'Had a go round the slag heaps on Ginger's bike,' I said. I daren't tell her I'd been back in Uncle John Temple's cellar. 'Had a go dirt-track riding.'

'Well keep away from them slag heaps. I've told you before – and about borrowing and lending bikes. I'll dirt-track your ear-hole if I catch you at it again.'

'Wouldn't need if I had a bike of my own.'

'When bikes grow on trees you can have one.' I chased the soap round the tin bowl until the water was a froth of suds.

'A lad at school found a bike on the tip,' I said. 'If I find one can I keep it?'

'No you can't,' Gran said. 'And keep away from that tip. You'll catch fever.'

'This lad at school, his mother let him keep it.'

'Well never mind.'

'Why couldn't I keep it. It's not fair.'

'Never mind why not. Just think on.'

'Well, it's not fair. Can I have a cuppa cocoa?'

'No, I haven't the time to be bothered making it. You can have cold milk.'

'It's not fair.'

'Never mind.'

I lay in bed. Rotten cold milk. Outside the street lamps came on and threw a shaft of light through a chink in the curtains.

The cast shadow from the little girl with her skirts up that stood on the windowsill was magnified into a huge horned head on the opposite wall. I pulled my head under the bed-clothes.

'I have four corners to my bed
and at each an angel spread . . .'

From downstairs came a mumble of voices and the front door kept opening and shutting.

'Lord keep us safe this night secure from all our fears . . .'

The kitchen door opened and there was the clink of teacups.
Still supping tea and I had to have cold milk. It wasn't fair. I
hated my Gran for a minute and then felt sorry about it.

'Please God bless Gran and keep her safe, and please God
bless my other Gran who's dead and both dead Grandads, and
Grans and Grandads everywhere.

Thank you for the food we eat,
Thank you for the world so sweet,
Thank you for the birds that sing,
Thank you Lord for everything.
Amen . . .
A-a-a-men . . .
Aaaaaaaaaaaaaaaaaaaaaaaamen.'

Safe until the morning, I curled into a tight ball. If there was
a tiger under the bed, it couldn't get at me and neither could
the dead man in the wardrobe.

The next day when I came home from school, Uncle John
Temple was showing the box to Gran. He'd finished it off a
deep mahogany and he'd lined the inside with padded stuff.

'It's very nice,' Gran was saying. 'It is, it's lovely.'

'It kept me occupied.' He closed the lid, tucked the box
underneath his arm and stood up.

'Where are you going, Uncle John?' I asked.

'Why, to see a man about a dog,' he told me.

I followed him to the door and called after him, 'What sort
of a dog, Uncle John? What sort of a dog?'

'Hush your clack!' Gran ordered.

'Is the box to bring the dog home in?' I asked her.

'Never you mind. Hush your clack.'

That night in bed, I heard the door opening and shutting
again and the same murmur of voices – this time with Uncle
John Temple's deep bass among them.

I dared the dead man in the wardrobe, the monsters behind
the doors on the landing and the zombie under the stairs. I
crept from the safety of my blankets and down to listen at the
kitchen door. It was ajar. Through the narrow crack between
the door and jamb I could see a slice of Gran's profile; her
jutting chin and serious, tight-lipped mouth. She was standing
against the press, her arms folded. The woman from next door
was neighbouring in the rocking chair and further away,

on the wooden chair with the broken back, sat Uncle John Temple, the box resting on his knees.

'Told me they'd had her burned,' he said. 'Told me that's what they always did in these circumstances – made immediate disposal.'

'Hospitals!' Gran sniffed.

'On account of her being still at birth and not baptised,' Uncle John said. 'Told me it was standard procedure.'

'Hospitals!' Gran sniffed again. 'When will they bring Grace home?' Fat lot Gran knew for all her pomp. Aunty Gracey wasn't coming home again, I could have told her that.

But Uncle John Temple had a surprise for me.

'Tomorrow,' he said.

I was leaning against the door and the wood murmured. Gran glanced in my direction at the noise and I quickly scuttled back upstairs in case I was discovered. I lay in bed wondering why Uncle John Temple had lied to me when he said Auntie Gracey wouldn't be coming home.

The following day there was no school for me in the afternoon. When I came home after the morning session I was forced into my Sunday clothes after a Sunday wash.

'Now you're to come up to your Uncle John Temple's and see your Aunty Gracey,' Gran said. 'And you're to be quiet and not keep agape with your everlasting questions.'

She led me by the hand. The same aunts who'd been at our house two days before were now sitting round my Uncle John's front parlour. The curtains were drawn, making the room gloomy. I stood, uncomfortable in my Sunday clothes, my eyes glued to my Sunday shoes. I only raised them once – when I was told to look at my Auntie Gracey. She was laid out in her wedding dress, the same dress I'd seen her churched in just about a year before. Her eyes were closed.

'Your Aunty Gracey's sleeping with Jesus and her little daughter in heaven,' Gran told me. She led me out. I spent the rest of the day with the next-door-neighbours.

Uncle John Temple Byrnie was a big, stolid man. Careful and easy by nature, he took life calmly as it came. No one ever knew him show any emotion.

I loved to watch him doing some job at the bench in his cellar workshop. One day I was down there, squatting by the coal shoot, watching him fix the door off Gran's meat safe.

He turned the door all ways, weighing up the job. Then he put it down and smoked a cigarette in slow, thoughtful puffs. He finished it as last, stubbed out the butt and picked up a gimlet.

'While I'm making the hole, see if you can find us a one-inch screw, will you, our Bobby?' he said. 'There should be one in the box under the bench.'

The box had once been polished a deep mahogany, but now it was dusty and chipped. I opened it.

It was lined with padded stuff, still white where it wasn't stained by rust from nails and screws, washers, bolts and various oddments that now filled it. I searched out the screw that Uncle John Temple Byrnie had asked me to find.

'That's a good box to keep screws in, Uncle John,' I said as I gave it to him.

'Aye,' my Uncle John Temple Byrnie said. 'It'll do.'